# THE PRINCE

Also by Dinitia Smith

*The Honeymoon*
*The Illusionist*
*Remember This*
*The Hard Rain*

# THE PRINCE

*a novel*

DINITIA SMITH

Arcade Publishing · New York

Arcade Publishing books may be purchased in bulk at special discounts for sales promotion, corporate gifts, fund-raising, or educational purposes. Special editions can also be created to specifications. For details, contact the Special Sales Department, Arcade Publishing, 307 West 36th Street, 11th Floor, New York, NY 10018 or arcade@skyhorsepublishing.com.

Arcade Publishing® is a registered trademark of Skyhorse Publishing, Inc.®, a Delaware corporation.

Visit our website at www.arcadepub.com.

10 9 8 7 6 5 4 3 2 1

Library of Congress Cataloging-in-Publication Data is available on file.

Jacket design by Brian Peterson
Cover photo credit: Getty Images

Print ISBN: 978-1-950994-19-9
Ebook ISBN: 978-1-950994-20-5

Printed in the United States of America

Dedicated to Henry James
All Honor . . . and Apologies
(See Endnote)

"It's terrible"—her memories prompted her to speak.
"I see it's always terrible for women."

The Prince looked down in his gravity.
"Everything's terrible, cara, in the heart of man."

—Henry James, *The Golden Bowl*

# Part One

# A Prenuptial Agreement

# One

THE TIME HAD COME FOR FEDERICO, THE PRINCE, TO SIGN THE prenuptial agreement. Should the marriage fail, which of course it wouldn't, he'd be a very rich man.

He was sitting at the conference table in the offices of the Woodford family's old law firm, opposite his future father-in-law, Henry Woodford, and Washburn, the Woodfords' austere and unfriendly attorney, who'd protected the family's interests for decades. Sitting next to him was his own representative, the elderly Accardi, who'd been flown in from Rome for the occasion, at his father-in-law's expense.

The huge glass windows of the skyscraper sealed them off from the outside world. The air conditioning was heavy, Federico cold. The only decoration in the place was an arrangement on a sideboard of unusually large, green calla lilies with chunks of black wire wound around the stems. It was ugly; Federico didn't understand it.

As he read through the document, he felt as if a film was descending over his eyes . . . "*One million dollars for every year of marriage . . . equal division of assets resulting from the sale of any artwork acquired during the marriage . . . any property jointly-acquired during the marriage or jointly-held will be deemed to be owned equally with each party entitled to fifty percent (50%) of the net equity of the property, regardless of the initial or ongoing proportion of each party's investment . . .*"

He'd offered no resistance to any of it. Neither had Accardi. Perhaps because they were dazzled by the terms. Was this his father-in-law's way of apologizing for requesting that he even sign a prenuptial agreement?

Emily had already signed hers. It would have been crass to have had to sit across the table from one another contemplating the end of their marriage before it had even begun. It would have made Emily, who was so sweet and so optimistic, weep, and no one could bear that.

Washburn slid the papers across the table one by one. There were red plastic tabs on those he was supposed to sign. Federico could feel that Washburn didn't trust him, even though he was now about to become a member of the family. What could he possibly not trust? Did he see something in Federico that he himself didn't see? There'd been hardly any negotiation at all because the terms Henry offered were so generous.

As Federico signed each of his allotted pages, Accardi watched with a weary gaze. At last, it was done, and Federico put down his pen.

"Well," Henry said, rising from his chair with a sigh of relief. He reached across the table to shake Federico's hand. Henry's handshake was crushingly strong. He was eager to confer his goodwill—*very American*, Federico thought. Henry was fair haired and blue eyed, much taller than his son-in-law-to-be, handsome and intimidating in his power and energy. Federico was slender, of medium height, with dark brown hair and olive skin, though his eyes—somewhat surprisingly, given his dark coloring—were a blue-hazel color.

Federico figured Henry had inherited his handsomeness from the generations of beautiful women who'd married the rich and unattractive Woodford men, most of whom, Federico judged from their family portraits, were pale people with small chins and protruding eyes. The women's good looks, after many generations, had permanently seeped into the family line and begun to dominate it. When Federico was with the Woodfords, he was always conscious of being dark amongst the light. There was no one in the Woodford family, or among their circle of friends, whose coloring was as dark as his, and he felt like an alien among them, a foreigner, which of course he was.

Outside in the hall, the group dispersed. Federico and Henry waited together in uneasy silence for the elevator, not looking at one another, except when Henry gave Federico a small, encouraging smile. As always, Federico was shy with Henry, with his largeness of spirit and movement. But despite his height and his wealth, Woodford had a certain hesitation about him, which Federico found endearing and a relief. He understood the awkwardness a future son-in-law would feel with his fiancée's father.

As they exited onto Third Avenue, Henry shouted over the din of traffic and construction next door, "I think we deserve a drink! Got time for a toast?"

"Sure," Federico said. "I'm not meeting Emily until seven." Whatever Henry wanted, Federico would politely agree to.

"We could go to my club," Henry said. "I never go there, but it's just ten blocks away and it's not crowded this time of day."

Henry led the way, pushing through the mass of people. Thank God for the noise, which made talking impossible. The prince never quite knew what to say to this man. They came from two different worlds: Federico from the stultifying culture of his elders in Rome, the younger, more contemporary crowd at the *Istituto*, and the gigs he'd played in clubs with his band (stupidly named "*I Giovani Stalloni*"); Henry from the educated, democratized, fourth-generation wealthy class of this country—quite another sort.

Henry's red brick club was on Fifth Avenue, on the corner

across from the park. They entered the cool black-and-white tiled marble lobby with its perfect, echoing quiet. The doorman, trained to recognize all members, even those who, like Henry, rarely came here, bowed his head. "Mr. Woodford, welcome."

Up the curved staircase they went, to the lounge. It was a huge room, deserted in the afternoon, extending into the shadows, with a coffered ceiling, deep leather chairs and couches, and oriental rugs. There was a human-sized fireplace framed by the ivory tusks of some immense animal. The prince was used to these sorts of spaces. In Rome, of course, they were grander, older, ancient upon ancient.

They took their seats, and a waiter came and stood over them, notebook poised.

"Champagne?" said Henry.

"It's a bit early for me for alcohol, I'm afraid," Federico replied. "Just a coffee, please."

"Well, I usually don't drink before five either," Henry said. "But I think I could use a whiskey today. Black Label," he told the waiter. "With ice. And some nuts or something, please."

Henry Woodford was, quietly, a very rich man. His wealth surrounded him, it was the air he breathed. The Woodford family's wealth was largely invisible these days, except for their big, impregnable houses and their private island far out in the middle of Long Island Sound. There were no buildings with their name on them, no websites with products they manufactured. The original sources of their wealth had long disappeared, leaving only their money, which had grown immensely over the years.

Yet, Henry, to his credit, was acutely conscious of the needs of others. He never forgot that most people were not as fortunate as he, and that he must do his best for them. He'd abjured the career paths sometimes taken by men of his wealth such as working in a white-shoe law firm. Instead, he'd founded his own law firm in Westchester, doing pro bono legal work and serving the desperate and the indigent. Through the Woodford Foundation, and from his own funds, he also contributed millions to health care organizations, to education, to groups helping immigrants, and lobbying for housing for the homeless.

"Woodford" wasn't a well-known American name, like "Rockefeller." The Woodfords were modest people, remaining extremely private for their own safety, and to protect themselves from fortune-hunters, thieves, swindlers, and people who constantly solicited them for money. Their name rarely appeared in newspapers, and the foundation often made its donations anonymously. The name could occasionally be found on the donor lists on the websites of nonprofit organizations, denoting old wealth that had faded into obscurity, and mostly unrecognized by the public.

Their fortune originated in the nineteenth century in a small West Virginia town actually called "Woodford" after Henry's great-grandfather, Ephraim Consider Woodford. Ephraim Consider built steel mills, and coal mines to feed them, and railroads and ships to transport his goods. Ephraim Consider was also a war profiteer, his fortune greatly enhanced during the Civil War by charging the government exorbitant prices for raw materials to manufacture munitions. His workers toiled twelve hours a day, with a half-day off Sunday to go to church. When they went on strike, Ephraim hired the Pinkertons, private security guards, and four workers were killed. Eventually, the family sold the business to the Japanese who closed the mills. Only a stamping plant and the hulking ruins of the factories remained. The town was a dying place. The old Woodford family mansion was now a small museum housing art that Henry's grandparents had collected. It was open only part time and the building was in disrepair.

Henry was appalled by the origins of his family wealth, and his great-grandfather's brutality. Over the years, the family had given money to the town for a hospital, a library, and a baseball field. Recently, Henry had retired from his law firm and decided to restore the old family home and make it into a real museum, hoping to attract tourists and revitalize the town.

Now, in the dim confines of the club, Henry turned to Federico and said, "I hope this prenuptial thing wasn't too difficult for you."

"Not at all," Federico replied. "It's only right that you look after your daughter. I completely understand."

"It's the best way. The Family Council decided years ago that everyone should do it as a standard thing. Not that anything would ever happen to you two. But it makes things easier."

For a moment, Federico said nothing. Then, "I cannot imagine anything that would necessitate it. I am—" he hesitated and then said softly, because his and Emily's relationship was a private thing and shouldn't be discussed with a father, "*Sono l'uomo più fortunato del mondo.*" He found the English words, "I'm the luckiest man in the world." Federico spoke English quite well, though when he was nervous, he reverted to Italian. He'd learned English in school from a British teacher, and spoke it with an English accent, occasionally using antiquated British constructions. Sometimes he couldn't even understand American English, with its truncated sentences and its slang.

"It must be very hard giving up your daughter," Federico said politely to Henry.

"It is hard," Henry admitted. "But the fact that she's so happy helps. She worries too much about me, and it's really time she lives her own life." He took a deep breath. "Everything's going to be fine, and congratulations to you!" he said, lifting his glass to Federico. Perhaps the man really did need a drink after the afternoon's events. "I couldn't be more pleased." Federico returned the toast with his coffee.

"Pardon me," Henry asked politely, "but I've always wondered. What does it mean in Italy these days to be a prince? Does the family own land?"

He'd never asked Federico about being a prince before, but now that he was marrying his daughter, he was of course entitled to. Federico never referred to himself as such, but he knew that people in this country mentioned it when they spoke about him, especially out of his earshot. The title was part of his identity, his bones. In Italy, people knew it, but his friends at school and university weren't impressed. They were mostly from upper class families too, and some were also titled.

"Everything was sold off after the War," Federico said. "There used to be lands in Pistoia, but that's long gone. And then came the tax reform and the cost of regulations governing *proprietà principesca*, 'princely properties,'" he said, as always a little embarrassed when the subject of the ancestral lands came up because they were so far from the reality of his family's situation now, and people always misunderstood that.

He didn't mention that his disreputable grandfather had squandered what was left of the family fortune in Monte Carlo. Federico's late father had worked for an import/export company but never earned much, and his parents had to scrape together the money for Federico's school tuition. His father was devoted to his son, but he was a sad, quiet man who spent his spare time researching the family history and trying to write a book about it. After he died, Federico had tried to get it published, but no one was interested. Family histories of the Italian aristocracy were a dime a dozen. To this day, all his father's years of work lay dormant and unread on his desk.

Federico was an only child, his parents' main focus in life. His mother, Isabella, was an aristocratic beauty with a fine, Roman nose and immaculate posture. Everything Federico did was "wonderful," and he was "a brilliant musician," though he wasn't. She constantly made suggestions about how he could use his "talents." During Federico's adolescence, her praise became an annoying background music. He'd achieved nothing of what she expected, her endlessly encouraging words were a lie. But in the last few years, he'd begun to understand how her love for him had given him protection and hope.

"Of course, there are still some families with money," Federico told Henry. "But a lot of people support their estates by giving tours and renting them out to tourists."

His father had left almost no money, and Federico worried that he wouldn't have the means to provide for his aging mother. They still had the big, old, dilapidated apartment in Rome, but they'd sold off all the art to make ends meet. Now there were only squares and rectangles visible on the faded walls where the paintings had hung, like ghosts documenting piece by piece the family's decline.

Though Federico felt no particular pride in being a prince, he was aware that the title gave him some advantage, an identity at least, and extra importance in some circles. It was a label. Still, he had nothing else, and he wondered if, even for Henry, a democrat in his most basic self, the fact of his title made up for his deficiencies. Would Henry have approved of his daughter's marriage to such a penniless man if he hadn't been a prince?

"Being a prince really doesn't mean a lot these days," he told Henry. "The Italian government doesn't recognize titles. There's a lot of minor nobility hanging around, doing various things. Most of us—we're just ordinary. I read that there's an Italian prince out in California who's selling pizza from a food truck. I even saw a place on the Internet where you can buy the title."

"You're kidding," said Henry.

"I don't know anything about it," Federico said, and chuckled. "I saw that you can pay for it with PayPal."

"But your family's very old, isn't it?" Henry asked.

"We've got a few Cardinals, a Pope. They often chose them from the nobility."

He could sense Henry was running out of conversation and was searching for some area of common interest between them. "Emily tells me you're a big soccer fan?" he said.

"Indeed. Yes," said Federico. "I was on my team at school. I'm a bit of—what they call a '*fanatico*.' But I'm not very good myself."

"Do you follow any one team?"

"My team is Juventus. Ever since I was in school."

"Emily says that you were volunteering to coach soccer to migrant children in Rome."

"Yes. Emily came to one of our games."

"She said she really admired you for what you were doing."

Federico felt a sudden pang. He missed the boys, Efrem and Ahmed and Amir and Jamal. Ten- and eleven-year olds, mostly North African, with tough, cold eyes and hard, stoic faces, arriving at the run-down field on the outskirts of the city in the battered black van that Padre Matteo had managed to secure for them. Skinny kids, but the muscles of their legs were surprisingly sinewy from running around, picking up odd jobs, and often doing heavy work, although they were children, just to survive. Padre Matteo had found them in the illegal migrant camps around the city, camped out along the walls of the Tiburtina train station and in abandoned office buildings and parking lots.

Federico had spotted a sign in front of a church seeking volunteer coaches for a soccer team for migrant children, and had gone inside to find out about it. Padre Matteo, the priest, was a young-looking man, his own age, though balding, with smooth, pale skin. He was a big soccer enthusiast, and amidst the religious paraphernalia in his office—the cross on the wall, the picture of Christ, and the statue of the Virgin—the priest had a poster of Cristiano Ronaldo, who was playing for Juventus that year. He happily enrolled Federico as a coach. He warned him that the boys were wary and self-protective, and told him not to ask them questions about their lives—the Romans hated the migrants, and the police were always routing them; their existence was perilous.

But out on the dusty soccer field, the boys were transformed. Within minutes, they lost themselves in the game with amazing focus. They flew back and forth at lightning speed. Federico tried to keep up with them, yelling instructions and blowing his whistle, while Padre Matteo, on the other side, yelled at *his* team. The boys knew some rudimentary Italian from the streets, but they swore vehemently at one another in their own languages, which Federico couldn't understand. At the end of the game, they came off the field smiling and breathless, their bodies gray with dust and dirt.

After a few weeks of coaching them, when Federico thought that they might have come to trust him, he demanded, man to man, that they translate the swearwords for him. Maybe because he was male, they told him. "*Halay!*" they said, giggling. That was supposed to be "Dumbass" in Tigrinya, apparently an Ethiopian language. "*Kes Emak!*" was an Arabic reference to "Your Mother's Vagina!" When they explained the words to him—in a mixture of street Italian and sign language—Federico laughed, and they'd loved it.

Gradually, he learned a little about their lives, about how fleeting their happiness on the field was. What he discovered appalled him. The children slept in abandoned buildings on concrete floors, if they were lucky enough not to have to sleep outside on the pavement, and foraged for food in the garbage. They lived without running water, or toilets. He learned about a sick grandmother with no doctor to care for her. Some of the children didn't appear to even have parents, although sometimes there was mention of a cousin or an older brother who had come with them on the boat across the Mediterranean. They were on their own, or they had only each other. They didn't trust Federico enough to tell him exactly where they were living, fearing that he might inform on them. Anyway, they had no fixed abode. The Roman police came in the middle of the night, tore down the doors, smashed the windows and toilets, routed them, and beat them like rats.

When Federico took the New York job, he'd had to leave them behind. He felt somehow guilty about it. He said now to Henry, "I don't know if I deserve Emily's admiration that much."

"I'm sure Emily's admiration for you is entirely justified," Henry said. He moved on to another topic. "I'm so sorry your mother can't make it. I'd like to have met her."

"I am too, of course. But the illness . . . is progressive, and my aunt can't leave her—" He stopped. Since his father's death, his mother's mind had deteriorated, and it frightened him. She was becoming more dependent on him, and running out of money. Soon, he'd have to support her totally. Aunt Celeste had moved into the apartment to look after her, but Aunt Celeste was older than his mother.

"What's wrong with your mother, exactly?" Henry asked.

"The doctors say it's a form of dementia. But for the moment, she's functioning okay, and I don't have to worry about her as much with my aunt there."

"I hope now that we can help out, from our end," Henry said.

He'd been aware, of course, that perhaps the Woodfords might help with the two old women, but he didn't acknowledge this to Henry. It would have been too obvious, that he was aware of how rich they were, and that he'd be willing to take money from them. He was already sending money home to Accardi to pay for a *badante* to look after them. But his bank salary would never be enough to live in New York and pay for a good, safe, permanent home for the two old women when they needed real care.

"That would be very kind," said Federico. "But I hope I can manage."

Henry took a breath. "So," he said, "everything's set. God, I hope the weather holds. We've got tents just in case. The boats for the guests are arranged for Friday. It's a forty-minute ride. We've got the rooms booked on the mainland for people we can't put up on the island." The wedding was to be held on the Woodfords' private island, which had been bought by Henry's ancestors in the late nineteenth century as a hunting preserve. It was a special place to both Henry and Emily, a natural spot for the wedding. "I think you'll really enjoy it," Henry said.

Nearly an hour had passed, and the prince had had enough of this closeness to Henry. It was difficult having a dialogue with your future father-in-law. Despite Henry's goodwill, Federico believed he was still scrutinizing him, still unsure of him. Possibly he thought that Emily's money was an attraction. Federico was in love with

Emily, but of course her father wanted to make sure his affection was honest, that he was good enough for his adored daughter.

The prince was awkwardly quiet for a moment, then he said, "Please don't think I'm taking her away from you. You will always be part of our lives."

"I know that," Henry said. Federico felt a burst of affection for the man, for his care and optimism, and his determination to like the person his daughter had chosen.

The waiter arrived with the bill. Henry signed for it. Federico was free to go.

Outside on the sidewalk, they shook hands. Henry pulled Federico toward him, held him for a second and patted him rhythmically on the back. It was the first time Henry had embraced him.

As Henry stepped away, the weight of the responsibility of what was going to happen in a week's time, forever, for the rest of his life, descended upon Federico—the act of marrying this man's precious daughter, this sweet, small woman with only goodness in her, rich and sheltered and adored by her father, and who, apart from her mother's death, had never known privation. That loss had colored her entire existence and fused her to her father and made her fearful of leaving him. When she went away to boarding school in Massachusetts, Emily had told Federico, she was so homesick that she'd begged her father to let her come home and finish up at the day school near them. At the age of twenty-seven, she still hadn't moved out of the house.

# Two

FEDERICO WATCHED HENRY'S TALL FIGURE WALK AWAY. HE HAD two hours to kill before he met Emily for dinner. There wasn't enough time to go downtown to his apartment in the Village and back.

Strolling along in the heat, he felt empty, devoid of all excitement about what was to come. It scared him. Was it normal to feel this way now, on the eve of such a great celebration? Most people in his situation would probably be counting the hours in anticipation of the time when the knot would be tied and they'd hold their bride in their arms. For the merest second, Federico had the sensation of a great steel door clamping down in front of him. Did he even realize what he was doing? He quickly banished the thought. The decision was irrevocable.

Yet, he thought, maybe this feeling wasn't so unusual, and perhaps it was natural for a man about to take this momentous step. Still, he felt as if he were moving through a tunnel of white light. He had no one in whom he could confide these feelings; these were not the sorts of emotions you could tell anyone about before your wedding.

It was late afternoon, the air was beginning to cool off, the hard gleam of sunlight on the pavement was softening. He walked up

Fifth Avenue, past the tall apartment buildings with narrow strips of heavily mulched, artificial-looking impatiens and begonias alongside them.

He took out his cell phone and dialed Jean. She was possibly his one true friend in New York. After Emily, of course.

"*Ciao*. It's Federico. I was passing by. We had our meeting about the prenuptial agreement. Would you like a visitor?"

"Oh," she said. She seemed to be wavering. Usually, she was glad to see him.

"Is this not a good time?" he said.

Then, "Absolutely, darling!" she cried. "Come right over."

Jean Gavron lived in an apartment building two blocks down. She was Henry Woodford's art advisor. It was mid-June but not everyone had departed for the country yet, and she was still in town because she had clients to see. Jean was an Italophile, and when her husband, Mike, retired, they'd taken an apartment in Rome. Jean had introduced Federico to Emily at a party there when the Woodfords were in town for the auctions.

Federico went up in the elevator which opened directly into her apartment. Jean was there to greet him, dressed all in white linen as she often was, and wearing a necklace made of delicate steel loops, probably designed by one of her artists. She was in her mid-fifties, her hair was gray and straight, cut at an angle to her cheekbones which were high and sharp. Dark red lipstick and nail polish were the only colors on her body. She was barefoot, her toenails perfectly groomed.

"Should I take off my shoes?" he asked. Jean usually liked people to do that.

"It's okay," she said. "You can leave them on. Come in, come in!" she said, giving him a hug. She seemed hyper today. "How was the meeting? How was Henry?" she asked. "Do you want something?"

"Just water, thank you," Federico said, following her into the kitchen. "Henry was great." Jean's maid, a Spanish woman, in a blue uniform and white apron, was there.

"Marienella, you remember my friend, Federico?" Jean said. Federico had observed that the American rich often introduced their friends to their servants by their first names.

Marienella nodded. "Yes. Of course," she said.

Jean's thin figure moved quickly to the refrigerator. He saw that she was agitated. Though she was customarily effusive, she seemed unusually nervous today. She poured him some ice water from the fridge and led him back down along the hall to the living room.

"Henry was wonderful," Federico said.

"How are you feeling now that the big day's near?" she asked.

"*Va bene*," he said.

"Only 'okay'?"

"I guess I'm feeling a bit strange. I don't know why. I know I should be grateful that Emily would have me. Maybe it's the responsibility."

"Feeling uneasy when one's about to get married is totally normal," Jean said. "In fact, I think if you *don't* feel a bit uneasy, it's bad. It means you're not fully aware of what you're taking on."

"Yes," he agreed. Jean was the only person in New York that he could confide in, though she was a generation older. She and Mike had no children of their own, much to Jean's regret, she'd told Federico. Obviously, the need to be a mother was great in her. Jean "collected" young people, welcoming them into her life with warmth. She loved learning about their little triumphs and sorrows and romances. Jean was always there for her protégés, the recipient of their confidences—safer than their natural parents perhaps, because she kept their secrets and didn't judge them. She was ready to offer advice, to reassure. Her willingness to listen was irresistible. But with this came the close scrutiny of her "children," the awareness of their doings and their moods, that a real mother might have. Mike was more restrained. He'd been an investment banker, and was a genial, confident man, more a spectator of his wife's enthusiasms, and her interest in art.

The apartment had been decorated to showcase the couple's art, and there was nothing to distract from its perfection. It was all a peaceful gray, in tones of light and dark, the couches pale gray velvet, the walls paler gray, bare except for the precisely chosen art. The art was mostly small pieces that Jean and Mike had been able to afford or had gotten at a discount from dealers who wanted Jean's business. On one wall there was a sort of box containing an etching of curved black and white lines; beside it, a framed sketch of lines and squares and animal forms. Various plastic objects were mounted on the walls. Each work was framed, sacred and revered, and hung precisely within the moldings.

As Federico looked around, Jean watched him, smiling—too brightly, he thought. He nodded at one of the pieces, a painting of a perfect red rectangle, within it two smaller rectangles, one yellow, one dark orange.

"Who's that by?" he asked.

"That's our newest 'child,'" she said. "It's a Donald Judd. We got it for a very good price. We were lucky."

"I'm rather ignorant about art," he said. "I know just a bit about the old stuff my family had."

"You're going to learn a lot now from Henry."

He sighed, holding the cool glass of water in his hands, watching the condensation run down the sides.

"I owe everything to you," he said.

"Not really. Just an introduction. You owe the rest to yourselves."

"I would never have known her without you."

"Well, thank you for that." She grew serious, glanced nervously at him, looked away.

"Something's happened," she said.

"What?"

"Did you know Christina's in New York?"

He felt his heart seize. "No," he said slowly.

"She's going to the wedding. She called me when she got in. I found out she was staying in some awful hotel in Midtown. I couldn't let her do that. I insisted that she stay here and go out to the island with us."

Federico hesitated. Why on earth had Jean done this?

Then, softly, he echoed the name, "Christina," he said. "I didn't know." As he had Emily, he'd also met Christina through Jean in Rome. Christina was half-Italian, and Jean had known her American mother there. People in the American expat community socialized with one another. And coincidentally, Christina had gone to boarding school in the States with Emily when they were girls.

"What's she up to these days?" he asked.

"She's been in Rome living with her mother, working in some vintage clothing store, trying to finish her degree. Emily wrote her and invited her to the wedding, but Christina wrote back and said she was sorry, but she wouldn't be able to come. She couldn't afford the ticket. So, Emily insisted on sending her a ticket."

Federico's shoulders slumped, he felt suddenly weighed down. "When is she coming?" His words came from far away. He could hardly hear himself.

Jean looked fearfully at him. "Any moment now. I couldn't avoid it. I'm sorry. She was already here when you called. She just went out to get something."

He faltered, "Is she still the same? As . . . beautiful?" the words escaping despite himself, his eyes now focused on Jean's front door.

She looked at him anxiously. "Yes," she said.

Just then, the house phone in the hall sounded. Jean went to answer it, and he heard her muffled tones as she spoke into it. She came back into the room, sat down, and stared at him. He gave back the look—there was almost the intimacy of mother and son between them now.

Federico tried to keep his face expressionless, to conceal his anticipation, although he knew Jean was aware of it.

The doorbell rang and Jean left the room again. He heard the gleeful sounds of greeting, and Jean lowering her voice. He was aware of them coming down the hall toward the living room.

And there she was, standing before him, tall, slender, long necked, her dark blonde hair pulled back today, her skin luminous in the heat. She wore a sleeveless blue cotton dress, loose-fitting and plain, with a low, square neck, which showed her slender arms and legs, and her thin feet and long toes.

Unmoving, she looked back at Federico, her head held high, amused. This was Christina, strong, defended, slightly mocking.

"Federico!" she said. "I didn't know you were here."

He went toward her. They kissed on both cheeks in the formal, European manner, and the familiar fragrance of her body enveloped him, the scent of the lavender shampoo and lotion which had always emanated from her. He stepped back. He saw that her pale green eyes were laughing at him, and yet he saw too, beneath that, the hardness and the hurt.

"What brought you here?" he asked.

"I'm coming to the wedding," she said.

"I heard."

"Emily couldn't bear that I wasn't coming. She sent me a ticket. I hated accepting it, but she kept saying that it was for her, not me, and I had to be there!" Emily had told him nothing about this, perhaps because she had no idea how well he knew Christina. He had never told her the full story.

"I'm so glad," he said, though he wasn't.

Jean was looking unhappily from one to the other. "Christina, are you hungry?" she said. "Have you had anything to eat yet?"

"No, no. I'm not very hungry in this heat. But maybe, if it's not too much trouble, I'd have some iced coffee if you've got it made?"

"Good. I'll run and fetch it," Jean said, hurrying out.

After she'd gone, Christina stood without speaking, eyebrows raised, her smile crooked, a question, a challenge on her face.

"Well?" she asked.

"Yes?" he said, pretending not to understand what she was asking.

"It's been over a year," she said.

"You haven't changed. How have you been?"

"I've been okay!" she replied, in her bright, arch way, smiling at him dazzlingly, daring him.

"That's good," he said nervously. And he felt the old, overwhelming heaviness that came to him whenever he saw her, as if his legs were made of sponge.

"*Emily lo sa?*" she said, reverting to the language of their intimacy. "Does Emily know?"

"Know what?" he asked deliberately in English, though he knew exactly "what." By asking the question, he could diminish the whole thing, as if he'd forgotten it. Or, more importantly, that *she* should have forgotten—he hoped. If so, he'd be less guilty.

She looked back at him with her unwavering eyes, glowing, her arms and legs uncovered, unbearable.

"I didn't know you were coming," he remarked, for want of anything better to say.

She raised her eyebrow. "Do you mind?" she asked.

"Of course not. Emily knows we knew each other in Rome."

"Did you tell her the rest?" she asked.

"No. Why should I?"

"You didn't think it was right to tell her?"

"Why? It was the past."

"Yes. But a big part of the past, don't you think?" she said. Another challenge.

"I didn't think it was necessary."

Now he could see the hurt. Her features set. For a moment, the shield had fallen away.

"I'm sorry," he said hastily. "You never told her yourself?"

"We used to be very close when we were in school. We've hardly seen each other since we graduated from school. And you know me. I'm very private."

She let this hang in the air between them. At last, she said, "I want to have one hour alone with you, before it happens."

For a moment, her audacity took his breath away. Then it all came rushing back to him, a sensation like an electrical current coursing across his skin. "Oh, Christina," he said. "No."

This time her smile was cold. "Very well."

He saw it, said nothing. Then he said, "Do you still have the same cell phone number?"

"Yes," she said.

And her smile became hope.

# Three

LATER, AS THE SUN FELL ACROSS THE CITY, GOLD AND ORANGE, making everything seem worthwhile again, Mike Gavron came home and found his wife sitting anxiously on the couch and twisting her fingers. Mike was a big, ruddy-looking man, with a head of bushy, white hair.

"What's up?" he asked, recognizing signs of trouble. He threw his keys into the dish on the table, took off his shoes, and went to kiss her.

"Federico was here," she said, as if announcing a death.

"Good," he said. "They must be very busy getting ready."

"Yes. But I think it's mostly in Emily and Henry's hands."

He looked at her. "So, what's wrong?" he asked.

"Christina Verano."

"What about her?"

"She's here. She's going to the wedding. I invited her to stay with us. She and Emily knew each other from boarding school. She was Federico's girlfriend before Emily. You've met her."

"Of course. Very attractive girl."

"She's too young for you," Jean said sharply.

"Silly woman," he said, putting his arm around his wife and kissing the top of her head. "So, what's the problem?"

"I introduced them."

"I remember that."

"They went out together. And then I introduced him to Emily."

"Yes. Of course."

"Christina arrived today and Federico came over."

"Okay?" said Mike.

"Now she's back and she's going to his wedding with Emily."

"Good."

"What do you mean, 'good'? You never pay attention to anything I say."

"I do! I do, my dear. Always. Every word you say, I pay attention to. It'll be good to have her. Where is she?"

"She's having drinks with some friends. I gave her a key and told Carlos she was staying with us."

"Oh," he said.

"Now you see," she told him.

"Does Emily know about the two of them?"

"I'm sure she knows they were acquainted in Rome. But the rest, I don't know what she knows."

"Well, it's been a while, right? He's not still interested in her or anything?"

"God—I hope not!"

"That's good," he said.

"Now you see," she said. "Now you're paying attention." She rubbed her forehead. "What am I going to do? I introduced him to my client's daughter."

Mike was a pragmatic person. He'd negotiated a good retirement from his firm, and now filled his days with racquetball and opera. Life had treated him well. He cherished his intelligent and nervous wife. She was his window on the world, exposing him to the joys of art. Jean's observations and insights always surprised and fascinated him. He himself accepted the world on its own terms. His wife made him feel safe. She looked out for both of them.

"Why would you even concern yourself with it?" he asked. "I don't see why you're worried. It'll be alright."

"I care about all of them. Emily's so good, that girl." She looked up at him, stricken. "What should I do? If it comes out that I introduced Federico to Christina, I'll lose Henry's friendship." Henry was her principal client, and now she'd been given the huge—and lucrative—task of advising him on the expansion of his art museum.

"His daughter's everything to him," Jean said.

"For goodness' sake. Henry's a modern man. Do you really believe he thinks that his future son-in-law—what is he—he's over thirty, right?—has never had another girlfriend?"

"He's very protective of Emily. He might be angry that I haven't told him."

"Why would you even bother to tell him? I mean, it's the past, right? It would be odd for you to talk to Henry about something as private as his son-in-law's previous relationships, his sex life."

She sighed. "I guess you're right."

"So, where's Christina in all this?"

"I think she'll be fine," Jean said. "Christina's a real survivor. They're three good young people."

"I think you give yourself too much credit, my dear," he said.

"I hope so," said Jean. "I need a drink."

"What'll it be?"

"Gin and tonic."

He went to the bar cart and mixed the drinks.

"Maybe we should think of someone for Christina to marry," she said.

"Do we know anyone?" he asked, bringing her drink to her.

"I can't think of anyone right now," Jean said glumly. "But it'd make everything safe, wouldn't it?"

" 'Safe'?"

"Yes. Safe," she said.

# Four

Federico arrived at the restaurant before Emily. He had to see her, to be reminded of who she was, that he loved her, that he was excited about the marriage. The restaurant was in the basement of a townhouse with steps leading down to the entrance. When she came in, he saw her look eagerly around for him with her quick, bird like movements. Because she was a small person, she always appeared to be looking up at the world. She spotted him and, beaming, hurried over to him. Emily's eyes were a radiant blue; they always expressed joy and hopefulness. Her skin was pale and perfect, but her cheeks were always pink. Emily was a natural beauty. No makeup for her. She had light blonde hair, cut short in no particular style, but it was curly, so it didn't matter and it formed its own style. Her long, smooth nose turned up at the tip. She was full-breasted, her clothes rather carelessly chosen, as if she just grabbed the nearest thing she saw in the morning to put on. Today, it was a white cotton blouse and a short denim skirt, no jewelry. One would never have known Emily was rich. She had either the confidence of not needing to care about her appearance, or she was innocent of any necessity to enhance it.

He rose, gathered her to him, and kissed her. Emily's breath always smelled of spring.

"Sorry I'm late!" she cried. "The subway was held up at Fourteenth Street. We just sat there. The air conditioning was broken. It was so incredibly hot, I could hardly breathe." She was five minutes late, but Emily was unfailingly polite and punctual. She hated to give offense in any way. That was one thing Federico understood about Emily, her old-world manners; they'd been part of his own upbringing as well.

"You should have taken a cab," he told her.

"I hate cabs. I'll do anything to avoid them. They're so ridiculously expensive now."

That was so like her, to think of something as too expensive, as if she weren't even aware of how much money she had, or was ashamed of having so much of it and believed it was the right thing to preserve the norms of public transportation.

"How was it?" she asked, settling into her chair. She screwed up her face. "I hope it wasn't too awful!"

"Of course not. It went by like a snap. And your father and I went out and had a drink afterwards."

"It's just the way the family does things," she said. "It doesn't mean anything."

"I certainly don't care," he said. "It's probably very sensible."

This was an old restaurant from another era that still served authentic Italian food, a small, snug space, with exposed brick walls and posters of Pompeii and the Bay of Naples. At home, Federico liked to cook Italian food himself for Emily. "You won my heart through your cooking," she'd laughed. Indeed, he was an excellent cook. It was one of the few things he thought he did well. The secret of good Italian cooking, of course, was everything must be totally fresh. Cooking good Italian food for Emily was something he could do that no one else could; a man cooking, other than a professional chef, was a new thing for her, an added gentleness and nurturance.

"How was work today?" she asked.

"Oh, a bit boring." He didn't want to acknowledge to her how much he hated it.

"Well, what did you do?"

"Well, let's see," he said. "We advised the client to invest in a broad market index, in two indices tracked by ETFs."

"What on earth are those?"

"Exchange traded funds, a collection of securities that tracks an underlying index."

"I'm afraid I have no idea about this stuff. I'm completely ignorant about money."

"Perhaps you should learn?" he said.

"Dad and The Office handle it all," she said. Federico had discovered that the Woodfords had something called "The Family Office" which managed their affairs. "The Office," as they called it, managed their trusts, kept their bank accounts filled, paid the maintenance on their co-ops—most of their bills, for that matter—prepared their tax returns, did background checks on their servants, and made their travel arrangements. If they needed medical attention, The Office could give them the names of the best doctors and dentists in New York and arrange hospitalizations in the luxury wings of institutions the Woodfords had donated money to.

Emily's lack of knowledge about worldly things, her indifference to them, astonished Federico. Perhaps it was a kind of efficiency on her part because she didn't *have* to understand. She was surrounded by money; it was all she'd ever known. Being poor or in need had no reality for her so she didn't have to worry about it.

"But what if something happened to your father?" Federico said.

"Nothing will ever happen to my father," Emily said firmly.

Emily was an intelligent person. She'd had an elite education and was very well-read in all the classics, books that Federico couldn't possibly understand himself. Her knowledge had impressed him. Once, after they made love, as she lay next to him, she'd recited a poem to him. He could only remember a couple of lines: "*Don't leave me even for an hour, because then the little drops of anguish will all run together.*" They were by a Chilean poet, Pablo Neruda, she told him. He was amazed that she knew it by heart.

Emily's innocence was a willed thing, he'd decided. If someone made a mean remark about a person, she'd cover her ears with her fists to stop them, didn't want to hear it. Maybe it was a way of imposing her will, of decreeing that the world was a safe and happy place, even if it wasn't. Perhaps someone who was as rich as Emily could afford to not see evil in the world.

That evening, as he had walked downtown to meet her at the restaurant, he'd made a decision. It was better to tell Emily himself that he'd seen Christina. Let her find out from him. It would make it seem unimportant.

He said now, "You'll never guess who I saw today."

"Oh. Who?"

"Your friend, Christina Verano. She's staying at Jean Gavron's. I dropped in to see Jean after your father and I had our meeting. She's staying there."

"How great," she said. "I haven't seen her yet. It's been ages and ages—we've only seen each other when I was in Rome or she came to the States to see her grandmother. When I drew up the guest list, I decided I wanted to have all the people who've ever been important to me, even when I was a child." The list of invitees to the wedding kept growing. Even Federico himself didn't know who was coming. They were almost all from Emily's side because his family was in Italy, and his mother and Aunt Celeste were too frail to make the journey.

"I was hoping we could have lunch before the wedding," Emily said. "But there just isn't going to be time."

She opened her menu. As her eyes scanned it, she asked, "Did you know her well in Rome?"

"I met her at one of Jean's parties." Not quite a lie. "Other than today, I haven't seen her since before you and I were together." That was a form of the truth.

He didn't say the rest. Not on the eve of their wedding, when everything had been settled, their huge decision had been made. This wasn't the time to cloud her happiness by bringing another woman into it, especially a woman he'd had sex with, and who happened by chance to be her childhood friend. Emily knew he'd had girlfriends before her, of course, though he never went into detail about them. She'd told him about her first boyfriend. He was a senior when she was a sophomore in college. Her first sexual experience was with him, and it had hurt a lot. After that, there'd been a couple of other boyfriends, but she'd been a fearful, reluctant lover.

Only with him, Federico, Emily said, had she discovered the true meaning of sex.

She looked up from her menu. "I'm surprised you didn't try to date her. I mean, she was always so amazing looking."

He could feel his face turn red. He prayed that in the dim light of the restaurant she wouldn't notice. He composed himself and tried to give back her open look. "I was waiting for you."

Emily focused on him a moment. She didn't say anything, as if pondering what he'd said. She smiled and went back to her menu. "Anyway, it'll be great to see her again," she said.

To tell her everything would be to reveal how powerful it had been. She'd ask more—had he been in love with Christina? And why hadn't he ever told her about it? And why had they broken up, she'd want to know? Because he wasn't ready for marriage. Then the question would be, why was he ready now? And the answer would be complex, would include of course that he loved her, Emily, more than he'd ever loved Christina. But there were reasons he didn't marry Christina that he didn't want to reveal.

He saw with relief that she was letting the matter of Christina pass.

"I like everything here," she said, happily studying the menu. "What're you going to have?"

After they ordered dinner and a bottle of wine, she reached into her backpack. "Look at this," she said. She took out her cell phone, scrolled through it and held it up to him.

It was a photo of herself, cross-legged on a mat surrounded by small children at the school where she worked. Emily was wearing a paper crown.

After she graduated from college, she couldn't bear to go on for an advanced degree and spend all those hours in the library, on some irrelevant thesis. "It's all theory now," she said. Federico only knew vaguely what she meant by "theory."

She'd found a job as a researcher at a foundation gathering statistics on child poverty and hunger, but she wanted to be "more hands on." Her father knew someone on the board at the St. Andrew's Church School and then she got an interview as an assistant to the head teacher.

But now, because of the wedding, she'd resigned. One day she hoped to take education courses at Bank Street, and eventually to teach, and maybe join Teach for America—though she might be too old. And she'd have to teach at a school in New York because that's where they were going to live. The picture on her cell phone was of her farewell party.

She put the cell phone in her backpack and took a breath. "I'm nervous," she said.

"About what?"

"That this is going to be so hard for Dad. My getting married, leaving him."

"But he seems so pleased about it," Federico said. "Has he said that?"

"No. Of course not. All he knows is how to be supportive of me. And he really, really likes you."

"But this is the natural course of things, surely? You can't live with your father all your life."

"No—no. I know I've lived at home far longer than I should. It was just too easy. The house was big enough." When Federico met her, he'd wondered at the fact that she still lived with her father in his great limestone mansion on the East Side. At college, she'd lived in a dorm and, she told, almost never invited friends home. "I just felt weird about it, sort of embarrassed." After she graduated, she'd taken a lease on an apartment with some friends. But when the lease was up, she'd moved back in with her father. "I mean, I basically had my own apartment on the top floor of the house," she explained. "Dad didn't care when I came and went. I just had to tell him when I'd be home for dinner so Adolfo would know." Adolfo took care of Henry's house, did the cooking, and supervised everything.

"It's weird," she said. "I feel like I'm *his* protector. I think that I'm the only thing between him and . . ." Her voice trailed. "I can't say it."

"But a daughter isn't really a protector of the father," Federico said. "It's the other way around, no?"

"I know, I know. It's wrong—even he knows it. I can't help it."

"He's sixty years old, yes?"

"Sixty-one."

"He can take care of himself, I think," Federico said.

"But he's had so much tragedy in his life." Henry's father had been a total alcoholic, she told Federico, and his mother committed suicide when he was nine. "And then," she went on, "there was Mummy's death."

"I'm sorry." He took her hand.

"My mom came from the same sort of family," Emily said. "But her parents, my grandparents, they were good people."

Emily's mother had been determined to create a normal life for them, Emily told him. They'd lived in the northern part of Westchester County, which was more like country, away from the noise and snobbishness of New York. They had a big, old, cozy farmhouse and two yellow labs, Dottie and Arnie, who were allowed to lie all over the furniture and shed their coats everywhere. Emily had a horse, Freckles, and her father commuted to his office in an old Volvo.

Her mother had been a lover of books. She read to Emily all the time, and it was from her that she got her love of literature. Her mother didn't have to work, but she opened a bookstore in town.

She adored being a saleswoman and was unrecognized by customers for the wealthy woman she really was. She started a children's book club in the shop and on Saturday it was crowded with townspeople and their children sitting on the rug at the back while she read to them—she had a gift for reading aloud, and acted out all the characters, and entranced parents and kids alike. "When I was a child, I used to play on the floor by the cash register," Emily said, "and I'd always hear her talking to customers about her favorite books. But all that stopped . . ."

She got cancer. It went fast, a dreadful deterioration. Toward the end, her father wouldn't let Emily go into her bedroom to see her. He didn't want her to die in the hospital, and he didn't want to frighten Emily with the sight of her. So, Emily would sit outside her mother's door straining to catch a glimpse of her as the nurse went in and out. She could hear, coming from inside, her mother moaning in pain.

When her death was drawing close, Emily's father took her into the bedroom to say goodbye to her. Her mother was unconscious, shrunken, almost unrecognizable, her breathing ragged. Emily was scared to touch her for fear she could hurt her, and that she might catch her illness. Her father said, "I think you should kiss her goodbye now, honey," and, gripping his hand, Emily leaned down and touched her lips to her mother's forehead.

When she finally died, "It was strange, I didn't cry at first. I didn't feel anything. I thought, 'I'll take care of my dad. It'll be just the two of us.' Ridiculous, of course."

Her father couldn't bear staying in the house in Westchester with all its memories and he sold it, retired from his law firm, and they moved to New York.

"He's never gotten over her death," Emily said. Then, abruptly, she stopped. Federico squeezed her hand. At that moment, he decided she was the nearest thing he'd ever known to unalloyed goodness.

"But we won't be that far away," Federico reminded her. The

tragedy had melded father and daughter together, and he'd have to accept it.

As a wedding present, Henry had bought them a house three blocks from his own on the Upper East Side. When he proclaimed his intention to do it, Federico protested, "Sir"—lapsing into the polite salutation of his upbringing—"I can't let you . . ."

"It's a practical matter," said Henry. "Think of it as, I'm able to do it, and most people can't afford a reasonable place in the city anymore. Real estate's out of control. Don't feel bad about it. I want you and Emily to lead a good life, and besides, I'd like to have you nearby."

Federico had, of course, given in. What Henry said was true—there was no way he could buy a decent house or apartment for his wife. But he'd felt unmanned by his generosity, even though he'd realized that this sort of thing might happen if he married Emily. All they'd had to do was look at some houses and choose one. In the end, there were two they liked equally and Emily was in a state, vacillating endlessly between them. Since Federico wasn't paying for it, he felt he had no right to make the final choice. Finally, Emily asked her father to choose for them.

The house was an old Victorian with three floors and a basement apartment for a servant. The Family Office arranged the inspection and the closing, and it was all cash, of course, no mortgage; Henry made sure that his daughter wouldn't be encumbered by such a thing as debt.

Henry was also paying to renovate it. Emily designated a room to be Federico's "office," for whatever he might want to do in it. She bought an exquisite French ormolu desk for it and a big nineteenth-century photograph of Roman ruins for the wall. For herself, she wanted a place to store all her books from college. A small room upstairs was set aside for her with floor to ceiling mahogany bookshelves installed. That would be her special place.

"It'll ease the transition for Dad," Emily said. "Having us near him."

"I wonder that your father hasn't remarried," Federico said.

"I know. All I want is for him to. Someone to take care of him." She sipped her wine.

"Surely, many women would be interested in him?" he asked.

"Of course," she said, shaking her head. "But he just avoids them!"

"Has there ever been anyone? I mean . . ."

"Not that I know of. Maybe there've been some, but he hasn't told me. Maybe he thinks I'd be upset."

"Perhaps now that you're getting married?"

"I really hope so. I so much want him to have someone." She smiled radiantly at him. "I love you so much," she said.

"And I love you too," he said. "Only more."

# Five

THE AFFAIR WITH CHRISTINA HAD STARTED AT A PARTY AT THE Gavrons' apartment in Rome. The apartment was in an old palazzo, a grand place with frescoes of angels and cherubs on the ceilings. Federico's bandmate, Rodolfo, was working in a gallery and Jean invited him to the party and told him to bring a friend "to lower the average age" of the guests. Among the guests was Christina. She was tall, her height nearly equal to his own. Her skin was golden, her breasts small and firm, her pale green eyes clear and wise.

After the party, they went to a bar, and that night they made love. Until that moment, he'd thought of sex as an urge attached only to the sight of an attractive woman. But with Christina he realized for the first time how lust could be accompanied by tenderness, curiosity, admiration, and respect—for her strength and independence, her ability to survive, her resourcefulness. At the time, he himself was only just making ends meet with a little money from his parents. Taking it from them only made him more depressed and guilty. They hardly had anything themselves. He was sharing an apartment with three roommates from his band, earning a pittance from gigs here and there. He was nearing thirty and he was scared.

The relationship with Christina progressed. She learned of all his weaknesses, yet she loved him. Her love gave him confidence; perhaps he could steal some of her strength.

She had no money either; she was taking classes at night, trying to finish her degree, working in a vintage clothing store, burdened by her hippie mother, who always offered him weed when they visited her. The mother had frittered away her small inheritance, going from boyfriend to boyfriend—usually younger, useless men—and from cult to cult. Christina observed her mother coolly, pragmatically, and didn't complain about her except to remark ruefully on her latest escapades. Christina had an utter lack of self-pity, a cool self-confidence.

When Federico's father died, she held him in her arms while he sobbed like a little boy at the loss of the man's great, good presence. It was she who had the idea that Aunt Celeste should move in with his mother to help take care of her, a good thing because his mother declined so quickly after the old *principe's* death.

Christina perceived something within him that he hadn't seen within himself, something fixed and firm that she could love, that she judged with her otherwise cold, uninflected perceptiveness and all-seeing gaze, that had come from her own hardship. She never complained and went about her day with energy and forcefulness. She didn't let him feel small and inadequate because he existed in a state of constant indecision about who he was and what he wanted to do in life.

For a year, she asked nothing of him. Then, one night they were in bed in her tiny studio apartment—she lived four flights up in a 1950s building in Pigneto that was already falling apart. "You know, when we make love like this, it makes me want a child to come out of it, like a tiny seed's been planted or something from all this."

He sat up. "But . . . you use something? Right?"

She looked up at him coldly. "Don't worry!" she answered finally, with a bitter laugh. "You've got nothing to worry about." There was a closed smile on her face.

He laid back in the pillows, relief washing over him.

But the moment lingered and left him on guard. They went on as usual, meeting for supper, and then he'd spend the night. She mentioned nothing more about having a child. His obvious panic had stopped her, he thought. He was safe. Yet, he felt a new distance from her.

A couple of weeks later, when again they arrived at her apartment, he was expecting to have sex and spend the night as usual. She locked the front door behind them and in his rush to embrace her, he flung his jacket to the floor. But she just stood there. She didn't reach out to kiss him fully and richly on the mouth as she usually did, didn't touch him in the urgency of her need. Instead, she sat down on her bed and looked up at him without saying anything, and he saw something in her he'd never seen before, a hard resolution. He bent down to kiss her. She didn't acknowledge the kiss and remained stiffly sitting there.

"What is it?" he asked. "What's the matter?" Though, somewhere, he knew.

"I want to know," she said, "what's going to happen to us?"

The question thrust him into turmoil. She'd never mentioned the future before. He said, "We'll keep on loving each other. Why do you ask?"

"It's been almost a year," she said.

"Yes."

He tried to deflect her, brought her to him and kissed her.

But she pulled away.

"Why is this coming up now?" he asked.

"Because I want to know if there's a future for us."

"Of course," he said.

For the first time since he'd known her, her voice was tentative. "I mean . . . a real future, something permanent."

"But . . . you're only twenty-six. Why do you want that now?"

"Because," she said, "I feel it in me now. Will we . . . are we ever going to get married?"

"Married?" He repeated the word as if it were completely foreign to him. He felt himself grow cold. "I don't know," he said.

"After all this time, you 'don't know'?"

"This is ridiculous, Christina. Why are we talking about this? How could I ever support a wife and family now?" It was impossible. Impossible! He saw an eternity before him, committed to an absolute thing, a marriage. He was practically a child himself. He didn't have the means to provide for a family, he had no idea what he was going to do in life.

Before this, he'd been thankful to her for never asking where their relationship was going. She'd said the words, "I love you," and he had too, and he meant them. He was angry at her for making this happen, for spoiling everything by confronting him. Why was she doing this now?

He sat down beside her on the bed in the hard, electric light. She got up and moved away. "You better go," she told him.

"Now? What?"

She stood there inflexibly, with her immaculate posture, her wide shoulders.

"But . . . I *do* love you," he said.

"That word has no meaning now."

"I—"

"Admit it. Don't be weak, Federico."

It had all happened so quickly.

"Why are you doing this?" he asked.

"Go," she cried, cutting him off clean, as if she were severing a limb.

He retrieved his jacket and fled.

As he hurried down the stairs of the apartment building, he too began to cry, tears he hadn't shed since his father died and Christina had held him as if he were a child.

He sought out Jean Gavron, who was in Rome at the time, for consolation. She'd been the one who introduced him, the only person who knew both of them, and he and Christina had been among Jean's "young people." He confided in her about his misery and guilt. If Jean forgave him for what he'd done, that would absolve him.

"How can I marry *anyone*?" he cried. "Look at me!"

"How old are you?" Jean said.

"I'm going to be thirty."

"Well, that's not so young."

"But she's only twenty-six!"

"Yes, but if she really loves you, she wants to know what's going to happen. She has a right to that."

"Maybe. I don't even have a job. I don't know what I want to do with my life."

"Maybe you just don't care for her enough," Jean said.

"But I *do*! That's the problem." He went on. "She shouldn't be talking about marriage now. *She*'s too young."

"Perhaps," Jean said. "But Christina is an amazing girl." She shook her head. She sighed. "We go on," she said.

He went home and slept for hours. When he awoke, the realization of what he'd lost descended over him. He reached for his cell. But it would be wrong to contact her. He'd be leading her on when he knew he couldn't give her what she needed. That would be cruel. He was able to hold himself back.

He tried to numb himself. He developed a method—whenever her image appeared in his mind, or he heard the sound of her voice in his head, he forced himself to banish it. It was an exercise in nullifying pain.

Three months passed. He spent much of it getting high, sleeping late, and waiting for night to come. His only surcease was coaching the boys' soccer team, running up and down after them in the exuberance of the open air, the intensity of the game—it was win or die for them. And at those moments, he felt he was healing them—and himself—at least temporarily.

Those ninety minutes each week were the highlight of his life. He was playing as wonderfully and fiercely as they did. He had a purpose, to nurture these feral boys and bestow on them just a little happiness, and make them feel like someone cared about them.

When he could, he slipped them money. If the other boys saw him give money to one of the group, they'd crowd around him, holding out their hands for some for themselves. He'd end up giving them the rest of what he had.

Most nights, he and his roommates gathered in their barely furnished living room—an inside room with no windows—lying around on the stained furniture and smoking weed, listening to American pop music in a haze of cannabis, nodding to the beat, not talking, trying to learn something from the music, to analyze it, though they were too stoned to grasp anything.

Then, through an old friend of his father's, he was offered the bank job in New York. It was a salvation. The salary seemed huge: $115,000 a year, they said, more than he'd ever earned in his life, and more than he could ever earn in Italy. He felt guilty leaving his mother and Aunt Celeste, but he would send money back to them, and fly back and forth to Rome to see them. Meanwhile, he'd leave old Accardi in charge. The bank job would be a real job, an actual career. The band had come to nothing. This job would make him responsible, a man. It would give him a definition. And New York would be an adventure. New York had a great music scene—you could achieve nothing professionally in Rome with music. He'd been to New York once and loved the excitement of it. Maybe he could start another band there. Eventually, he was sure, the bank would give him a raise, and that would be great.

He broke the news to his mother. He was her only child, and he was leaving her. But he had to do this. "I understand," she said, grasping his hand. "You must do what's necessary. We will be all right. I don't want you to worry about me. I will be fine."

"And I will be back soon to see you," he promised.

"You have my blessing," she said. How could he have a more sainted woman for a mother?

Soon after that, while he was still in Rome—the bank had given him six weeks to prepare before his start date in New York—Jean gave another of her parties (whenever an American was in town, she gave a party) and invited him, though, tactfully, not Christina. "It'll be good for you to be with people," she said. "It'll take your mind off things." One of her clients, Henry Woodford and his pretty young daughter, Emily, were visiting from New York for the auctions. Henry Woodford, Jean said, was an important collector, a nice man, and very rich. "You'll get to meet some New York people in advance," she told him.

Anyone would have been taken by Emily's natural beauty, her radiance, her bright, eager manner. Everything about the young woman belied her wealth. She seemed entirely unaware of her beauty and there wasn't a hint of snobbery in her. It hadn't even come up that he was a prince, though no doubt Jean had mentioned it before to the father and daughter. The night after the party, Jean phoned him and asked if he'd like to join her and her husband, Mike, and Henry and Emily Woodford for dinner.

After dinner, with the city grown quiet, he walked Emily along the dark cobblestone streets back to the Hassler where the Woodfords were staying. They trailed behind her father and the Gavrons. The others, glancing back at them, and no doubt perceiving they were deep in conversation, tactfully let them go at their own pace, finally disappearing ahead. As they talked, Emily looked up at him with a tilt of her chin, like a bird, he thought for the first time. She was small, and quite a bit shorter than he was, which he rather liked. At one point she nearly tripped on the cobblestones and Federico grabbed her hand to steady her. She didn't disengage her hand from his.

The next day, he invited her to dinner, and every day from there on they saw each other.

On the third night, they went back to his place. It smelled of weed and his stoned roommates barely looked up when they came in. But she seemed not to notice. He led her by the hand into his bedroom—fortunately, he had his own room—and he made love to her.

Afterward she gazed up at him and said, "Your eyes are light, sort of a bluish-green color. I always thought Italians had dark eyes. They really stand out with your dark skin."

"My northern blood," he told her.

"And your eyelashes are so long and curly. Not fair for a man!"

"Thank you," he laughed. "I hope you don't love me just for the way I look."

"Of course I do," she said, laughing too.

On the following day, he took her out on the Metro to see one of the boys' soccer games. He worried she'd be scared of the disreputable neighborhood; she'd probably never in her life been in a place like this. He sat her on the bench at a distance from the field while the boys played, and he forgot about her as he ran up and down yelling instructions at them.

In the middle of the game, a fight broke out among them and suddenly they were in a heap on top of each other. These fights among the boys happened without warning. You could never tell exactly how they'd started. Padre Matteo blew his whistle and stopped the game. One of the boys, Efrem, emerged from the pile of players, furious and crying and wiping his eyes with his fists.

Federico led him to the bench, put his arm around his shoulders, and asked him what had happened. Efrem, shoulders heaving, complained indignantly that Jamel had fouled him. In retaliation he'd taken a swipe at him. His voice was rough at the edges, just beginning to break, but his tears were those of a little boy. As Federico tried to calm him, he saw up close the tender skin of the boy's neck and the soft curls of his hair. For a moment, he was no longer the tough, slightly scary pre-adolescent who'd arrived at the field earlier. The boys always seemed older than they actually were, but underneath it all they were still children. Federico patted him on the back, "*Calmati, calmati . . .* " Efrem heard the comfort in his words and glanced up at him, and his tears increased. Probably, no one had tried to comfort him for a long while.

Finally, he ceased crying, Padre Matteo blew his whistle, and the game resumed.

At the end, when Federico came off the field, Emily said, "I saw you with that boy. You were so wonderful to him. I was very moved."

"I wish I could do more for them," he said.

"But don't you think just giving them a little kindness helps?"

"Not enough," he said.

One night, Emily came to see his band play at the tiny club where they'd managed to get a gig. Federico played guitar and was mostly back-up. Marco was the lead singer. Federico had one solo and while he sang and played, Emily sat at her table, chin in her fist, and never took her eyes off him.

"You've got such a sweet tenor," she told him at the end of the set. But the music wasn't good, and he knew that his voice was merely adequate, not strong enough to be heard over the instruments. But she didn't know the difference.

Emily didn't seem to be impressed that he was a prince. In the world of the rich such as hers, perhaps that was of little importance. Maybe to her the title was just part of his exoticism. Or simply a label. Anyway, he certainly wouldn't seem like a real prince living in his dingy apartment.

It was Emily who said the word "love" first. Federico wasn't sure if he was ready for that. She was almost childlike in her adoration, in her wonder that he would even be attracted to her, and he responded that he loved her too. And he did.

He learned very quickly about her intense attachment to her father. It was time she moved out of the house, she admitted.

Her utter trust in him was frightening. Her unworldliness made him want to shelter her, even though she was the one who came with all the wealth and the deep roots in America, with a father who looked after her. She made Federico feel strong. She seemed drunk on him, perhaps because he was so foreign to her. He was undeserving, not an interesting person. But there was something about Emily's hopefulness, no doubt the result of her privilege and her great wealth, that drew him to her.

At one point during that time in Rome, she mentioned to Federico that she'd seen an old friend from school in America, Christina Verano. "I told her about you and that we were going out," she said shyly. "She said she'd met you at Jean's."

Obviously, Christina hadn't told Emily what had happened between them. And he didn't tell her the whole story either. They were on the verge of a new relationship. To reveal to her that he'd been with someone she actually knew would add a complication, spoil it, and interfere with their newborn love. He couldn't tell her that he'd broken up with someone because he wasn't ready for marriage, when now he was making a commitment to her, not only because of the lovely way she looked up to him, but yes, because her great wealth and her background made it possible when he had nothing. Except that he was a prince.

When Emily finally departed from Rome, they knew that in just a few weeks they'd come together again in New York when he started his new job. They texted one another and emailed messages of affection and missing each other. By the time he finally moved to New York, their relationship had grown.

The ocean's separation between himself and Christina helped him to forget her; his concentration on Emily, his absorption into her life, became total.

# Six

IT WAS HE WHO MADE THE PHONE CALL THE NEXT MORNING. HE suggested that they meet at 11 a.m. at the 79th Street entrance to the park. That would be "safe," a public location. He didn't propose lunch, because then they'd be across the table from one another, and he'd have to look into her eyes.

He emailed Ricardo, his boss at the bank, and said he had a doctor's appointment that morning and would be late. The man didn't seem to care when Federico came in as long as he was there for meetings with clients. He'd been hired as a decoration, so his bosses could introduce him as "My associate Prince Pallavicino," to reassure them about investing in Italian companies, securities, and debt. Inevitably, the client would pause and look at him curiously, taken back at the presence of an actual prince in the room. Following that, Federico would sit there saying nothing while Ricardo wooed the client.

Now, as he waited for Christina at the edge of the park, the trees were a fresh, brilliant green, the daffodils were beginning to brown, the tulips about to open. He sat on the bench, waiting.

At last he spotted her. She was wearing a wide-brimmed straw hat today, and the same summer dress as the day before. As she came toward him, he felt dread; his whole being was concentrated on her, on her magnificence.

Again, he gave her a brief, chaste kiss on the cheek, hardly touching her flesh with his lips, not wanting to draw close.

"Should we go into the park?" she asked.

"Let's just walk up toward the Museum," he said. There would be too many enclosed areas in the park, too many private places. He preferred the public space of the street.

They went a block or so and she stopped. She smiled. "I want to buy Emily a wedding present!"

Tentatively, he said, "That would be nice."

"Will you help me?" she asked him brightly.

"Well, I—"

"You know her better than anyone," she said.

He didn't respond. He didn't want to acknowledge their shared past, that they were familiar with each other's lives—and that now he was intimate with the same person with whom she had once been a close friend.

"I've got this vision in my mind," Christina said. "It should be timeless, though not necessarily perfect. Very unusual, that no one else would think of. Like I'm saying to her, 'I realize I can't buy you anything really expensive. But here's something pretty, something unique, that only I could think of, maybe. Because I'm so original!' " She laughed at herself.

"But . . . can you afford—?" He knew she didn't have any money.

"Don't you remember?" Christina replied. "I always manage."

That was frighteningly true. She was strong, a survivor. She always found a way. When he first encountered her, he was a lost soul, he didn't know what to do with his life, and he had needed her firmness and her bright self-confidence.

Christina led the way, crossing Fifth, turning into a side street and onto Madison. Her sudden excitement overtook his nervousness. As usual, it was her energy, her great moods, that dominated him, got him out of himself, and propelled him into action.

They strolled along the street while she searched the shops.

"Okay—there!" she said, pointing to the second floor of a building where a sign in the window said EDOUARD GAMAL, ANTIQUITIES in flowing cursive.

Without waiting for the light, as soon as there was a gap in the traffic, she hurried across the street and he went after her. Inside the doorway, she pressed the button for "Gamal."

Christina gave her their names, and they were buzzed in.

At the top of the stairs there was a glass door and an office within. An older woman, her hair pulled back in a bun and wearing a business dress and high heels, looked them over. Apparently satisfied they weren't there to rob the place, she opened it and led them through another doorway into a gallery.

In the gallery waited a dark-skinned man in a finely tailored suit, a silk tie, and pocket square. "I am Mr. Gamal," he said. "How can I be of help?" He appeared Middle Eastern, and he had a French accent.

The shelves of the gallery were filled with busts and statuettes and vases, and there were glass cases containing ancient jewelry and relics.

Christina said to the man, "I know this is silly—I'm looking for a gift. I know you don't have anything I could possibly afford, but I thought I'd give it a try anyway. Just to look."

Mr. Gamal smiled. "My pleasure," he said. "What can I show you?"

"As I said to my friend here, I've got this vision in my mind. It's a wedding present for a friend. I want it to be old—unusual. It can be very small."

Christina gave him one of her dazzling smiles, begging his forgiveness for her foolish hopes of affording anything in his obviously expensive store, and taking up his time.

Christina spotted a big sculpture of the head of a woman

mounted on a plinth, the marble scuffed with age, and with what looked like a chipped diadem. "That!" she said. "That's lovely. For example, how much would that be?"

Mr. Gamal peered at a label on it. It had a number written in calligraphy. He went to a ledger on the counter and paged through it, showing not the slightest irritation at his time being taken up by a person who probably couldn't afford anything in his shop. He'd succumbed to Christina's vitality and self-confidence and good looks, Federico thought. People always did.

"Isn't it great?" she said to Federico. "Doesn't it look sort of like Emily?"

The head was staring out, sightless with an unearthly serenity. The face was oval, the lips bow shaped.

"I'm not sure," Federico said.

"See how the nose turns up just a bit at the tip? Like Emily's. No?"

"Possibly," he said.

"But how much is it?" Christina asked Mr. Gamal.

He didn't answer, but instead said, "She's probably a Queen or a goddess. It's late Hellenistic, about the first century BC." The prince was familiar with this style of salesmanship: whet the appetite of the potential purchaser first, before you disclose the price.

"The price," said Mr. Gamal, "is two hundred thousand." He left out "dollars."

"Heavens," said Christina. "But she's worth it, of course," she added quickly, politely. She sighed. "I see this isn't possible. Maybe there's something smaller, more realistic in price for me?"

Mr. Gamal proceeded to take various objects from the cabinets for their perusal, unlocking and relocking the doors as he removed and replaced them, no doubt in case his attention was diverted by the strangers and they tried to steal his treasures. He showed them a ring with a carnelian intaglio stone, first to third century, four thousand dollars; a necklace of green glass beads with gold links. Two thousand.

"Can I touch it?" Christina asked.

"*Bien sûr*," Mr. Gamal replied.

Christina held it around her neck and studied herself in the mirror on the wall.

Federico, watching her, said quietly, "Perhaps I should buy *you* a present."

She laughed. "You know you couldn't afford it! Don't tease me." She smiled contemptuously. "Are you guilty about something?"

Federico's mouth tightened.

Mr. Gamal showed them a small clay statuette of a dancing figure, also Roman, third century, $4,500. From a drawer he removed a big, battered nail.

"What's that?" Federico asked.

"It's a crucifixion nail," Mr. Gamal said.

"How awful!" Christina cried. "Not from—?"

"Of course not," Mr. Gamal said. "But it dates from the first century. It was a common form of execution then."

Christina twisted around to Federico. "This is hopeless." Then, back to Mr. Gamal. "I'm so sorry we've taken your time. But we've learned a lot."

Mr. Gamal said, "I do have one idea . . ." He unlocked a drawer, produced a red leather box, and opened it. Embedded in a dark blue satin mold was a small glass vase, about eight inches tall. It was spindle shaped, with a thin neck. The glass was clouded by age, but it was shot through with a green and gold light.

"It's dear!" Christina cried. "But how much is it?"

Mr. Gamal went to his ledger, sifted through the pages. "This is only five hundred."

"Still too much," she said. "I don't know what I was thinking. What is it?"

"It's what they call an '*unguentarium*,' or a '*lachrymatory*,'" he said. "It's Roman, found in Egypt. From the second century."

"What's an . . . '*unguentarium*'?" she asked.

"They think it may have been used to hold oil, or perfume.

They've found them in tombs so the deceased would have them in the Afterlife."

"And that other word you said?"

"Some scholars think that they were used at funerals to catch the tears of mourners. There's a dispute about it. This one is bigger than usual so it might have had a commercial use."

Federico remained silent behind her. Christina said, "She could put it on her dressing table and look at it and always be reminded of me."

"It's very inexpensive for what it is," said Mr. Gamal. "I got it at a much lower price than usual."

"Yes? Why?"

"It has a flaw."

"A flaw?" She studied it. "I don't see it."

"Then, it doesn't matter, I think, at this price. If you can't see it."

"*Guarda qui*," she said to Federico, switching to Italian to conceal the discussion from Mr. Gamal. "*C'è un difetto*."

Federico took the object from her and examined it. Quickly, he handed it back to the man. "*Aspetterò fuori*," he said, coldly.

Then he turned abruptly and left the gallery. Christina hurried after him. "*Che cosa c'è?*"

"*Fa quello che vuoi*," he said angrily. Mr. Gamal had come out and was watching them. Federico went toward the glass door and the woman sitting at the desk, seeing his haste, buzzed him out.

Christina looked after him, then back at Mr. Gamal. "Pardon us. My friend has a lot on his mind at the moment. Even with your generous price, I can't do it."

Down on the sidewalk, Federico lit a cigarette and began pacing back and forth.

"What's the matter?" she asked.

"The thing is useless. There's a crack in it."

"He said that's why it's so cheap."

"It's too expensive as it is."

"But it's so sweet."

"No, it isn't."

"You think the fact it has a crack means bad luck?"

"Yes. At a time like this?"

"Are you scared the crack could mean something?" She laughed mockingly, a laugh he'd heard before, when he, terrified, had asked her if she might be pregnant with his child. "That it would mean unhappiness in your marriage?" she said. "I can't believe you'd believe that!"

He started to walk away. "I've had enough," he said.

"You're angry," she said.

She caught up with him and took his arm. He wrenched it away.

"Don't worry, I'm not going to touch you," she said, and released it.

He stopped, tormented. "One day," he said, "I will buy you a present."

"One day?" she said.

"Yes," he said. "I'll buy you a present when you get married."

"You want me to get married?"

"Yes."

"So, you won't be guilty?" she asked.

And with that, he left her there.

# Part Two

# A Wedding and an Island

# Seven

He sleepwalked through the ceremony in a daze, as if it had nothing to do with him. There was whiteness everywhere, a mist of white, the tent, the flowers, Emily's white dress, and so true to her nature, her simple crown of daisies. He hardly heard the minister's words, only enough to say, when he asked if Federico would take Emily as his wife, "I do," and then to reach over and kiss her. All the while, he was aware of Christina on the edge of the crowd of guests intently observing the proceedings, not mingling with them but visible to him because of her height. He tried not to look at her, to be attentive only to his bride.

After the ceremony, there was the reception and the toasts. Emily stood up and prepared to give hers, her cheeks flushed, and with an expression of great seriousness. He knew she'd spent much time sequestered with all her books, searching for the right words. She lifted her glass to him. "Federico, my love for you is '*an ever fixed mark, / that looks on tempests and is never shaken.*' " There were cheers and applause from everyone at the intelligence and articulateness of the small, angelic-looking woman's words.

Federico's own toast was short, rather formal. "To Emily. I can say no more than that I'm honored that you have chosen me. *Ti voglio bene*." But as he said those words that he believed, he knew that across the tent Christina was watching him with her steady gaze. He knew, as he said them, that they would cut into her. He wanted to punish her for coming, to affirm that it really was all over. But Christina would never cry because she almost never did. Except once.

During the evening on the dance floor, they passed close to one another, he holding his new wife in his arms, and Christina with some man he didn't recognize. She rested her pale green eyes on him, expressionless, but penetrating in their focus. He looked away, and within her line of vision, he deliberately nestled his lips into Emily's neck, knowing that this would pierce her heart, and meaning to, to make her keep away.

Immediately after the wedding, Christina disappeared, to Boston, Emily told him, to visit her grandmother. And for a long time, he didn't see her again.

They spent their honeymoon in Rome. As soon as they'd checked into their suite at the Hassler, they went to see his mother and Aunt Celeste. They arrived unexpectedly and what they found dismayed him. His mother had lost weight, and Aunt Celeste was very withdrawn. The apartment was in disarray, dirty dishes lying around, a stale smell in the air, and the *badante,* who was supposed to be caring for them, was just sitting there knitting.

"This has got to end," he muttered to Emily. He introduced her to his mother and Aunt Celeste and she kissed each on the forehead. "*Sei troppo magra!*" Federico told his mother. She only beamed at him, alight at seeing him.

"Are you getting enough to eat?" he asked Aunt Celeste.

Aunt Celeste grunted and glanced malevolently at the *badante*.

"I'm not happy with your care for them," he told the woman.

"I do everything!" she said indignantly. "Your aunt, she is very difficult, very demanding."

"I'm going to clean this place up," he said. He searched for a broom and began to sweep the floor. Emily joined him, working hard alongside him, wiping off the kitchen counter and washing the dirty dishes. He hadn't known that Emily even knew how to clean. Perhaps she'd learned it during her time living in a college dorm.

Afterward, he went out to the corner store and bought food. With Emily's help, he made a simple, filling meal of pasta for them.

On their way back to the hotel, he said, "How can I leave them like this? They've got to be in a better place."

"We'll find a place," she said. "You are so sweet with your mother. It shows me who you really are."

"Yes," he said absently, trying to think through what to do. "I don't know."

In the morning he phoned Accardi and asked his help in finding a place for the two women. The government-funded places were awful, Accardi said. They were filthy and the residents were neglected, and there were scandals about them in the newspapers all the time. The private places were extraordinarily expensive.

Emily, sitting in the living room of the suite, overheard him, and when he hung up, asked what he'd been talking about. When he told her, she said, "Let us help with the money."

"But how can I let you do that?"

"We won't know the difference," she said calmly, acknowledging, absently, their enormous wealth. "I'll speak to Dad. They're part of our family now."

She called her father in New York and explained the situation to him. He asked to speak to Federico.

"You can't let them go on like this," Henry said to Federico over the phone. "You need to find a good place for them, and we'll take care of it."

"You are very generous," Federico said. "But I feel we can't accept it."

"Then, call it 'a loan' if you want," Henry replied. Federico, and surely Henry, knew the "loan" would never, and could never, be repaid.

He had no choice but to take their money. Within days, Accardi found a *casa di riposo* for the two women, a luxurious place, modern and clean, with prints of birds and flowers on the walls, a library, a television room, excellent cuisine, and courteous attendants bustling about attending to the residents' every need.

His mother would probably not even notice the food by now, but the staff would make sure she ate. They would be safe here. Federico signed a *procura* giving Accardi power of attorney over their affairs, and Henry arranged for The Office to make payments directly to it.

After their honeymoon, they moved into their new house and Federico went back to work at the bank, waiting for Ricardo to summon him to a meeting with a client. Their words floated past him . . . "international reference points for advanced production capacities with automation processes . . . generic improvement of microorganisms, fermentation extractions . . ." and a dull headache filled his skull.

In the intervals between meetings, he sat in his office staring at the rooftops, or tried to teach himself about the stock market, but he'd never know enough to be of real use to Ricardo. He watched Italian soccer on his computer, quickly switching to another screen when the secretary came in. Sometimes, he'd fall asleep, then force himself awake and there would be a bitter taste in his mouth.

At night, he came home, empty and irritable. He tried not to complain to Emily, but she'd ask him what the matter was, and the complaints would slip out.

"Why don't you just quit?" she said.

"How can I do that? Don't be ridiculous." He was a husband and his job was to provide, at least partially. He couldn't be a complete parasite on her family.

"But you don't need the money," she said.

"Of course, I need the money." That was a lie. He used his earnings for his clothes, for his gym membership, for little luxuries for himself, and as a matter of principle, gifts for Emily. His earnings were his small independence from them.

"I can't just live off *you*," he said irritably. He already was. Every month, The Office automatically put money into their joint bank account, and no one paid any attention to what he spent out of it.

Almost every night, he and Emily had dinner with Henry. It was as if Henry lived with them. Federico was daunted by Henry, by his self-confidence. He was always interesting, with his intricate plans for his museum, his vast knowledge of art, his reminiscences of his career as a lawyer, the awful situations of his clients, and his efforts to help them. Sometimes he'd succeed, he said, though he didn't want praise because he said these people were only a few among many who desperately needed help.

Federico imagined Henry, tall, blond-haired, sitting across his desk from those smaller, darker, frightened people, reassuring them in their desperation to obtain green cards, bringing suits against their landlords to force them to provide heat in winter. They probably didn't fathom who he was, though they recognized he belonged somewhere else. They were at their rope's end, time was running out, and they were exhausted and panicked and probably didn't ask themselves what this man was really about. When local judges beheld this unusual lawyer standing before them, who obviously had a superior social position and a legal education from some prestigious law school, it often helped him win his case. Though, Henry said, sometimes the municipal judges resented him because of how different he was from the lot of them. They were political appointees and often corrupt.

Around Henry, Federico was literally tongue-tied. And of course, when he and Emily were with him, the couple couldn't enjoy the easy intimacy of marriage, the back-and-forth they had when they were alone together.

Though Henry lived only three blocks away, Emily was on the

phone with him at least once a day. When Federico came home from the bank and heard her laughing and talking in the other room, he knew it was her father on the other end of the line. He was surprised to find himself irritated. Perhaps she got a reassurance and strength from her father, that he, Federico, couldn't give her. Henry seemed utterly unconscious of the fact that perhaps now that his daughter was married they should separate themselves from one another, and Emily should transfer her dependence to her husband. In the end perhaps, Federico thought, he wasn't strong enough, he wasn't dependable enough.

One evening, Federico arrived at the house and went to pour himself his usual Scotch. Dinner would be soon, and then he could lose himself in television, and go to bed.

The depression weighed on him.

Tonight, they were alone, for once without Henry. The housekeeper, Mrs. Evans, served the meal and left. He felt Emily watching him.

Out of nowhere, she said, "Federico, it's just time."

He looked up from his food. "Time?"

"You've got to quit. We can't go on like this. You're miserable. I can't stand it anymore."

His thoughts were churning; he didn't answer her. He sighed. But this time he didn't protest.

The next day he did it. When he called her from the office to give her the news, she was jubilant. "I'm so relieved! You did the right thing. Now we can be together all the time."

For Emily, there was nothing strange about the situation. In her world, there were many husbands who didn't have real jobs. They travelled around to polo matches, yachting races, and charity events that were mostly an excuse to have parties. They played squash. The older men spent their days in front of their computers watching over their investments and phoning instructions to their brokers. But to Federico many of the men seemed like idiots.

Nonetheless, a weight had been lifted from his shoulders. He was free. His days were his own, to discover what he really wanted to do with his life. He could go to the gym more often. Through a friend, he'd gotten to know some other Italian expats, and they formed an impromptu band. They'd designated Luca, whose day job was as a translator at the UN, as the lead singer. They hoped to make a video, maybe get some music industry person, intrigued by American-style music sung by Italians with American accents, to come and hear them. Federico suggested they get together at least once a week to rehearse, but unlike him, they all had full-time jobs.

Early on, Emily, in particular, had wanted a baby, and soon she was pregnant. The pregnancy rescued him from his life of uselessness. There were doctor's visits, the blurry pictures of their daughter on the sonograms (they knew pretty early it was a girl), the childbirth classes, the wonder of this bundle of cells ever dividing and growing inside her, soon visible in the bump on her stomach, that he'd actually helped create. It felt like the first substantial, grown-up thing he'd ever done: He was capable of being a father! And they both had the luxury of devoting themselves full-time to the pregnancy. As an expectant father without a job, he was able to go with her to all her doctor visits and childbirth classes.

After her water broke, her labor went on for fifteen hours and was very difficult. She wanted Federico by her side constantly to hold her hand and wipe her brow. Only *he* had the ability to soothe her and reassure her. But oh, seeing the tiny red being emerge, her hair matted to her scalp, and, holding her swaddled in his arms for the first time and gazing into her dark eyes. Emily agreed to name her "Isabella," after his mother.

Two days later, there was the excitement of the homecoming: watching over the bassinet together to be sure she was still breathing, waking up in the night to make sure she was still alive. His task was to change her and bring her to Emily so that she could breastfeed. Emily was nervous about breastfeeding at first, anxious that Isabella wasn't getting enough, or that she'd develop an awful breast infection as one of her friends had. But after a day or so, her milk began to flow, the breastfeeding occurred perfectly naturally, and it was easy to carry the baby everywhere and feed her whenever she wanted it.

Henry arrived with a gift, carefully wrapped. It was a small, very old painting of a Madonna and child, in an ornate gold frame, by an unknown Flemish artist, and clearly very valuable, a tribute to his daughter's new motherhood. The Madonna had long, curly yellow hair and a veil transparent in the light of the candle behind her, her big, confident child at her breast. Her skin was like ivory, her cheeks rosy. She bore a resemblance to Emily, Federico thought. Perhaps Henry had deliberately chosen it because of that.

Emily refused to have a nanny. Anyway, Federico was always there. They never went anywhere without Isabella in her Baby Wrap, which resembled a shawl in which African women carried their infants, and which Emily had bought because it was said to bring the baby even closer to the mother. They rarely went out at night because Emily didn't trust anyone to babysit. Federico felt indispensable. He had an important and vital task as husband and father. At first, he was the only person that Emily would let hold the baby, except for Henry. Mrs. Evans, the housekeeper, who came from the island of St. Vincent in the Caribbean and had raised two sons who were now adults, stayed in the background, gently offering advice when asked. Emily missed her own mother so much, she said. It wasn't fair that she wasn't there to see her newborn granddaughter, and to teach her how to be a mother. Nearly every day when Federico came back from some errand, Henry was at the house, a love-struck grandfather, watching over mother and child.

The baby grew and began to smile and roll over. Emily weaned her and nervously agreed to allow Mrs. Evans to babysit at night. Their outings lasted only a couple of hours, and they'd rush home and up to the nursery to check on Isabella.

Federico watched with relief as his daughter grew, began to put on weight, and developed an appealing plumpness, which they were glad of because it would guard her from illness. Like any devoted father, he registered her daily progress and her every response to the world.

That first summer the whole family went out to the island. Emily hired an au pair, "so you and I can have some time together," she said.

# Eight

Woodford Island was one of the largest islands in the country still in private hands. It was six miles long, just under four miles off the mainland, and owned by the family through a series of interlocking trusts. "It's a bit like what we in the United States call a 'time share,'" Henry explained to Federico. For most of the extended family, the place was too remote, and they had their own summer houses, so its upkeep fell mainly to Henry, who was devoted to the place. The taxes on it were too high even for the Woodfords, so the family had obtained a conservation easement from the state, which significantly reduced the tax burden.

No one but the family and their guests and the workers was allowed there. The Audubon Society did an annual bird count in December, and every year Henry held a benefit tour for the local Historical Society. The caretaker, Devlin, and his crew patrolled year-round with shotguns to keep trespassers away. Every now and then some boater succeeded in landing on the island and the Marine Patrol was called in to arrest them.

The island had a private airstrip, but Henry and Emily preferred arriving by boat, the Woodford pennant (a brown "W" on gold) flying silkily in the wind, the sea spray cooling them after the heat of the mainland, anticipating the romance of the place. The ride was hypnotic, the expectation of their arrival temporarily wiping away all troubles and gradually releasing them from the tensions of city life and preparing them for the peace to come. Watching ahead at the horizon, they were mostly silent as the vague blue form of the island slowly began to take shape. As they drew nearer, they could see the outline of the cliffs and the windmill on the headland, and at last, the big wooden sign anchored in the sand warning in red letters, NO TRESPASSING RESTRICTED AREA VIOLATORS WILL BE PROSECUTED.

The boat bumped against the dock and the engine sputtered to a stop, followed by a moment of utter quiet. On the shore, the Jeeps, which also had the "W" logo on the side, were waiting to take them up to the house.

They disembarked and paused, taking it all in. During the wedding, Federico had been so busy greeting all the guests, most of them strangers, and reassuring Emily who was nervous that something might go wrong, and with his own nervousness about the marriage, that he had hardly noticed the island's magnificence. It was a private paradise, transparent waters swirling onto the pristine shore, primeval forests of first-growth white oak and beech, ponds with graceful white egrets skimming along the surface, osprey nests dotting the grounds.

"This is one of the few locations left on the eastern seaboard where they make their nests close to the ground," Henry had proudly told Federico. "There are no natural predators."

Flocks of white-tailed deer grazed heedlessly. "Every fall Devlin and his guys cull the herd, or they die of starvation. Be careful," Henry warned, "they spread Lyme disease." There were cans of insect repellent so guests could spray themselves.

On a rise in the middle of the island stood a red brick Georgian manor house, with views of the Atlantic Ocean on one side and the Bay on the other. Though the house looked old it was actually quite new. The previous manor had burned down in the 1950s—when a drunken guest had fallen asleep with a lit cigarette in his hand; a new house resembling the old one had been built. It could accommodate an endless number of guests.

The house was high-ceilinged and filled with a pale light. There was a curved staircase leading to the upper floor. But Federico thought it an oddly vacant place, perhaps because it was only lived in part of the year, and there was no single presence presiding over it. On the walls hung stiff portraits of various Woodford ancestors, men with watch chains stretched across their vests, and women in ball gowns and ropes of pearls. There'd been an effort to make the place homey through benign neglect, to let the slip-covered couches and chairs grow faded and worn. There were battered family antiques, and in the drawing room was a grand piano, perhaps in hope of family sing-alongs, its wood housing chipped, its keys yellowed like old teeth.

The house was encircled by a flagstone terrace. Steps led down from it to a grassy slope and a path—and then an allée of hornbeam trees leading to a walled garden and a maze and a marble-columned gazebo. Henry called it "Grandma Gracie's folly." It had been built by his grandmother as her private abode and was rather formal for a seaside estate. The plantings were expensive to keep up in the ocean climate, but it was maintained because it was part of the family's history.

There were small frame houses for the workers. In winter, they had the place to themselves until the warm weather came and the various branches of the Woodford family arrived. The Woodfords always said they envied the workers, whom they held in special regard because some of their ancestors had worked for the family and because they were able to live here all year round. The Woodfords themselves never came in winter because the island was so bleak, with freezing winds sweeping in from the sea, the landscape gray and brown, the trees bereft of leaves.

Although life on the island was largely informal, at five o'clock each afternoon everyone showered and washed off the salt from the beach, dressed up a bit, and gathered on the terrace for cocktails, a reunion at the end of the day after their separate pursuits. At dinner, the food was excellent—fresh lobster and fish caught by Devlin, with vegetables from the kitchen garden, which was planted in the spring for the family. Meals were prepared by Devlin's wife, Maureen, who acted as cook and maid during the season.

For Federico, the untouched isolation was unreal. So too, the fact that this family owned it all by themselves. There was a chapel in a clearing in the woods, a small, white frame structure built for the workers when the place was a farm. The chapel had a starkness and simplicity, but was a ruin now, vegetation growing up through the slats in the floor. Once you stepped inside and smelled the old wood, you'd seen the whole thing. Out on the headland was the windmill. It was built in the eighteenth century and was now on the National Register of Historic Places, though this was a private island and no one but the family could visit it. You couldn't go inside. There were wooden beams nailed across the door because the stairs leading to the top had rotted out and it was unsafe to climb them.

Federico knew he should be grateful to be here. Although it was hot now in the summer, it wasn't the intense heat of the Italian Riviera in the season. And of course, there were none of the horrible crowds of Italian beaches, or indeed, of the beaches on the mainland.

Henry adored it here. It was where he had had his few happy childhood moments: summers playing with his cousin, Everett, who was his age, and with the caretaker's children. His father was usually away somewhere, or drying out. Everett's parents were dashing partygoers who also left him in the care of nannies most of the time. By the time the two boys were ten or so, after Henry's mother's suicide, they'd had the island pretty much to themselves, except for the workers and college students hired as tutor-companions for them for the summer.

On the island, Henry was the undeclared king.

Federico noticed that Henry seemed to prefer to be with Isabella, his fat-cheeked granddaughter, to anyone else. He watched her as closely as Federico and Emily did.

"She looks so much like Emily's mother," he said to Federico. "And just like Emily did when she was little. The same blonde hair, the same blue eyes. She does have your same-shaped face." And she was Italian too, thought Federico. She was from *him*, from *his* family.

Federico longed to absorb himself completely in his child, to catch every moment of her progress, to breathe in the warm perfume of her hair, and admire the texture of her perfect, silken skin, to delight in her new recognitions, her willfulness. He couldn't quite believe she'd come from him—at last, something perfect that proved his adulthood. He didn't want the day to end. She was an object of worship adored by them all. She'd kick her little foot up at them, knowing that they'd be delighted to put it in their mouths and give it a bite because they loved her so much they could eat her.

If you put her down, you couldn't look away from her for one moment or she'd swallow anything she found—a pebble, a fragment of sea glass, some poisonous plant. But it was often Grandpa who stepped forward to rescue her, faster than Federico or her mother, and took it away and pacified her when she cried at losing it.

Federico knew Henry didn't mean to be intrusive, but his height, the force and energy of his movements blocked him. And Isabella adored her grandfather. When he appeared, she held out her arms to him, demanding to be picked up. Despite his age and great intellect, he was an endless source of silly games, and happily gave her the non-stop attention she craved. Federico had never before seen a grown man who wasn't the father so attached to a child. He wondered, was it natural for a sixty-two-year-old grandfather to want to spend so much time with a baby? Though Federico had adored his own gentle father, he came from a culture where men, especially grandfathers, didn't spend much time with infants.

With all of them vying for Isabella, there was nothing for the au pair, Justine, to do. Justine was eighteen, a student at Wesleyan. She soon gave up trying to help with Isabella and spent her days on the beach, reading, or trying to call her boyfriend on her iPhone. The cellular service on the island was terrible. There was no landline or electricity, just generators. The poor girl seemed bored and depressed, and held herself away from everyone, though they were careful to try to make her part of the family at meals and include her in their outings.

Federico tried to forgive Henry for taking over his daughter. He realized the man still carried within himself the pain of his wife's loss, and now there was her likeness in Isabella, and the memory of Emily herself as a baby. The rhythms and warmth and noise of her childhood, when his wife was still alive, given flesh again in the form of this delightful girl. Out of politeness, Federico didn't fight him but stepped back and let Henry take over. He felt obliged to; after all, he'd provided Federico with this grand existence.

But couldn't they see what was happening? Didn't Emily realize it? *Federico* was Isabella's father. Did he have no importance? Now that he'd done his job and helped produce Isabella, he had no function.

Night was one of the few times when he and Emily were alone. They were sitting up in bed reading, the insects playing around the light, he with an Italian soccer magazine and she with her novel.

He put his magazine down and was looking straight ahead, pondering.

"Is everything all right?" she asked. "You seem preoccupied?"

"It's nothing." He could never say anything critical of her father. And it was partly his own fault that he had nothing other than his daughter to occupy himself with.

She sat up in the bed. "I feel there is," she said.

He hesitated, then took a breath. "Well. I must tell you, I feel your dad is taking over Isabella. It's as if *he's* her father, not me."

Emily looked stricken and he immediately regretted saying it.

Reality had been thrust at her and she couldn't ignore it. "Oh dear! I guess I haven't seen it. I feel awful."

"You shouldn't feel awful," he said quickly.

"It's so good to see him so happy."

"We're fortunate," he said.

"Yes, but it's bothering you." She asked slowly, "Do you want me to talk to him?" He could hear her reluctance.

"No. Leave it alone," he replied.

"But . . . I can't bear to think of you unhappy."

"You hadn't noticed?" he asked her.

"Only that he adores her."

"Well, then," he said, grimly. He couldn't believe himself, that he had dared to criticize her father to her.

"I'll speak to him," Emily said.

But he knew how much she didn't want to say anything to her father. It would be agony for her to confront him. Federico knew she understood their relationship was too close. But the tie ran so deep that even knowing that, she couldn't extricate herself.

"I forbid it," Federico said. "Don't say anything."

Emily sighed with relief.

He switched off the light beside the bed, slid down under the covers, rolled over with his back to her. "I so want you to be happy," she said.

"I am," he muttered.

She switched off her own light and snuggled up behind him.

Now when Federico succeeded in getting to Isabella before Henry, he saw Emily smile with approval. See, she was saying, it's going to be all right. It's all working out. We don't have to say anything to him. She wanted to affirm it to Federico, and to herself.

Federico had brought his guitar with him to the island, and when he started to play for Isabella, her attention was riveted on him. She stopped everything as he sang to her the nursery rhymes from his own childhood, verses neither Henry nor Emily could understand. "*Le cose d'ogni giorno raccontano segreti /A chi le sa guardare ed ascoltare* . . ." She moved her body to the music and gazed up at him, transfixed. Then she was his.

When he did manage to take Isabella to the beach by himself, they couldn't stay too long because she'd get sunburned. Then, there were her afternoon naps, and the long period in the house with nothing to do, the only sound the distant waves breaking on the ocean side of the island. Emily quickly seized the time to read, her favorite activity which she'd been largely denied because of the baby.

Emily's reading was completely foreign to Federico. He tried to read a few of her books, but it was a struggle. English wasn't his native tongue, and he wasn't a great reader anyway. The Wi-Fi on the island was spotty and he couldn't watch soccer on his computer. Henry deliberately had no television here. It had to do with going "back to nature," taking a rest from "all the devices," and having a true country experience, a respite from modern life.

Once in a while, Federico took over the kitchen and cooked, watched over by Maureen to be sure he didn't create a disaster. But his meals worked out, and it was a big occasion for everyone, the guests *ooh*ing and *aah*ing over his talent as a chef, charmed that he could make such a delicious meal for so many people. They were not used to it in men. Federico was a symbol of the new, younger generation, where young men cooked. It made them feel "in touch."

There was his morning swim, and Henry invited him to play tennis. Every spring, a company came and restored the court for the family after the depredations of winter, repainting the lines, repairing the net, and so on. Federico had been a reasonably good soccer player at school, but he was no good at tennis and no match for Henry, who was bigger, stronger, and a far superior player. Though Henry was always gracious when he won, Federico soon declined to play with him.

"Darling, you're bored," Emily said. He knew she dreaded that he'd say "yes." She felt guilty for taking him away from his own life and imposing her own on him, and she couldn't extricate herself from it.

"I'm fine," he told her.

But more than ever, in the vacancy and vastness of the island, the realization swept over him that he had no skills, no talents. Nothing was going to come of the band—in fact, they'd "disbanded" for the summer, mainly because Federico had to leave the city for the Woodfords' island. In the evenings, when the family asked, he played the guitar for them and sang, softly, for he felt awkward singing in front of Henry. Henry and Emily said they loved it.

At least, now that he had the luxury of not working, he should try to do something to help other people, to be of some use to those less privileged than him. Perhaps he could volunteer to coach soccer for underprivileged kids as he had in Rome. He'd loved that time, forgetting his own anxieties by helping others. He'd called an acquaintance in New York who coached soccer in a private school and asked if he knew of some way Federico could volunteer. But it was different here in the States, the man explained. Most of the kids' teams had professional coaches, and to get a job he'd have to go through all sorts of rigmarole, work permits, and background checks, and so on.

So, where did this leave *him*? He was a dark-skinned man (or olive-skinned), exotic-looking to people in some circles, who spoke English with an Italian accent and a British inflection, which Emily and other Americans seemed to like.

He had no job, no obligations, other than to his family. By relieving him of the need to make a living, though he'd hated his job at the bank, they'd taken a great chunk out of him. What would he do with his life? He knew few people his age in this predicament. His friends in Italy had gone on to law school or jobs in tech. When he went out at night for drinks with his expat friends, they talked about their jobs, but he had nothing to contribute.

Before him stretched the future, without definition or boundaries. He no longer knew who he was. But then, had he *ever* known? He longed to go somewhere and smoke a joint. But he'd given up weed out of concern for Henry's disapproval.

The arrival of guests provided a distraction, gave him something to do, to help entertain them. Henry's cousin, Everett, arrived with his wife, Fran. Everett was a thin, gentle, wan-looking man with pale, watery blue eyes. Emily called them "aunt" and "uncle," and the two of them happily filled the roles. Uncle Everett, in particular, had always been ready with a comforting word, Emily said, attending her birthday parties and graduations to help make a family for her. Everett seemed never to have had a real job. He was a recovering alcoholic, frail, reserved, but always smiling, hollow-cheeked, his chest almost concave, though he had a pot-belly because of his damaged liver, the result of years of drinking. Emily had told Federico she remembered, as a child, looking up from the garden one night at a second-floor window of the house and witnessing Everett bent over the bathroom sink, vomiting.

Aunt Fran had bleached-blonde hair and careful makeup. She had a gravelly voice and slurred her words, and talking seemed almost an effort. It was known, but not spoken about, that she was still drinking.

Seeing "Uncle Everett" always made her father happy, Emily said. Although he was her father's cousin, he was the facsimile of a sibling for him. Henry took a sentimental pleasure at reminiscing with him about their boyhood summers on the island, a respite from the chaos of life with his father, and his mother, when she was still alive, memories he savored even in middle age. Uncle Everett had been a fellow traveler on their journeys from estate to estate with neglectful parents. It was perhaps proof to her father, Emily thought, that his childhood hadn't been all misery.

In July, Mike and Jean Gavron came. They brought with them a friend, Celia, to stay for a few days. Celia was one of the dealers Jean did business with for Henry's project. Nothing had been said about why Celia had been invited, but it seemed to Federico that everyone must know. Her husband, a prominent financier and a scoundrel, had left her for a younger woman after seventeen years of marriage and two children. Jean had told them that Celia was by herself for the summer for the first time while the children were away at camp, and had asked Henry if she could invite her to the island along with them. "Of course!" he said. Henry loved showing people the island and the house was so big guests could get lost in it.

The woman was pretty and immaculate, in her forties, with smooth, dark hair that fell to her shoulders, her skin tanned and oiled. She had a sweet manner, and a slender figure. Henry was still a youngish man, just sixty-two years old. A widower. Healthy. Rich. Obviously, Jean thought of Henry as a good match. She was a motherly sort and couldn't bear to see someone like him without a woman. Celia didn't need Henry's money, which Jean no doubt figured would be a plus as far as he was concerned.

Celia came to dinner freshly bathed and made-up, clothed in form-fitting pants, the buttons of her blouse opened to her breast. It was clear she was not an immodest woman, but perhaps she'd unbuttoned the blouse because she thought she ought to in order to attract a man. You could see the hurt still lingering in her eyes, Federico thought, the bafflement at what her husband had done. She was shyly eager, hanging politely on to Henry's every word, laughing at his every mild joke, now and then venturing well-conceived remarks about art and the art world. Henry said, "I'm hoping to buy a Thomas Hart Benton. There are a lot of lithographs for sale, but I want an actual painting."

"That's a good idea," Celia ventured. She touched her hair nervously as she spoke; it seemed an effort for her to come forward. "I think I may know of a piece. Benton's wonderful," she said, her voice soft, rushed. "He's not quite as 'hot' right now and the prices are vaguely reasonable. The one I'm thinking of isn't on the market yet, but the owner is interested in selling. He's going through a divorce." She smiled wryly. "I can make some calls."

"That would be great," Henry said. "Let Jean know what you come up with."

Federico saw that the woman hoped. She hoped.

# Part Three

# Henry Nearly Escapes

# Nine

In the late afternoon heat, Henry escaped to the library. It was one of the few cool, shady rooms in the house, lined with glass cases full of disintegrating volumes that no one ever read. The house was at a lull. Isabella had gone down for her nap, and Emily and Federico were in their own room resting. He wanted to sort through his catalogues.

Nothing made him happier than to plan it all here on the island, in this place he loved, and he loved having Jean here to help him. He trusted her to be always honest with him. The range of her knowledge and contacts with dealers was extraordinary. He had her on an annual contract as his art advisor, always on call. She'd never let him buy anything that wasn't of value from the most reliable dealers, never pressured him to buy a piece he wasn't sure of, or imposed her own likes and dislikes on him. She deferred to his own taste, which was, she assured him, very sophisticated, and she tactfully cultivated it. She taught him to see, to recognize good work.

They'd gone together to the European auctions, to Rome, Basel, and Maastricht. All the dealers knew he was rich, and sometimes they tried to overcharge or cheat him. She protected him. Last year at Basel, she had saved him from buying a fake Ellsworth Kelly. Jean's integrity was unassailable, and Mike was well-off; Henry's money wasn't necessary.

Right now, all the art they'd purchased was in storage in an industrial area up in the Bronx, in a huge, highly secure fireproof warehouse, waiting to be transported to West Virginia when the museum was completed.

Henry spread his catalogues out on the old library table. He opened the Sotheby's catalogue and browsed through upcoming contemporary sales. Three Francis Bacons—studies of George Dyer—were up. There was a Jenny Holzer, a Calder gouache, an oil by Elaine de Kooning, an Alex Katz . . .

The library door opened. It was the woman, Celia, fresh from a shower, her dark hair damp and pleasing. "Oh, hi!" she said nervously. "I didn't know you were here."

He knew that she knew he was here, and that she'd had to summon up courage to open the door. He realized this might be the first time she'd approached a man since her husband left her.

She said shyly, "I thought I'd walk to the old chapel. Jean told me about it and said it's great. I'd like to see it."

"Yes," he said. "The old workers' chapel. It's a ruin but we keep it because it's really part of the history of the place."

He wished Jean hadn't invited her. The whole thing unnerved him. She was obviously attractive and intelligent, but it wasn't going to happen. And what was he supposed to do, flirt with her in front of everyone, in front of his daughter? To not respond to her made him feel guilty and rude, and was humiliating for the poor woman.

She didn't move, but stood tentatively in front of him as if she was about to say something.

Henry had long believed his ability to love another woman had been sealed forever by Margaret's death, like a scar from an old burn. He'd met Margaret their freshman year in college. He was a depressed, aimless soul then. She'd introduced herself at a meeting of a campus group that did community organizing called Seeds of Justice. She was small, athletic looking, with a big, friendly smile, her blonde hair boyishly cut, fresh, pretty, and very self-confident. Margaret had said that when she first knew him, he never smiled. She couldn't understand it, she'd said, he was so good-looking.

With her spark and optimism, Margaret challenged him, showed him the way. She recognized the basics of his upbringing—because she too came from an incredibly wealthy family. With sex, with tenderness, with laughter, her matter-of-fact common sense and lack of sympathy for his depression, she roused him from his sorrow. Enough moping! she cried.

By the sheer force of her being, she dragged him away from his memories of that day when he was a nine-year-old in boarding school and the headmaster's secretary summoned him to the headmaster. As the woman led him along the hallway, he'd wondered what he'd done wrong, what his punishment would be? When he entered the headmaster's office, he found his father sitting there waiting, sober for once. His father took him in his arms and told him that his mother had died. To this day, Henry remembered the stink of stale alcohol on his body.

As they rode back to the city, he informed Henry that his mother had hung herself in the bathroom. Then he removed a silver flask from his pocket and offered some whiskey to Henry. His father often offered him a drink as if encouraging him to like alcohol. Henry thought his father wanted to justify his own alcoholism by making his son into an alcoholic too, but he was a child and the alcohol made him sick.

His father had had enough money to stay drunk, and to let other people take care of him, feed him, keep the house clean, and pay the bills and eventually he sent the boy away to boarding school to relieve himself of the tasks of fatherhood and to spare Federico the sight of his mother lying upstairs in bed for days at a time in her sorrow.

The memory of those times stayed with him, of course. He could never completely stop them from returning, even when he was older. Then, he met Margaret who said, "It was horrible, but it's over. You've got a life ahead of you, and you have *me*, and us. I'm here."

He'd confided his dreams to her, his unformed desire to "help people," and she encouraged him to go to law school. Henry was the only person in the family, as far as he knew, who had actually worked for a living. Later, when he became a lawyer, the tragedies he'd suffered gave him an added sympathy for the plight of the poor people he represented, an added urgency to help them.

Along the way, Henry had learned to be reticent and to observe. His wealth gave him power, of course. The people around him were always trying to discern his wishes and opinions. He developed his good-natured, optimistic manner as a kind of shield. He knew his power, and he wanted to live a moral life. Along with the power came the ability to forgive. And he exercised that power, and he did forgive. He began to see his father as "just a poor soul." His alcoholism was "a disease" and his father couldn't help himself.

Above all, Margaret gave him his daughter, a small, fresh-faced person just like her, with her rosy cheeks, and her long nose with the little tip at the end. They tried to have another child. None came, and they'd begun to worry.

Then she got sick, and the doctor said it could be fatal if she got pregnant again.

Why had she not at least had one of the treatable cancers? She'd led a healthy life, she'd never smoked, and she was athletic.

The doctors promised them she wouldn't suffer, just to soften the blow of what was to come. They tried one ghastly treatment after another but, one by one, the cancer destroyed her bodily functions. She begged for more morphine, but they'd only give it to her at intervals so she wouldn't become addicted. Addicted! He'd wanted to kill them, to steal the morphine and inject it into her himself. At the end, she was always cold; she shivered so violently you could feel her bones rattling in her skin. All he could do was climb onto the bed with her and wrap his arms around her fragile body, trying not to break her bones, which had become as brittle as sticks from the illness. He held her close and tried desperately to infuse her with his own life force, the warmth of his own blood. He couldn't save her. Thank God, he had his daughter. The new museum was to be named "The Margaret M. Woodford Memorial Museum."

Since Margaret's death, he'd been with other women, but only for very brief relationships. They'd begun about a year after her death, in response to the need within him, not just for sex, but also simply to be held, for the warmth of someone's arms. The encounters were occasional, almost experiments, to see if it was possible to achieve healing from his loss. They were good, pretty women, but he never called them again. Instead, the next morning, he sent a lavish bouquet of flowers, with a note thanking them for a wonderful evening. He couldn't imagine sharing a life with any of the women, or even being with them for more than a few hours. Of course, he never told Emily about them. He wanted her to think that he remained loyal only to her mother.

Now, here in the library, Jean's friend, Celia, took a step toward him. "Would you like to come with me to the chapel perhaps?" she asked.

He was abashed. He didn't want to embarrass this woman whose eyes were still full of the pain of her husband's desertion.

"That's a very nice offer," he said. "But I've got to go over these catalogues. I think we're going to the sale."

He did rather like her shyness. Again, he felt the force of Jean's well-meaning manipulations. But if he went with her for a walk, and didn't give her what she wanted, he'd be the cause of further hurt to her. Better to cut it off now.

"But you should go yourself," he told her. "You just make a left at the foot of the driveway, it's through the woods. It's a ten-minute walk. It's very nice there."

He saw her blink, her eyelashes flutter. Another defeat. Jean

Gavron's plan hadn't worked. And again, he felt guilty, and he desperately wanted her to go away.

Fortunately, at that moment, he spotted Emily through the window down on the lawn with Isabella. "Would you excuse me?" he said to Celia McKay. "I think my daughter needs me." And, before she had a chance to reply, he rushed out, leaving her there in the library.

# Ten

"EMILY!" HENRY HURRIED UP TO HER AND MUTTERED UNDER HIS breath. "Honey, can you go with me? Let's go down to the maze. I've got to get out of there."

She laughed at him. "What's the matter with you?"

"Can you just get the baby and let's go? I'll tell you later."

She picked up Isabella, who protested. The child was trying to crawl now.

"She's getting heavy," Emily said. Indeed, the baby's cheeks were fat and rosy, and there were creases in the folds of her plump little legs.

Emily followed him down to the walled garden. They crossed the grass to the allée, sheltered by the branches of the hornbeams. "What is it?" she asked.

"That woman."

"What woman?"

"Jean's friend, Celia."

"What's wrong with her?"

"I don't know. She's too much."

"What do you mean? She seems very gentle." She glanced at him. "And pretty, too."

"Yes."

"Are you afraid of her?" She let out another laugh.

"No. Of course not. It's just that—"

Isabella was struggling to get down. Emily lowered her and they paused and watched as she picked at the grass. She found a twig.

"I can't imagine you being afraid of a woman," Emily said teasingly.

He didn't smile. "I suppose not. I think she's been through a lot. But . . . I don't think I'm quite the one for her."

"Maybe it's time you thought about being with someone?"

He said nothing.

"I've deserted you," she said. "Now that I'm a married woman." She'd always had the idea that somehow, she had to protect *him*, her father.

"Please! You didn't desert me. That's silly. You're three blocks away. You got married—as you should. And you and Federico created *her*." He smiled at his granddaughter, who was now examining a leaf.

Yes, he was glad she'd married Federico, even if he wasn't rich. Federico's title didn't impress him particularly, but his daughter deserved to be a "*principessa*." It gave her even more status, an added strength, a weapon against the world. And Federico had turned out to be a very good father to their child. True, he didn't have a job, but Henry didn't care about that. All that mattered was that his daughter loved him, and he her.

He knew that Emily was still too dependent on him. He shouldn't have encouraged her to live with him after college. But he'd wanted the comfort of her presence, and the image of Margaret in her, like her ghost. Still, he knew he'd been selfish and deprived her of knowledge of the world that she needed to protect herself from hurt and harm.

Emily's trust in everyone—family, friends, servants—troubled him. He'd never known her to say an unkind word about anyone. If she didn't learn the reality of things, what would happen when he was dead and gone? She'd be in charge of the money, and she'd have to keep an eye on the operations at The Office. The people who worked there were good, but you never knew, one day the temptation to find a way to steal from the family could overcome them. And the finances were very complicated, the way the trusts worked. If something happened to him, Everett would help her of course—though Everett's brain was softening because of the drink. He'd probably die before Henry because of its effects.

Gazing at his granddaughter, Henry murmured, "The little Princess."

"Isn't it funny?" Emily said. "She's actually, by heredity, a princess."

"And so are you, by marriage," he said.

"You know," she said, "I never say it to anyone. It's ridiculously snobbish. Anyway, we live in a society where princes aren't important."

"Not true. People always react to the title. They can't help it, as if being royalty is some sort of—magical state."

"I suppose. Anyway, she *is* authentically a princess, isn't she?" Emily said.

"That she is."

"But, Dad, what about it? Isn't it time to think about your own future? Federico and I've been discussing it. And I know Jean thinks about it."

"That's clear," he said dryly. He walked on thoughtfully. "There's never been another right one, after your mother," he said.

"I know. But don't you think she'd want you to be happy? Dad, it would make me and Federico happy if you were happy too."

"I am happy."

"I'm worried I've abandoned you," she said.

"Well, don't be worried. I'm fine."

"You're still a young man. You're only sixty-two."

He smiled grimly.

"So, Dad, what *would* be the right sort of woman for you?"

"I don't know!" he said irritably.

"You must have some idea."

"I don't."

"Do you mind my asking you about this?" she asked.

"Maybe."

"After all, I'm your only custodian," she said, with a laugh. "I have to look after your welfare."

"You shouldn't. You've got your own life to lead."

Isabella put a leaf in her mouth and was about to eat it. Henry bent down and snatched it from her. Her face crumpled and she began to protest. He found a pebble and handed it to her to distract her.

He stood up. "I hope Federico's not bored with our quiet life."

"Oh dear, have you noticed that?" she said. "I guess I've seen that too lately. He doesn't complain. Though, sometimes he tells me some wonderful story about growing up in Rome. He's said a couple of times that he doesn't think he can ever really feel at home in New York. But he'd never burden me with it."

Henry picked Isabella up and swung her around and she giggled. They walked on.

"But you didn't answer me," Emily said. "Who'll take care of *you*, Dad?"

" 'Take care of me?' " he echoed.

"When you're old?"

"You think I'm old?"

"No! Of course not."

She studied him a moment, and then, she took a breath. "I got an email the other day from my friend, Christina Verano. You remember her? She's here in the States and she wants to come and visit us." She looked doubtful. "But I'm not sure about it. We've had so many visitors."

"If you want her to come," Henry said, "that's fine. I don't care."

"She was at the wedding." She sounded uncertain.

"Yes, I saw her," he said. "There was such a crowd, I didn't have a chance to talk to everyone. How's she doing?"

"I don't know. We haven't really spent any time together for years. She wrote me out of the blue. I hadn't heard from her for over a year, since the wedding."

"Where's she now?"

"In Boston, visiting her grandmother."

"What's she doing with herself?"

"Still living in Rome, I guess. Trying to get her degree. She lives a very peripatetic existence. She doesn't have any money." Emily caught herself. "What am I saying? That not having money is an unnatural state . . ." She grew quiet. "It *would* be a strange person coming in," she said. "It's so perfect with just us, the family. And Jean and Mike, of course."

"You seem doubtful," Henry said. "If you'd rather not have her come, you can make up an excuse, can't you?"

She didn't counter him.

"If you don't want another person, that's fine," he said.

"You don't mind a stranger?" she asked.

"No. Why should I?"

"I feel bad turning her down. She seems to really want to come," Emily said. "She said she wants to see the island again. She hasn't been here since we were children. And I feel guilty. We've got this lovely place, our own resort. I feel we should share it. She doesn't have anywhere to go except her grandmother's."

"I remember her as a pretty girl," Henry said. "She's tall, right?"

"Yes. I always felt daunted by her," Emily said. "She's really gorgeous. Boys always loved her." She looked thoughtful. "I guess I feel a little threatened by her."

"Why should you feel threatened? You're my beautiful girl."

"Thank you, Dad. She's had a hard time, but she's very strong. She really knows how to get what she wants. When she wanted to go to the school in America to escape her mother, she wrote to Mr. Wrigley—remember, the headmaster at The Falls? Her mom went there. She told him her father had left the family and wasn't supporting them, and she wanted more than anything to attend her mother's alma mater. Mr. Wrigley was so impressed by the letter he gave her an emergency scholarship." She walked on quietly. "I wish I were as strong as she is."

"What is this!" her father cried. "You're as strong as anyone, a very strong little girl."

"Dad, I'm not 'little'! Well . . . only in height."

"Your mother was small too, and she was very strong."

"I know. But apart from Mom's death, I've never really been tested."

"And I hope you never are," he said.

"I suspect she's known a lot of hurt from men," Emily said suddenly.

"Hurt? With whom?"

"When I had a chance to talk to her for a minute at the wedding, she said there'd been a man a little while back, and the relationship had ended, and she was still devastated by it." Emily seemed to be deliberating. "She refused to tell me who it was. She's always been incredibly private. You'd think she'd have someone by now," she said.

"Look, if you don't want her to come, don't invite her. Otherwise, do what you want."

She didn't answer.

Henry crouched down next to Isabella, wiggled his fingers at her and growled, pretending to be a monster, and she laughed delightedly. Because of course, the monster wasn't real.

# Eleven

SHE WAS TO ARRIVE IN THE LATE AFTERNOON. CELIA MCKAY, her hopes failed, was leaving, going back to the mainland and the train. Christina would be coming on the return boat.

Emily told Federico, "I'm going down to the dock in the Jeep with Dad and Isabella to meet her. She'll want to see Isabella right away."

"That's fine," he said. "There's not enough room for everyone. I'll stay here." He didn't want to see her.

When she'd told him that Christina was coming, he'd simply stared at her, unable to speak. Frighteningly, out of the blue, she was back again.

Emily looked hard at him. "Is something wrong? You don't want her here?"

"No. Not at all. It'll be nice to see her again."

"You knew her before, in Rome, right?" she said. "And she was at the wedding."

"Oh yes," he said. "I remember, of course. We met at Jean and Mike's."

When Emily and Isabella and Henry had left for the dock, he went up to the bedroom. It would take awhile; the boat could be a bit late. Nonetheless, he stood at the window, waiting, looking out for it. The bay was calm and blue; two huge white clouds floated in the sky above it. The house was temporarily quiet, with only the distant cry of a bird somewhere; a faint breeze stirred the curtains.

Presently, he heard the purr of the motor, and the Jeep came into view. It drew nearer, making its way up the curved driveway, and pulled to a stop at the front door. He watched as Henry leaped from the driver's seat and walked around to let the others out.

First, he saw her long, tanned leg, the white cloth of her dress pulled up over her knee, and finally, her shroud of long hair hiding her face. Henry helped Emily untangle the car seat and lifted the baby out.

He couldn't go down there. He went over to the bed, lay down and buried his head in the pillow. From below came the sound of their voices and laughter.

The bedroom door burst open. "There you are," Emily said. "I didn't know where you were. Come say hello." She frowned. "You okay? You don't usually nap." She sat down on the edge of the bed and stroked his forehead and kissed it.

He pretended she'd woken him up. "I'm fine. It was the swim this morning."

"Don't you want to come and say hello?" she asked. "We're having drinks on the terrace so Christina can see the sunset."

Wearily, he raised himself. There could be no more delay. He showered and put on a clean shirt and pants.

He descended the stairs. What was she doing? Why had she asked to come? Maybe his anger would purge him. Why didn't Jean stop her?

# Twelve

"This is my friend Christina," Emily said. Her voice was hesitant. "I think you two met in Rome. She was at the wedding." Christina was sitting in a wicker chair, drink in hand, receding back into it, so he didn't have to see her full body and feel the absoluteness of her presence.

"Of course," he said. He bent forward and briefly brushed her hand with his fingertips.

She glanced at him. "Hi," she said, cheerful, friendly, and then looked away. She was pretending she didn't know him. What was she doing?

He took a seat on the other side of the group next to Henry. He caught Jean looking from him to Christina. Jean would cooperate, he thought. Mike, sitting genially by, was a good-natured man, and he'd take his cue from his wife.

Fortunately, Isabella was on the floor playing with her dollhouse. She was still too young to really understand what a dollhouse was but kept putting the little plastic figure in and out of it. Emily had bought it for her because she was nostalgic for her own dollhouse she'd had when she was little. Federico got down on the floor with her, his back to Christina, and played with her. It was socially acceptable to pay intense attention to one's baby—they were demanding anyway. Federico made the doll go up the stairs in the open side, into the bedroom, onto the bed. "There," he said to Isabella. "She's going to bed. *Guarda, sta per dormire,*" he whispered. "See, she's going sleepy-sleepy . . ." He made a practice of talking to her in Italian in the hope she'd learn to speak *his* language.

Christina's voice wafted over to him. "I can't believe how beautiful she is! She looks just like you, Federico." It was the first time she'd said his name. So, she was aware of him, though he had his back to her. Federico saw Emily look at Christina as if surprised that Christina knew Federico's face so well she could see his daughter's resemblance to him. He thought he saw a question form on her face, but then it disappeared. Of course, everyone was always trying to find a resemblance in a child to a parent.

Through drinks, he was aware of Henry telling Christina about his museum. "It's going along well, thanks to Jean. We're adding a whole new wing, and we're busy shopping for art." Christina was focused entirely on him. "How long do you expect the whole thing to take?" she asked.

"It could be another year. They're starting to dig the foundation for the new wing. They want to at least get it up before the weather changes."

From the floor, Isabella gave a cry. She was tired, ready for bed. Tears were imminent. Emily scooped her up. "Time for bed! Say 'night-night,' honey. Can you wave?" The child made an approximation of a wave. "See, she knows how to wave," Emily said.

Federico got up from the floor. "I'll come with you." Isabella liked both parents to put her down. It was a drawn-out process, both singing the same three lullabies to her while she watched them, thumb in mouth, from her crib. If they hurried and missed a word, she protested—she was precocious, and seemed to know the words, or at least the sounds of them, and they'd have to repeat the whole thing.

When she'd finally gone to sleep, dinner was served: lobster that Devlin had caught in his traps. Christina was seated at the other end of the long table from Federico, next to Henry, still talking animatedly to him. She seemed completely fascinated by him, Federico thought, or she was sucking up to him. But Henry was the most interesting person among them, the only one who really had anything to talk about—his museum, his art, his career as a lawyer. He was handsome and intelligent, and he ruled the place.

She wanted to make him jealous, Federico thought. But how could he dare to be jealous? He tried not to look at her, but when Jean or Mike bent forward in their seats and their bodies hid her, he was annoyed, then relieved that she'd momentarily disappeared.

Thankfully, everyone went to bed early on the island; the pure sea air did that to people. That night, he made love to Emily. He tried to bury himself in her, to not think about Christina in her own bed in the guest wing on the other side of the house.

On the second day, Henry and Christina seemed to find one another again. Henry hoisted Isabella onto his shoulders and suggested he give Christina a tour of the island, and off they went, chatting animatedly, absorbed in each other.

Afterward, Christina recounted excitedly what she'd seen, while Henry looked on smiling, seemingly entranced by her. "The lighthouse and that sweet old chapel. And we saw the egrets. They're so marvelously graceful." She directed her remarks at Jean and Mike and Emily, and hardly looked at Federico.

He'd noticed that at first Emily seemed unusually reserved around Christina. But now Federico saw that Christina was drawing Emily in, taking the lead, remembering their times at school together. Christina spoke of one spring vacation when she stayed with them in Westchester; she was riding Freckles, when something startled him and he bolted. But Christina gripped the saddle and held tight to the reins and let him have his head and gallop until she managed to get him to stop.

Emily, after initially hesitating, got caught up too in the reminiscences. "Freckles was so strong, sometimes even I couldn't control him. You were a really good rider."

Then, Emily said, "Remember those fifth grade dances with St. Theodore's?" They'd called it "St. Testosterone's." The boys used to line up on one side of the gym and the girls on the other. Then, as soon as the headmistress gave the signal, they would charge at each other. "Christina, remember how we used to sneak 'out of bounds' to the chestnut tree at the end of the driveway and smoke?" That was their idea of being bad. Miss Clayborne, the tennis teacher, caught them once, but she didn't report them. She just said, "You guys better be careful next time." Miss Clayborne was probably a lesbian, Emily and Christina agreed, but it wasn't okay to be "out" then.

Federico declared that he was going on a hike to explore the island. It was a big enough place that he hadn't even been everywhere on it. Nobody seemed to mind that he was leaving.

He headed inland—he'd be less likely to run into anyone there. He came to a meadow. It was hot and dry; the grass was uncut. There was a pond in the middle and Federico made his way across to it, the high grass cutting into his skin. The pond was surrounded by reeds and wet, gray sand, and he found a rock where he could perch. On the far side, there was a flock of egrets and he sat in the stillness watching them. A slender, white bird was poised at the edge of the water and looking down at something. In a sudden motion, it speared the water with its orange beak and came up again with the silvery flash of a fish in its mouth. It swallowed it and then took flight, gliding in a perfect straight line parallel to the water, its wings beating rhythmically, trailing its black legs behind itself.

Federico knew that he was lucky to be here, in this primeval place, to see these magnificent birds so otherworldly in their grace, in a place no strangers were allowed to come and spoil. He should be filled with wonder and gratitude. But he wasn't. At least he'd made it through the second, full day of her visit.

On the morning of the third day, he decided to go for a swim. The beach roses had come into bloom a vivid pink, and the succulents were full and rich. From up on the dunes, he spotted a solitary figure standing at the waterline looking out at the bay. It was Christina, assessing the water. She was wearing a bikini. Her skin was golden, her limbs long and slender. There was a line of pale skin just above her waist where her bikini had slipped down. He could see the dimples at the base of her spine, just above her buttocks, her *fossette di Venere*, her Venus dimples.

He wanted to go down there, to pull her into the shelter of the dunes and down onto the sand with him and make love to her. But a voice within him warned—it would be fatal.

Christina stepped into the water and waded in until she was waist deep, then plunged into the indolent blue-green waves. Federico stayed out of sight, watching her graceful, confident crawl. But—she shouldn't be swimming here by herself. Even here, in these calm, clear waters, it could be treacherous; there could be an unseen riptide, or some harmful undersea creature. What if she were to drown? There flashed in his mind the thought that this would be the end of his struggle, the torture of her presence.

He felt the temptation to go in after her drop away; it was almost physically painful. She would go farther out, she would swim far, he knew. She was brave, bless her. If he were a religious man, which he wasn't, he'd pray for her.

He went back to the house, and up to the bedroom. The shades were drawn in the afternoon heat. He had to sleep.

# Thirteen

HE WAS CONSTANTLY AWARE OF HER PRESENCE, AS A SHAPE, BUT without features. He was only vaguely conscious of the undertone of the chatter around him. If he let himself look at her, he wouldn't be able to take his eyes off her. Emily would notice, or Jean, whom he sensed lurking primed and electric with worry. When he was compelled to say something to Christina, he spoke only briefly, in bland, empty tones.

In those moments when he couldn't help it and found himself looking directly at her, he quickly averted his eyes, frightened that she'd look back at him and it would acknowledge to everyone their shared past. Isabella fussing on the floor and wanting to be picked up forced him to come awake and pay attention to *her*.

Emily seemed not to have detected that her husband and her friend were avoiding one another. But when she saw her father and Christina together, she smiled approvingly.

Christina, so dazzling, so voluble and charming, held everyone's attention. She was putting on a performance, he thought, calling on all her resources. He wondered why Emily hadn't asked him again why he'd never gone out with her in Rome. Perhaps she really did believe him when he implied that he hardly knew her. Anyway, if she had any worry about it, the main thing was that her father and Christina now seemed to be enjoying one another so much.

Jean and Mike finally departed. That pushed the four of them, Henry, Emily, himself, and Christina, closer together and left him on edge. Jean's warning presence, the fact that she and Mike were the only other people who knew about them, made it harder for him to keep away from her.

He noticed Christina playing with Isabella more and more. She was always with Henry and the baby and Emily, exclaiming delightedly about the child's every move. Was this some way of getting closer to him, pretending *she* was the mother of his child? She'd wanted his baby. He'd deprived her of it, he'd taken up her time, he'd let her squander herself with him.

Isabella seemed to have developed an ear infection. She was rubbing her ear; her fever shot up to a hundred and one. She was red and sweaty, crying and moaning, "Ma-a-a . . ." This wasn't her first ear infection, but Emily, a first-time mother, was always frantic when she got even a little cold. Her hysteria was worse because they were so far away from doctors out here on the island. "We've got to get her to the doctor!" she insisted. "But we don't know anybody on the mainland."

They consulted Devlin, who'd grown up in the town on the mainland. He knew a pediatrician, he said. His mother had taken the five of them there when they were children. The doctor had cared for all of them through their childhood illnesses. Devlin swore he was a good man. But Federico and Emily were used to New York doctors. Someone from out here couldn't be the best. She asked Federico, "Do you think he'd be okay?"

"I think," Federico said, "that the man can probably deal with an ear infection. And if he doesn't cure it, we'll fly back to New York."

"But if she has an ear infection, we can't fly!"

"Why don't you just let him look at her?" Federico suggested.

"You're just her father!" Emily said accusingly.

"That I am," he said firmly. "She is my child."

She realized she'd insulted him. "I'm sorry."

They ordered the boat and were rushing to pack up Isabella's diaper bag, when Christina asked, "Could I go with you to help? I'd like to learn more about babies." Still, she wanted a child, Federico thought.

"I was going," said Federico. Devlin was taking them in the fast boat which only seated four.

"Is that all right?" Emily asked him.

"Fine," he said. Even if there had been room in the boat, he couldn't have borne being in close quarters with Christina. She'd be away from the island, at least for a time. A relief.

"Your father and I will stay here together and wait," Federico said.

"Okay," Emily agreed.

Later in the afternoon, when they all came back, Isabella, having gotten her first drops of Amoxicillin, was already better and laughing and smiling. Federico took her in his arms and kissed her, reassured.

Then, in an awful way, he was saved again. A call came on his cell phone. "*Federico, sono Accardi . . .* " Through the static and the dropped signal, Federico heard the *avvocato* on the other end. Maddeningly, his voice kept going in and out and disappearing. He hated this fucking island! He stepped outside into the garden to get better reception and heard, sporadically, Accardi's words coming across the ocean. "*Tua madre*," Accardi said. Then, "*un infarto*."

Again, the signal faded. "*É un condizione grave . . .* " he yelled.

"*Vengo subito*!" Federico shouted, praying Accardi would hear him.

He gave up trying to talk to him, and stepped back into the drawing room where Emily, who'd heard him shouting into the phone, had come running to see what the matter was.

"Mama," he told her. "They think she's had a heart attack. I couldn't hear a damn thing." He paced around the room. "I've got to go right away."

"Of course, darling. I'll come with you."

"What about the baby?"

"We'll take her." Then, she touched her forehead and looked doubtful. "I don't know. How will she do on the plane ride, running around Rome in the heat? . . . "

"I can go without you," he said.

"No! No! I won't let you do that."

"I don't even know if she's conscious." He looked apprehensively about the room as if somehow help would be there. "How can I book a flight?" he said to no one. "There's no fucking connection!" He was not only desperate about his mother, but now all his pent-up anger at this place was emerging.

Henry entered carrying Isabella, followed by Christina. In Henry's presence, Federico stopped himself from saying "fuck" again.

The crisis was discussed. As the others talked, Federico resumed walking up and down, hardly hearing them. "All I want to do is go," he said.

"We're going to figure it out right now," Emily said.

"Leave Isabella here with us," Henry said. "We'd like that, wouldn't we, Christina?"

Emily stopped, startled, as if momentarily diverted from the crisis by her father's "we."

"That would be wonderful!" Christina said.

"But Justine's gone," said Emily—the girl had departed the island to prepare for the new semester at Wesleyan. "I've never left Isabella!"

Christina said calmly, "Of course you should both go. I think she's sort of used to me now."

"I guess we could have Devlin's mother Nora come in," Emily said. "She's a very experienced mother."

"And she's got me," Henry said. He smiled at Christina. "I think we'll manage together won't we, Christina?"

Henry wanted this. Federico felt his body emptying out. It would be like a play marriage for them.

"Of course!" Christina said. "How could we go wrong?"

Henry told Federico, "I'll try and reach The Office. They can always get a good flight."

It was arranged. Devlin ferried Federico and Emily over to the mainland, Emily weeping in his arms at leaving the baby.

And Henry and Christina were left behind with Isabella.

# Fourteen

In the beginning, Christina and Henry attended to Isabella during the day, with Mrs. Devlin there if they needed help. Mrs. Devlin brought her granddaughter Molly over from the mainland. The girl was about the same age as Isabella and the two children sat on the floor side by side playing with their toys, until both were settled in for their afternoon naps.

The first evening, they ate by themselves in the dining room opposite one another in the candlelight, at either end of the long table. As always, Christina asked him eager questions about his new museum.

"How many employees will you have?"

"I think we'll need twenty or more there," he told her. "Right now, we've got five. A part-time curator, his assistant, a couple of office staff, and a maintenance man. We'll try and have volunteer docents to help out."

"Have you decided where everything's going to go?"

"For a while I weighed hanging it all thematically. Or, at least, with paintings that relate visually to one another, but Jean's recommended a more traditional, historical approach."

"What artists are you thinking of?" she asked. He was touched by her interest. He'd been concerned he was beginning to bore everyone around him with his plans for the museum.

"A lot of artists painted pictures of workers," he told her. "Thomas Hart Benton, Winslow Homer, Ben Shahn, Rockwell. There are other less well-known artists, Bumpei Usui—he was Japanese American. I saw this amazing painting of his at the Met, *The Furniture Factory*. I don't know what else he did. Rice Pereira—he did some big semi-abstract paintings of machinery. I've got some books in the other room I can show you."

After dinner, they went into the library, and he sifted through the pages commenting on the art while she sat next to him and paid close attention. "It's interesting how the workers are always glorified," he said, "even though the work they did was so brutal. It's ironic that a lot of this stuff was commissioned by wealthy industrialists. Maybe they wanted to make the work seem noble and make themselves feel better about what they made people do."

As he spoke, he was conscious of her nearness, her shoulder momentarily brushing his while she studied the pictures, the fresh fragrance of shampoo radiating from her hair. She seemed totally fascinated listening to him, learning from him. She wore a necklace, not precious stones, just beads of variegated colors, coral, turquoise, with a small, gilded pendant, the type of thing that young women wore nowadays as sort of a tribute to the natural environment. Precious jewels were decidedly out of fashion. Emily never wore them, except for the old family engagement ring Federico had given her, the gold shining and malleable-looking and dented with age, with a pillow-cut diamond in the center. It had belonged to his grandmother, who'd been a *principessa* herself.

When they'd finished browsing through the books, Christina got up and walked into the living room and he followed. She sat down at the old grand piano and lifted the lid. "Do you mind?" she asked.

"Of course not. It's really out of tune. Nobody ever uses it."

She began to play. It was a Chopin étude. Henry sat back in

an easy chair listening. The piano was rusty, but he could tell she could play quite well; the melody and the rhythms of the piece came through. "Very nice," he said. "You can play it without the music."

"Just years of lessons," she said with a self-deprecatory laugh.

"If you'll play for me, I'll have the piano tuner come over from the mainland."

She beamed at him, then looked down again and concentrated on the piece. Despite the bad condition of the instrument, under her hands the notes seemed to ripple across the keyboard.

As she bent over it, her long-stemmed body swayed, and her sun-streaked hair hid her face. Out of the cloud of the past, a different image of her came to him, of the tall, thin, fleeting child visiting Emily in Westchester on school holidays, hurrying up the stairs after her, and out to the stables to go riding, with just a backward glance and a smile at him. He'd hardly seen the two of them all day, they were so busy with their private adventures, able to occupy themselves for hours up in Emily's room.

She finished and sat up. There was a momentary silence. At that point, he perceived her body as if for the first time, the shape of her breasts under the clean white T-shirt she'd changed into for dinner. He realized that he'd never paid attention to her body in this way before. He was taken aback by himself and averted his eyes.

She closed the lid. "I suppose I should get to bed."

He stood up from his chair. "Good night," he said. She smiled softly at him and went out into the hall.

At the foot of the staircase, she paused. Moving toward her, he touched her arms lightly and leaned down to kiss her. Before this, they'd exchanged only brief kisses on the cheek at the end of the day. Now she waited, head poised, as if there might be more, as if she were drawn to him. He could have kissed her on the lips. But he didn't. This was his daughter's friend, a girl his daughter's age. He stepped back. She gave him a wise, enigmatic smile. "Good night," she said. "And thank you."

" 'Thank you?' For what?"

"For a really good evening," she said.

He watched her tall figure climb the stairs. At the top, she made a left to the guest wing, and disappeared. The encounter had left him in turmoil. He felt uncharacteristically helpless.

He walked out through the French doors and onto the terrace. There was a clear view of the sea tonight, the waves gently swelling, stippled with moonlight. The sweet, briny fragrance of the ocean floated up to him on the breeze. For the first time in a long time, hope filled him, and wonder. Above him, the sky was blue-black, the stars flawlessly bright.

When he was little, his mother used to take him out here to look at the stars. For that brief moment, she'd seemed happy and interested in something beyond her own suffering. She would put her arm around him, and he would lean up against her hip and she held him close. "Look for the brightest star in the sky," she'd said. "That's Polaris, the North Star. Now, look up to the right. See those stars that make a kind of cup, and then those other stars that make a handle above it. That's the big dipper . . . "

He'd been impressed that she knew the stars, never having thought of his mother as knowing anything, and was so pleased to have her attention, to be close to her, that he didn't dare speak or move in case it would stop her.

# Fifteen

Another call to the island from Rome, staticky, the signal infuriatingly dropped again. Federico's mother had died. Emily got on the phone and wept for Federico's loss, and because she couldn't bear being away from Isabella any longer. And now they were going to be gone longer, she said.

Henry shouted into the phone, "Couldn't you come home? And let Federico take care of things? Settling his aunt?"

"I can't leave him. He's just devastated, though he knew it was coming. He's so guilty for leaving her to go to New York. He needs me. And it's all so complicated, he's got to clear out the apartment, and they have to process her will, and we've got to make sure Aunt Celeste is okay. I feel I have to stay, at least for a few more days."

"I see," he said. "Anyway, Isabella's flourishing. She's having a grand time with Mrs. Devlin's granddaughter. She just lights up when she sees her."

"Does she miss me?"

He laughed and reassured her. "Well," he said, "not too much."

"No?" She sounded disappointed.

"I'm sure she misses you very much."

"Is she eating okay?" Emily asked.

"She's a little tank. She's getting lots of attention from Christina and me."

"Are things going well with Christina?" Emily said.

The thought flitted through Henry's mind that the question might mean more. That she was pushing them and wanted them to grow close.

"Oh, she seems to be having a good time, too. She really enjoys playing with Isabella. She swims, she reads."

"I hope she's being a good companion for you," Emily said.

"Absolutely!" he said heartily. "A great companion."

"I feel guilty leaving all of you."

"My dear, you needn't burden yourself about that in the slightest," he said, and realized he didn't want her to come home now.

There was a new tension between Henry and Christina. They spoke of course, but fewer words—about the weather, about Isabella. He was moved by her attention to the baby. He wouldn't have expected that from a young woman like her, an unmarried woman.

At dinner, when the distractions of the day had ceased, there was a new constraint, a strange shyness. The piano tuner came over from the mainland and fixed the instrument, and she continued to play for him in the evening, leafing through the old sheet music she found in the bench, searching for a repertoire she knew. The piano notes were purer, delicate. Increasingly, the music moved him, and he was entranced—Chopin, Schubert, performed by this beautiful young woman, here in this, his most beloved of places. As he listened to the silvery notes, he was transported.

After a half hour or so, she would close the lid, rise from the bench and smile. "Thank you," she said, as if she never forgot, every day, that this was all his, that she was here with his permission and grateful to him for making it possible. Then, before he could go after her, she disappeared up the stairs to the floor above.

After two days, the unspoken question, the tension, couldn't continue. She played her pieces, stood up ready to leave, and he said, "Don't go."

She stopped, her back to him, waiting for him to tell her what to do.

"It's a lovely night," he said. "There won't be many left. We should go down to the beach and take a walk."

She shrugged, and said, "It's probably a bit cold down there. I'll get my wrap."

A minute later she was back, her blue Pashmina wound around her shoulders.

Outside, they went down the steps of the terrace, along the allée, past the walled garden, and onto the path down to the beach. As they drew near the water, there was a full wind. Above them, the sky was dense and starless, and yet there was still light.

The tide was coming in, the waves full and loud. Christina's hair blew across her face in the wind. She bent down and removed her sandals, revealing her slender feet, her long toes. He took his shoes and socks off and rolled up his trousers to keep them dry.

They walked in silence along the sand; the wind made it hard to hear one another anyway. It was a soft, warm wind, lovely to feel. As they made their way north on the narrow strip of beach, the kelp and shell fragments wedged between their toes.

The full luck of his life filled Henry, this island that he ruled, at least for a few weeks a year, this untouched place, given to few people on earth, preserved because they'd hung on to it. Often during the summer, he got caught up in the minutiae of daily life, making sure repairs were done during the season while he was here to supervise, new tiles put on the roof where they'd blown off in the winter storms, cracked windowpanes replaced, grocery orders brought over from the mainland. Now, under the dark blue sky, he was in the moment, here with Christina, following behind her slender figure. And he knew that they would go forward.

"Shall we sit?" he suggested. In the shelter of a dune she laid her shawl on the sand and they sat. They were close together, and it seemed so natural; he turned instinctively to her and kissed her. For a moment, he was scared she'd be shocked and run from him.

But she gave back the kiss.

Afterward, in the house, he rested on her bed and watched her long-limbed body move naked about the room, and he saw a vision of youth and perfection. For the next days, it was as if he was a young man again in his eagerness and his enjoyment of her. And always, she seemed to give back his affection; her lovemaking was as passionate as if she hadn't done this for a very long time and something had been released in her. He'd come home at last, and he'd discovered in this young body the peace he'd craved for so long, without having realized how much he craved it.

One night he said to her, "What will Emily say when she finds out?"

She hesitated. "I know. I worry about that too. But . . . somehow I've been feeling that she wanted it."

Yes, he'd felt that too, that Emily somehow wanted it.

But then she said suddenly, "Maybe she just wants me out of the way."

"What on earth do you mean by that?" he said.

"She could kill two birds with one stone."

Her remarked distressed him. "That's a strange thing to say. I don't know what you mean."

"I don't know what I mean either," she said.

He took a breath and lay back on the bed.

"I didn't mean it," she replied. He could tell she didn't want to say anything further, so he didn't press her. But still, it lingered in him—what *had* she meant? She seemed to forget about it, and once again she was her loving, happy self.

Still, the worry came back. "But, why *me*?" he asked her. He felt like a child importuning her. For once, he wasn't the one in control of the world.

"Why not?" she said.

"I'm an old man."

"You're sixty-two," she laughed. "That's hardly old these days."

Was it the money? The suspicion had been bred into him; it was part of his DNA. He'd learned to watch for it when people sought him out. But to ask her that would insult her and destroy this brief time of happiness. Then, again, desire for her flooded through him and drowned out the question.

But he couldn't help himself. "I mean, why *do* you want me?" he asked again.

She paused as if considering the question. "How could I *not* love you?" she said at last. "You're the most intelligent man I've ever known, the kindest, most generous person. I feel like I'm learning from you all the time."

She went on listing his attributes: "You only want to do good. You could have done anything with your life, but you chose to help others. How could I not love that?"

"But," he said, "is it because you just want someone?" He was reduced to being like a boy in love. "You've been with people—" He paused, not wanting to ask about other men. "Other people, I presume. You didn't stay with any one person. And now I'm here and you've made me that person." As he said this, he realized how pathetic the question was coming from him, a grown-up man, who had everything . . . nearly.

He watched her closely for an answer. He noticed her uncertainty and it scared him. Maybe he'd hit on a truth.

"Can't you tell," she said, "by the way I am with you?"

If he wanted to keep her, he had no choice but to accept that.

At night, when they went in to check on Isabella before they went to bed, they stood together over her crib looking down at her. The child lay peacefully on her back. Her hair was stuck to her forehead in the heat.

Christina touched her forehead. "Do you think she's too hot?"

He lay the palm of his hand on her forehead. "I think she's

okay. But I'm going to move the fan closer." He did so and it ruffled her hair.

"You don't want her to get a chill," said Christina.

"You're right," he said, moving the fan back. He said softly to her, "It's almost like she's ours."

She replied gently, "Not 'ours.' She isn't mine. She's yours, though—at least partly. She's Federico's and Emily's."

"Yes," he said. "I sometimes forget that, now that they're away."

"But they'll be coming back," she said.

They were never apart. One morning when they went to the beach, they saw Devlin on his tractor up on the rise and he waved down at them.

"I wonder if he realizes what's going on?" Henry said. "Oh, dear."

"But why would you care?" she asked. "You're an adult. You're not married."

"But you're my daughter's friend."

"If he's a good man, I think he'll be happy for you. Right? You've gone for years being alone."

"That's true," he said. "I hope he won't think it's odd."

The news from Rome dribbled in. Federico, deeply sad, was focused on the funeral. Almost no friends of his mother were alive to attend. She would be buried in the family plot, next to his father, surrounded by the remains of centuries of *principi* and *principesse.* Aunt Celeste would stay in the assisted living facility. They still had to meet with the *avvocato*, Accardi, to discuss the will, though there was hardly any money to dispose of; mostly the problem of getting rid of the apartment, a few antiques, and some jewelry. Emily was desperate to come home, and so was Federico, to be reunited with the baby.

That time was drawing near. Henry and Christina could no longer hide what had happened from Emily. The events of the past days had cascaded together. His relationship with Christina was inevitable now, beyond anyone's disapproval.

He had to capture it, encompass it, give it permanency—in case she changed her mind. The urgency brewed in him until, late one night, he said, "I want you to be my wife."

She let out a laugh.

It hurt him. "How could you laugh?"

"It's just so—oh, I'm not laughing at you, at all." She kissed him. "I mean—I'm just—surprised." But she looked unnerved.

"How could you be surprised after these past few days?" he asked.

"But it's—sudden. It's only been—what? —ten days or so."

"Sudden? I've known you practically your whole life."

She grew serious, she looked worried. "But maybe you don't really know me."

He said gently, "I don't have forever, Christina. I know this is what I want."

She frowned. "I'm just . . ."

"Is it because I'm too old?"

Once more, she said to him, "You're not old." She stroked his hair fondly. "Only a few gray hairs. You've got the body of a young man."

"What is it, then?"

"It's just . . . as I said, we don't really know each other."

"Then, I'd like to know you more."

"What if you don't like what you discover?"

The question cast a darkness over him. What more could he discover about her? What didn't he know about her?

His brow knit and he asked her, "How could there be anything about you I didn't like?"

She seemed to be deliberating on this. At length, she said, "Why can't I just be your mistress?"

"Mistress? How could we do that? I mean . . . Emily . . . I couldn't do that. No. I don't want that." He hesitated. "You can do it for Emily."

She walked away and stood with her back to him.

"I think Emily would be delighted," he said. "She wants me to be happy more than anything else. I think she feels guilty—

ridiculously—for getting married and leaving me. Now that she's safely taken care of, I'm ready to be happy too."

"But I'm her friend. She's used to thinking of me that way. Not as a stepmother."

"If you're worried, let's ask her permission."

She nodded apprehensively.

"I'm going to send an email," he said.

She looked at him without smiling.

"They're what—six hours ahead there?" he said. "They're probably still up."

She nodded.

He took his drink in hand and said, "Let's hope it goes through." He went up to his bedroom, sat down at the desk with his computer and composed the email, telling Emily of his happiness, acknowledging this was all sudden. Still, he pointed out, he had known Christina for many years.

He pressed "Send," sat back, and the message whooshed across the ocean. He confirmed on the "Sent" column that it had gone through.

Outside, there was a high wind, a magical late summer wind, coming through the big, open window. The voile curtains billowed. Henry sipped his drink and waited. A minute later, the computer beeped. A jubilant reply: "Nothing could make us happier! Oh, Dad, congratulations, congratulations! We love you." This was followed by a string of emojis with hearts floating above the heads.

He carried the computer downstairs and showed Christina the message. "Here."

She read it and smiled. Then her smile disappeared.

"What?" he asked. "What more could we want?"

"But she wrote to *you*, not me."

"Oh, c'mon. Obviously, she's speaking to both of us."

She was solemn. "What about Federico?"

"What about him? I'm assuming Emily's speaking for both of them."

"He's part of the family," she said. "I'd like to know that it's all right with him."

"How could he possibly not be delighted for us?"

"I don't know. But I'd like to know that he approves, too."

"Okay, do you want me to write to him?" he said. "I'll be happy to do it if that'll relieve you."

She contemplated this. Then, "I think I should write to him myself," she said. "After all, we'd both be on the same side, in-laws."

He shrugged. "Fine."

She went to her own room, and in solitude wrote a message, then rejoined him.

"Want another drink?" he asked, smiling.

"Yes," she said with relief. "That would be good."

A few minutes later, she went to her room to check the computer. She came back agitated. "He didn't write back."

"We don't know if he even got it."

"I checked 'Sent.' It went out. Emily got yours."

When they went to bed, she lay stiffly on her back beside him, and he didn't reach out for her. He respected her concern. It was only natural. It was a big step for a young woman to agree to marry an older man after such a brief time. He took her hand and she squeezed it, acknowledging him.

As far as he knew, when he did finally fall asleep, she was still awake and alert beside him in the dark, thinking thoughts unknown to him, but which troubled him.

Just as dawn was breaking, she stirred beside him, and he woke. "I'm just going to see if he wrote back," she said. She put on her robe and disappeared to her own room on the other side of the house.

A few moments later, she came back. "He offers us his sincerest congratulations." She wasn't smiling.

"Great!" he cried. "Now there's nothing to be concerned about."

"Do you want to see it?"

"No, it's fine."

She sat down on the edge of the bed, deliberating.

"Was he very happy?" he asked.

She said nothing. Then, "It was just a brief note. Congratulating us and sending us best wishes."

He smiled happily. "What more could we want?"

Slowly, she said, "Nothing."

# Part Four

# A First and Only Marriage

# Sixteen

CHRISTINA INSISTED ON A SMALL WEDDING, BUT A PROPER ONE. It would be her first and only marriage, she said, and she wanted to wear a veil and carry a bouquet, with only the immediate family there: Emily, Federico (who would have to be there of course), Uncle Everett, Aunt Fran, and Jean and Mike, who were sort of like family—but not her mother from Rome. Henry didn't press her on why she didn't want her mother. She said they'd see her soon anyway.

Before the ceremony, Henry said nervously, "You know, we have a sort of tradition. I apologize, but we always ask those marrying into the family to sign a prenuptial agreement. I hate to ask you. It's just our way of doing things . . ."

"It seems like a strange thing to do when you love someone," she said.

"I know. But really, it's worked well for everyone." He looked anxiously at her. "Of course, you should get your own lawyer to represent you. That's the way it's usually done. I'll pay for one if you can't afford it, of course, but he'll be there to protect your interests."

"I don't need a lawyer," she replied. "Whatever you give me is more than enough."

"Are you sure? It would make me easier to know you were properly represented. You really should think about it."

"No," she said again. "I can't imagine it. I feel safe." She took his hand and looked up at him. "I know our marriage will never end."

He kissed her forehead. "Well, think it over. There's still time."

She did think about it. To have a lawyer would seem greedy on her part, as if she didn't really love him and only cared about his money. Anyway, there seemed to be no choice.

After she'd agreed to marry him, she'd taken a deep breath and dared to ask him about the so-called "Woodford fortune." How much was it, actually? What did it mean? After all, she was going to be his wife. It seemed reasonable that she know. She'd framed the question as "the Woodford fortune," to make it seem less personal, more businesslike, acknowledging the money wasn't all his, but spread out amongst the family.

But when she asked the question, his mouth tightened. "It's hard to know the whole amount," he said. "It's all tied up in trusts. It changes with the market." He deflected her. Maybe he was embarrassed, knowing that for an ordinary human being the amount was unreal, impossible to conceive of, even shameful.

And she *did* love him. She would call it love. Yes.

The pain of what Federico had done to her had nearly destroyed her. She'd created a wall around herself, like bone. At first, when she arrived at the island, she wanted to make him worry, make him wonder what she was doing there and why. He'd be forced to confront the reality of her again, and remember the passion between them. And by keeping him wondering, she'd punish him. She saw how frightened he was, how unnerved he was by her reappearance. It was the only revenge she had. It gave her an awful satisfaction.

And then Henry Woodford had come into her life in an entirely new way, with a sudden clarity. He was no longer just the kindly father in the background when she visited Emily in the house in Westchester. She'd never known anyone like him, a person so big in body and spirit. Henry knew so much, he'd done so much. And he was a sexual being. No one had ever loved her the way he did. Yes, there was his money, but that wasn't his main attraction, it was simply intrinsic to the safety he offered her after all the perilous years of her childhood.

She hardly remembered her own father. He had left when she was three, and her mother had joined a commune. Then they moved out of the commune, and after that, there was only chaos, with landlords hammering on the door of the flat demanding the back rent, and her mother's frantic phone calls to her own mother in Boston, begging for some money to tide them over. Christina's grandmother was a dry, cold woman from a distinguished New England family, with meager means. She was eternally exasperated with her daughter. But she sent her a little money for the sake of her granddaughter, she said.

Christina's mother had held various odd jobs, occasionally translating for American authors and writers. But they were short-lived. She got a job as the assistant to a guru with whom she was having an affair. Then he broke up with her, said he was out of money, and couldn't afford to pay her anymore. Periodically, on the mornings of Christina's childhood as she sat in the kitchen eating her cereal, a strange man would emerge from her mother's bedroom, morning stubble on his cheeks and wearing only his pants, and he'd make himself some coffee. Finding the young daughter of the woman he'd spent the night with there, the man would smile embarrassedly and hurry back to the bedroom, sometimes carrying a second cup of coffee for her mother.

Christina didn't understand her mother, only that she seemed always to be desperately searching for affection and peace. Her mother cared about her, she knew, but she was essentially helpless, a child herself. Early on, Christina had learned to cook for herself, and to clean the flat when the mess became unbearable. Her mother, she thought, was beautiful, but as time passed, her skin grew deeply lined from the sun and smoking. There were experiments with different drugs, for happiness, for transcendence, for relaxation. Christina watched all this nervously, and with irritation, but as she grew older, she learned to watch out for herself, and to anticipate the patterns of her mother's behavior. She was at least predictable.

With Henry and his wealth and knowledge and authority, a whole new and magnificent world had opened before her. He was such a good man, so kind and generous. She was determined to be happy with him.

After the wedding, she was always aware of Federico in the background. She tried to ignore him, to not even see him—just as she realized he was trying to screen her out. She encouraged Henry to go and visit Emily and Federico without her. In the excitement of her new marriage, it seemed to work. She felt no attraction for him, only lingering fury at what he'd done, and contempt for him, that he'd managed to end up in a marriage with a rich woman on whom he was totally dependent, taking her money.

In the past, when they were together, Federico's every word and gesture, his every movement, had been alive with interest to her. There was his physical being, of course, but also his complexity. He was a prince in the modern world, but with none of the pretensions of a prince, and a deep uncertainty. She wanted to help him, to bolster him with her own strength and competence, to save him. More than anything, she wanted to make him be happy, to be the agent of his happiness. It was a challenge she couldn't let go. She was determined to succeed, and through that, to possess him forever.

When he left her that night in Rome, she thought she wouldn't survive. She imagined killing herself. She'd steal her mother's pills, but to swallow them one after the other and for them to take effect would take time and, if she changed her mind, it would be too late to go back. She imagined throwing herself off the Ponte

Fabricio. The current was very violent there because the Isola Tiberina blocked the river and forced the water around it. Then she remembered the sensation of choking on water when she swam, how painfully it singed the throat.

For weeks after Federico left, she hoped he'd come back, and she kept her cell at her side day and night. A week passed, then two weeks, and he didn't contact her.

Gradually, she hardened and resumed her bright toughness, her determined ability to survive. Eighteen months after he left, Emily's wedding invitation arrived. The coincidence hit her, made her stomach churn. This was impossible; two people, both of whom she'd known, somehow coming together. She wrote to Emily that she couldn't afford the ticket.

She'd barely seen Emily Woodford over the years. Once, when she was in the US to visit her grandmother and was passing through New York, they had had lunch. She'd cherished Emily as a girlhood friend, their merry, heedless times together, the unspoken communications of childhood. But as they grew up, during the few times Christina saw her again, she realized that they'd become profoundly different. It had been one of those girlhood friendships that had simply faded away because they'd gone on separate paths. Emily was intelligent—she'd graduated with honors from college and had an education that Christina envied. She knew about literature; she could have gone on to teach or write. But the way Emily hid her intelligence, and developed that girlish manner, was so ridiculously naïve and removed from the exigencies of ordinary life, so immune from its hardships, that it had annoyed Christina. It was as if Emily was afraid of her own intelligence and didn't want to grow up and confront the world. Christina had learned much about the world—too much—fending for herself, having to work in the shop, scrounging for money for her university fees.

Still, when Emily offered to buy her a ticket to the wedding, the idea of going pressed upon Christina. For a split second, there was the thought that Federico would see her and abandon the marriage. If not, she'd torture him with her presence, remind him of what they had together—something, she was sure, he'd never have with Emily.

That day two years ago, in New York at Jean Gavron's before the wedding, when she encountered Federico again, this man every inch of whose body she knew, she'd seen right away that he was determined to hold his ground and give nothing away. She could only smile, and play with him, sadistically, like a cat with a half-dead mouse, knowing that he, too, remembered. Making him go with her to buy a wedding present, veering close to him on the sidewalk as they walked together . . . but he was cold to her and stepped away. She was angry that he'd ignored her during the wedding ceremony. She wanted to remind him of what he'd done to her.

That contact with him in New York pushed it all back at her again. For a year, nearly two years, the need wouldn't go away, and intruded on her daily life. She was obsessed, and her obsession lasted through her brief affairs with other men, all of which were unsuccessful.

The need built up in her, and finally, on the spur of the moment, she contacted Emily. She told her she'd saved up the plane fare to take a summer vacation in the US and was planning to see her grandmother in Boston. She'd really love to come and visit her on the island. It was perilous, but once she'd made the decision, she refused to think of anything other than seeing him again.

And then, when she arrived on the island, he ignored her again. He refused to meet her eyes and left the room whenever there was the slightest possibility they'd be alone together. He acted as if he hated her. He told her, without words, that there was no way it would ever happen again.

# Seventeen

THE WEDDING TOOK PLACE IN THE WOODFORD FAMILY'S OLD church, a narrow Gothic Revival building set high above the street, built a hundred years ago as a summer chapel for the wealthy who had country houses along the East River. The Woodfords rarely attended services anymore. As a child, Henry told her, he'd been forced to go to Sunday School there, and now the family attended rarely, on Christmas and Easter, and for his parents' funerals, which had been held there. The Reverend Mr. Pomeroy was only too pleased to perform the marriage and have this rare visit from the family.

It was a brief ceremony, only a single row of guests in the nave, dwarfed by the vaulted ceiling and the big Tiffany windows. Emily smiled joyously, perhaps because at last her father had found happiness. The thought crossed Christina's mind that Emily, perhaps without fully realizing it, was happy that Christina was no longer a threat to her.

During the service, Christina held herself solemnly, smiling faintly when Mr. Pomeroy pronounced them man and wife.

On their wedding night, she and Henry left immediately for their honeymoon in Paris and Rome. They visited her mother in Rome. She had long gray hair now, and she was wearing her beads and a *kurta*. The tiny apartment was filled with the aroma of burning incense, which had been placed under a statue of Buddha. She gave Christina a big hug. "Darling, I've missed you so!" And then to Henry, speaking rapidly, "It's so wonderful to meet you, and to know that you are taking care of my daughter." With that she gave Christina yet another kiss and hug.

She went on to explain quickly that she'd embraced Buddhism and was now meditating twice a day. She was a disciple of someone called Ajahn Chah and had come to Buddhism through her new boyfriend, Reg—Reg was celibate, she quickly added, an American in Rome who'd introduced her to the practice. Ajahn Chah was in the Thai forest tradition, her mother told them. "It's all about reaching the Buddha Dharma which you achieve through morality, concentration, and wisdom. But I'm talking too much," she said. And then went on to talk more.

All the while, Christina sat unhappily, saying hardly a word. It was as if Henry and Christina weren't even there in the room with her mother; there was only her enthusiastic chatter, her wide smile, and glittering eyes. Her mother wanted her approval for her new craze, but Christina couldn't bring herself to give it, to see yet again another new plan fall through, as had all her plans in the past.

"We have to go now, Mummy," Christina said. "Henry wants to go to the Borghese before it closes."

"Oh no!" her mother cried. "You've just gotten here. I don't even know what *you've* been up to!"

"I'll be back," Christina told her. "Perhaps tomorrow while Henry goes to visit some other museums."

Down on the street, Christina said grimly, "Well, now you've met her."

"She was so glad to see you," Henry said, obviously not wanting to be hurtful about the woman.

"Not glad enough to come out of herself for just a minute to care about how I really am."

"I think she knows you're okay and that pleases her," Henry said.

"Yes," Christina said, without inflection.

"You *are* happy, aren't you?" Henry said.

She quickly smiled at him. "Of course! How could I not be?"

As they walked on, he asked tentatively, "Was she always like this?"

"Yes, only now she's more so. It's always been about somehow trying to heal herself. There's always a new fad."

"Maybe all of that made you the strong person you are."

"Maybe." She proceeded on, troubled.

They flew back from Europe and saw Federico and Emily briefly for dinner. The table talk was mostly between Henry and Emily, about Isabella's doings, while she and Federico sat politely by. They'd found a play group for Isabella. "She really likes being with other children," Emily said. "I think it's unnatural for her to spend her whole day with one person."

As Christina sat there, her scorn for Federico burned within her, smothering everything.

She and Henry were flying to Pittsburgh the next morning and then going straight to Woodford—Henry wanted to show Christina the town, "not a very great place," he warned her. "You have to be prepared."

"I'm really interested," she told him. "I've never been to West Virginia. I want to be involved. I want to help you."

And he'd drawn her to him in gratitude. Light had washed through his existence with her arrival in his life. She was tender toward him, aware of his every wish and hastening to fulfill them, sometimes before he seemed to even understand them himself.

The core of the new museum's collection, Henry told her, was to be the art his grandparents, Richard and Grace Woodford, had collected, most of which had been purchased from impoverished noble families during their summer trips to Europe in the twenties and thirties. Supposedly, Bernard Berenson had advised them. They had an Ingres, *Paolo and Francesca*, a Botticelli tempera of *The Annunciation*, and a Rembrandt etching of his mother. Some of the stuff was valuable; some of doubtful provenance. There was a reworked Leonardo drawing for the *Mona Lisa*, and a Rembrandt oil sketch of an African, but it wasn't certain whether Rembrandt had painted it himself or it had been done by an apprentice.

As a child, Henry had been forced to spend two miserable and boring weeks a year at his grandmother's house. Grandma Gracie was both silly and intimidating. She had a kind of primitive, biting intelligence, insisting that everyone dress for dinner and stick to her rigorous schedule. Henry's depressive mother was unhappy under the thumb of her overbearingly cheerful and sharp-tongued mother-in-law, who controlled the Woodford trusts that provided the income for Henry's father.

Grandma Gracie was much younger than her husband, and after he died, she continued collecting, buying a signed, original Picasso lithograph of a carnival figure, and a Monet, vaguely affordable then—and had her bedroom redecorated to match the colors.

She was also a maniacal collector of strange and inconsequential objects: Hummel figures, Czechoslovakian glass candlesticks, and, after her children grew up, toys. During his forced visits to her, Henry's only salvation were those toys stored upstairs in the old nursery, such as the child-sized Bugatti car, the rocking horse and train set, the Paddington bear. His grandmother had established a charitable trust mandating that the mansion be turned into a museum when she died. So at least something came of her soulless collecting.

The museum's charter decreed that her toys be exhibited in perpetuity alongside her art. Thus, among the Old Masters was displayed her old doll with its torn white dress propped up on a frayed silk chair. In recent years, the toys had acquired value as collectibles. The museum would have to continue exhibiting them because of the charter. Henry had always hated toy exhibits because children could only look at the toys but weren't allowed to play with them. He'd planned on the museum having a gift shop with copies of the old toys for sale for them.

Henry also wanted a section on Woodford's industrial history. There were old photographs of the steel mills in their heyday, fire and smoke pouring from the stacks, and of old Ephraim Consider Woodford in a top hat, standing in front of a factory in the middle of a line of forlorn and grimy workers. Local schoolchildren could come and learn about the town's industrial past. The museum would honor their forebears who had done such hard and terrible work for the benefit of Henry's family, and perhaps it would bring the town back to life.

"You have to prepare yourself," he said to Christina again.

"Please!" she laughed.

These days there were no hotels or places to stay in the town, so Henry and Christina would have to spend the night in Pittsburgh.

In the morning, a limousine pulled up to take them to the museum, an hour away.

She'd never been in this part of America. At first it was a beautiful drive. It was autumn, the leaves were beginning to turn a brilliant red, and they drove along narrow roads between tree-covered hills with riverbeds below.

But eventually, the hills became rocky and barren, gouged out by past mining. Alongside the road, there were pits and streams filled with strange orange water, and the hulking ruins of mills, with hollowed-out windows and smokestacks and silos gone dead. A rusted iron bridge was stretched over the highway.

Then they came to the town itself. It was nearly deserted, the main street lined with boarded-up shops and darkened storefronts. There was the City Hall, a big, gray building with a cupola. A man in a cowboy hat and a thin woman with long, scraggly hair sat on the steps of the building, smoking. A plump teenage girl wearing pajama bottoms pushed a baby in a stroller along the sidewalk. As the big black limousine passed them, they gaped at the strange sight.

"It's so sad," said Christina. She couldn't help saying it. She'd seen poverty before, of course, in the garbage-strewn migrant encampments right in the middle of Rome, with their plastic-covered tents and ragged children, and the gypsies begging on the streets, but she'd never seen emptiness and decay like this.

"There's just nothing here for people," Henry said. "It's awful. Though, sometimes in spring it's a little better when the green comes out. Maybe the museum will help things. People around here don't care about art, but they need jobs. I think when we finish the museum, tourists will come. There'll be a hotel, and restaurants, all local employment."

If she had to live here, Christina thought, she would die. But this was Henry's focus in life, his project and daily occupation, and of course, she would do what she could to help him.

The old Woodford mansion stood on a bluff overlooking the mills and the town. It had been designed to resemble a Florentine palazzo, with gray stucco and a flat roof—an anomaly after the broken-down buildings and clapboard houses of the town. It was a construction site now, surrounded by huge machines, piles of lumber and stone, and workers in yellow helmets.

As they pulled up, the architect, a young man in a suit and yellow helmet, was waiting for them. Henry had hired him from Pittsburgh. He was recently out of architecture school and full of the latest ideas about architecture and its social consequences. He'd designed the Museum renovation and the new wing that would adjoin the mansion. It was to be a simple, one-story rectangle, constructed of gray stucco to match the mansion, but set back from it so it wouldn't intrude on its lines. The new wing would also be "green" and incorporate the latest ideas in sustainability, materials, energy sources, etc.

The architect, whose name was Nick, hurried forward to meet them. This was his first big commission, and he was eager to show it off. He handed them hard hats and led them on a tour. The foundation for the new wing had been dug into the wet, orange earth. "You can see from the footprint how big it'll be," he said.

"It does seem big when you actually walk it," Henry said. "I was concerned from the drawings it wouldn't be big enough."

"There'll be the flexible exhibition areas for just that reason," Nick said. This was where the contemporary art would probably hang. There'd be a café, a gift shop, and a storage area in the basement. "The windows are on the eastern side to get the natural light—all UV glass, of course, but no windows on the western side, to give us more exhibition space."

"I got another bill," Henry said. "It's way over what we thought, Nick."

"I know," he replied. "Because of all the rock. They had to dynamite it."

"Shouldn't you have foreseen that?"

"You can't help the surprises sometimes," Nick said.

Henry glanced at the workmen in their yellow hats. "I don't want to be ripped off."

"I can assure you, Mr. Woodford, you won't be."

They followed Nick to the old house. It was empty now, but there were still vestiges of its former grandeur, the ballroom with its carved moldings and pilasters, the inlaid wood floors, all covered in dust now, and all to be restored.

Christina tried to ask insightful questions, about the museum's lighting and where the art would hang. Two hours passed, and she began to slow down.

"Why don't you sit and wait?" Henry suggested.

"Do you mind, just for a bit?"

She found a place on a bench in the entrance hall. She could taste the dust on her tongue. As she waited, the vast emptiness of the place, the grayness of it all descended over her.

When Henry finished with the architect, as they were walking back to the car she remarked, "It must be costing millions."

"I'm not going to tell you," he replied. This was only the second time since she'd known him that Henry had ever been terse with her like that. The other time had been before the wedding when she'd asked him about money too, about the extent of the Woodford fortune. She didn't ask him anything further, and he said nothing more.

As they drove back to Pittsburgh in the limousine, Henry said, "I've just got to come down here more now to supervise things. There's too much over-run. They think I've got an endless budget." Christina felt her heart sink. To live here would be a hell.

Then Henry brightened up. "I'm so grateful to you for coming," he said. "It means so much that you're interested in the whole thing. I know it must be boring."

"No." Christina rested her head on his shoulder. "It can never be boring. Nothing you do can ever bore me."

# Part Five

# In the Autumn Rain

# Eighteen

THE FIRST BIG EVENT OF THE FALL SEASON WAS OPENING NIGHT at the opera. Christina knew she was in her full glory that night; it was a transformation that she could effect when needed. She'd planned what she would wear for Henry, to be an ornament on his arm for this important occasion. She'd chosen a pale green charmeuse dress, the rich fabric glowing and gently brushing the curves of her body. Her hair was swept up, and she wore the diamond necklace Henry had given her as a wedding present. On the night before the wedding, he'd nervously handed her a dark blue velvet box.

"Goodness," she'd cried when she opened it. "It's amazing." She looked up at him with a panicked expression. "But . . . I mean . . . I've never worn anything like this. I don't know if I can . . ."

"I was worried about that," he said. "I know you don't like flashy things, but I wanted to give you something special, and lasting." He smiled shyly. "You don't have to wear it if you don't want to."

"Oh, God. Of course, I'll wear it. I'm so lucky! I'll wear it for you, on special occasions." She draped it around her neck, and he fastened the clasp for her and kissed her shoulder. She would wear it without any other jewelry for the opera. Anything else would have been too much.

But this morning, Henry had woken up feverish with the flu. His fever had broken, but he was still drained, and he'd insisted that she go to the opera without him.

"I'm not leaving you," she told him.

"You've got to go as my representative," he said. The family had had a box at the opera as far back as the old Met, and they'd always been major supporters. Tonight was opening night and traditionally they attended.

"For goodness' sake!" he laughed. "You're fifteen minutes away, and if I need you, I can phone you. But I won't need you. Go on, now," he commanded, lying back in the bed, reaching for the remote and flicking on the TV. "Besides, I want to watch the game. Anyway, Federico and Emily will be there to keep you company."

"You're just saying this because you hate opera!" she teased. "You're trying to get out of it." In fact, he was always averse to big social occasions, and he did hate opera. Opening night was a duty he went along with, passively. It was an annual Woodford event with other members of the family who shared the box.

He laughed and pointed at himself. "Look! I'm an invalid."

She bent over, kissed him, and went on without him.

When the usher opened the door of the family box for her, she stopped. The others, seated on their red velvet chairs, caught sight of her and ceased talking. She saw Federico's eyes flicker over her body, and she felt herself rise up, like a plant drawn to the light.

She bent toward him and he kissed the air beyond her cheek. For a brief moment, he would feel the warmth of her body, and she was glad to make him miserable. She gave Emily a hug. Emily was simply dressed as usual, in an old, black velvet gown with a ruffle at the breast, stiff and un-ironed as if she'd just snatched the first thing she found in her closet. Christina kissed Fran, and caught the whiff of alcohol beneath her perfume. Finally, there was sweet, watery-eyed Everett.

The house lights dimmed. The crystal chandeliers began their slow rise. The overture commenced. At first, there was a martial beat, and then the intimations of the sorrow and tragedy to come. She could make out Federico's profile in the light reflected from the stage.

The opera tonight was *Norma*. Onstage, the Roman proconsul Pollione was singing that he no longer loved the high priestess, Norma, who'd broken her vow of chastity to bear his children. He was in love with the young priestess, Adalgisa. "*Ma nel cuore è spenta la prima fiamma . . .* " The flame of his passion for Norma had been spent. At the end of the first act, Adalgisa realized the awfulness of what she'd done in taking Pollione away from Norma. "*Mi lascia scostati! Sposo sei tu infedele!*" She couldn't bear that she'd caused her such pain.

It was intermission, the lights went up and Emily announced, "I feel so guilty with Dad there by himself. I think I'm just going to look in on him."

"He wouldn't let me stay," Christina said. "I wanted to. His fever's broken—you're making me feel guilty now."

"Really, I don't mind. I'll go. I haven't seen him anyway since he came down with it. I didn't want to give it to Isabella."

"I'll take you down to the car," Federico said.

"The intermission's thirty minutes. I'll be back in time for the second act," and they quickly left.

Christina made the excuse of going to the restroom and left too. She strolled through the lobby among the crowd of attendees, the women in ballgowns, and the white-haired men in tuxedos and tails. She was among the youngest people there. The women were well made-up, their skin pulled across their cheeks, and they wore big, elaborate jewelry. The men's faces were ruddy, as if their skin had been treated and massaged. It was the women who were eager to greet one another—"Call me! It's been forever!"—while the men exchanged nods and handshakes.

Jean Gavron came toward her, dressed in gray velvet for the evening, and wearing big, irregularly shaped mother-of-pearl earrings.

Only her dark red lipstick interrupted the clean angles of her straight gray hair. "Where's Henry?" she asked.

She explained Henry's flu, his not liking opera anyway, and that Emily was concerned about him and had left to check up on him.

"But shouldn't you be with him yourself?" Jean asked.

"He absolutely insisted I come. He feels someone's got to represent him. And he doesn't have a fever anymore. You know how he is about these things. It's just an excuse to watch the game," she said, smiling fondly.

"You'd think now that he's got you to take care of him, Emily would be less worried about him," Jean said.

"You would, wouldn't you? But she's more so these days, if that's possible. She's always over at our house with the baby." Christina laughed. "Maybe she doesn't trust me."

"That's absurd," Jean said.

Christina smiled and sighed. "Oh well, what can I do? She'll be at the house when I get home, I promise you. You'd think it was kind of hard on Federico that she's always with her father."

Jean looked at her peculiarly. "Is it hard on *you* that Emily's in your lives so much?"

"Of course not. She's my friend."

"Well, they're good people," Jean said finally.

Christina paused for a moment. "Sometimes, I think he just married me to please her," she said. "He knew she felt guilty getting married and leaving him. He knew it was time for her to grow up and separate from him."

"That's utterly ridiculous. Henry married you because he loves you."

"Maybe that came afterwards."

"I doubt it." Jean looked nervous.

For a long moment, Christina studied her. "I feel you're deserting me," she said. "I thought you were my friend."

"What are you talking about?"

"I don't know." Christina smiled. "Are you on their side now?"

" 'Side'? What on earth's come over you? Is something wrong?"

"Just saying," Christina said. "Absolutely nothing is wrong."

She spotted Federico across the lobby, back from taking Emily to the car. He'd seen her too, and he was coming toward them.

As Federico approached, everything around her seemed to grow quiet, the crowd of people were but wisps, their lips moving soundlessly. Only *he* was fully formed. Watching him come toward her, his eyes intent upon her, though he'd been gone only a few minutes, was as if she were seeing him anew.

He reached them. "Hello, Jean." He kissed Jean, but not Christina.

"Darling," said Jean.

"Emily's on her way," Federico said. "She's a big worrier, as you know."

Jean looked from him to Christina. "I think I'll just get a glass of champagne before it starts up again."

They watched Jean move away, and they were left standing together amid the crowd.

Hardly thinking about it, Christina took his arm. He didn't resist but held himself stiffly.

She led the way, and they began to stroll through the lobby. It was alright for a woman to link arms with her son-in-law even though he was her same age—they were in public after all. She could rightly take his arm for support.

For the first time in months, in years, she was close to him for more than a second. His body brushed against hers, the material of his tuxedo against her bare shoulders, his thigh against hers. They'd had no contact with one another except for their polite family kisses, always in the presence of the others.

Christina felt a rush of something powerful and frightening, sweeping up through her body. She didn't want him to move away from her.

"It's good for Jean to see us together," she said.

He stopped. "Why?"

She continued looking out at the crowd, smiling unflinchingly. "She'll realize we're not afraid to be seen together, that everything's normal. Nothing to worry about."

"Of course, 'everything's normal'!" he said. "What do you mean? There's *nothing* going on between us," he said angrily under his breath.

"Oh, you know how she is," Christina said. "She's always sort of in other peoples' business. She knows about us from before."

"Why are you bringing this up tonight? There *is* no 'business.'" He grimaced and began looking wildly around him. "That's my old boss," he said. "Ricardo. I'd better say hello."

He broke away. Her eyes followed him as he hurried over to a gray-haired man with a neat beard standing with a group of other men.

Federico began chatting with them. The older man glanced over at Christina and said something to him, and Federico came back toward her. "Ricardo would like to meet you."

"How nice."

He touched her elbow but didn't hold it. She followed him across the floor and Federico made an introduction, then left her laughing gaily with him. Laughing to make him jealous.

Jean returned to Federico's side with her glass of champagne. "I saw you introduce Christina to them?" she said to Federico.

"She caught the old man's eye." He watched Christina encircled by Ricardo and his friends and talking animatedly with them. "She is sort of amazing, I suppose."

"Did they think you're together?"

"Well, obviously we're acquainted," he said. "We were standing with each other."

"They do know you have a wife, don't they?"

"Of course."

His eyes still on Christina, Federico said under his breath, "We are sort of in this together, she and I."

"What do you mean?" Jean asked. "She's Henry's."

"I am too," Federico said flatly.

He couldn't concentrate on what Jean was saying. He couldn't take his eyes off Christina. She was taller than Ricardo, and the old man was obviously captivated. He watched her smile and toss her head, holding herself high and proud.

He turned back to Jean, and said desperately, "I try to give back to Henry for everything he's done for us. I hope I can." He tried to calm himself. "Sometimes I just need to escape a bit. His generosity's overwhelming. For all of us. At least for me. Maybe even for her . . ." He nodded toward Christina.

Jean said, "Christina said Emily seems worried about him?"

"Yes." His brow knit.

"It was really time Henry got married," Jean said. "I know it's made Emily very relieved."

Federico was still distracted. Then, realizing he hadn't been paying attention, he said, "What?"

"Henry's my friend," said Jean.

"I know."

"Have you told Emily about Christina?"

"She knows we met before. The rest is irrelevant." He turned to her. "I need your advice."

"Please, Federico, I can't. Don't get me involved in this."

He nodded curtly. The bell was ringing. Intermission was ending and the next act was about to begin.

# Nineteen

Pollione, in his guilt, followed Norma to the funeral pyre. There was the curtain call and applause, and Mike and Jean exited into the warm September night. It was the beginning of fall, and a soft breeze underlay the balmy air.

"What a performance," Mike said of Radvanovsky, the evening's Norma.

"A bit rough at the top," Jean remarked absently as they strolled across the brightly lit plaza.

"But she was basically marvelous," he said. "There it is." He indicated their car waiting for them at the foot of the steps, the uniformed driver standing at attention beside it.

The man opened the door and, as they settled into their seats, the scent of new leather rose up to them. The car pulled out and made its way, stopping and starting in the line of traffic leaving the complex.

They turned onto Broadway, drove past the big windows of the chain stores and vacant storefronts, and then the car made a right into Central Park.

"The sets were a disappointment, though," Mike said as they proceeded smoothly along between the high walls of the transverse.

"Probably," Jean said absently, staring out at the darkness. "You saw them together," she said suddenly.

"Who?"

"Christina and Federico," she said, irritated at his utter disinterest.

"Yeah. I guess Emily went to see Henry."

"I don't think they'd do anything," Jean said.

"Do what?" he said, his attention straying again.

They were on Madison now, the shops lit up in the darkness, the mannequins in the windows pale and still and otherworldly.

"Anything," she said. "I can't say it. It's too awful to imagine."

"What are you talking about?"

"You know what I mean."

They could see the back of the driver's head through the plexiglass barrier. You could draw the curtain across it if you wanted privacy, but that would call attention to their conversation, as if it *had* to be private. Jean always wondered if these chauffeurs deliberately left their intercoms on so they could eavesdrop on the conversations in the back. What they must know, she thought; the gossip, the heedless embraces.

"Christina and Federico," she said firmly.

"Oh, come on!" Jean could just make out Mike's smile in the dark interior. "Well, the guy doesn't have a job. He doesn't have much else to do."

"Please! How can you joke about it? He's so wonderful to Emily. And he's the best father. He's crazy about that child."

"He sure is," Mike answered. "Why are you so suspicious?"

"The way they were standing together."

"Like I said before, it was in the past, a youthful thing, right?"

"Yes. Two or three years ago," Jean said. "I mean, once you and I had sex, everything was changed forever."

"I should hope so." He chuckled, no doubt remembering years ago when they first had sex and he won Jean's heart. After that, there'd never been anyone else for either of them. They'd gone in a straight line from that point to marriage.

Next to him, Jean was quiet.

Mike said, "You think Federico's told Emily that they went out together in Rome?"

"He can't have. Emily and Christina seem like such good friends. I know he didn't."

"Do you think Emily senses something anyway?"

"I don't know," Jean said. "Emily's very mysterious. You never quite know what she's thinking. She's always got this cheerful, optimistic front, as if there's nothing wrong in the whole world. I'm not sure I believe it. She does seem worried about Henry, though."

"Does *he* know?" Mike asked.

"Who?"

"Henry," Mike said.

"I don't think he could know about Christina and Federico," Jean replied. "Maybe he *should* know."

"Maybe he wouldn't even care."

"Of course he would," she said. "His son-in-law's old girlfriend—and he didn't know it when he married her!"

"Well, you can't do anything about it. It's none of your business."

"But it *is* my business. I didn't tell Emily about Christina and Federico. I never said anything to Henry. I didn't warn him."

"That's good," said Mike.

"I wonder if Christina even loves Henry," Jean said. "If she ever did?" She looked at Mike, her eyes wide. "You think it was just so she could be close to Federico again? And make him jealous?"

"That's dark," said Mike. "What a thought."

She went on, "Christina's got to let him be."

"You think Christina's trying to get him back?" he asked.

"Sometimes I think she's calling attention to herself. Tempting him."

They came to Fifth Avenue, and the reassuring solidity of the great apartment buildings and the old mansions, the elaborate cornices and gilded art of the lower floors visible in the lit windows.

"Jean, for Christ's sake, leave them be," Mike said. "Let them work it out. You're playing with fire."

"You mean, I should just let them . . . do what they want?"

"Yes," Mike said. "Look, I'm telling you, hon. You can't control these things. Only they can."

"*If* they can," she replied.

With that, the car pulled up under the portico of their building, in front of the big double door with its swirling iron fretwork. Beyond was the warm, safe light of the lobby and the guarded world within, and Carlos the doorman was hurrying to help them out.

# Twenty

THE AUTUMN RAINS CAME, POURING DOWN OVER THE CITY, sheets of water flooding the sidewalks and gutters. Isabella, understandably, was restless. She'd been cooped up inside all day and had exhausted her interest in all her toys in the nursery, and she was irritable. Emily bundled her up and took her over to her father's to give her a change of scenery. Henry's house was fully equipped with a nursery ready to receive her, with a crib and a set of toys, which would, at least for a while, seem new to her. There was even a room next to the nursery for Emily's own use—if she was exhausted from caring for Isabella, she could take a nap while Henry played with the child. Occasionally, if Federico was going out for the evening with his Italian friends, Emily and Isabella even spent the night there, though her own house was only three blocks away.

Federico had been left alone in the house, as was often the case when Emily was at her father's. He'd built a fire in the grate fireplace, refusing to ask Mrs. Evans, who lived in the basement apartment near the kitchen, to do it for him. Mrs. Evans was in her late fifties and he couldn't bring himself to make a woman of her age carry logs up the stairs, kneel down on the hard floor, and set a fire. He'd given her the afternoon off.

The room was gloomy in the rain. The firelight flickered on the walls and the brass sconces. The house was soundless, padded against the outside world by the heavy satin drapes. When they bought the house, Emily, who didn't care about such things, had left its decoration to a professional, asking only that it be simple and functional. The decorator had wanted to preserve the original Victorian elements, the stained-glass panels in the leaded windows and the oak half-paneling, which made the house even darker. It was a "grown-up house," muted, dignified, the colors tasteful soft browns, beiges, greens. Vaguely impersonal, Federico thought.

The heavy atmosphere oppressed him, and he felt a depression descending upon him. He'd read *La Repubblica* and *Corriere della Sera* cover to cover. There was no soccer on TV, his usual way of losing himself and forgetting the world around him. With this rain, he couldn't even go out for a walk and get some exercise. There were no trips, no parties, or other plans to give his agreement to.

Isabella, his dearest charge and preoccupation, who could always hold his focus and give him joy, wasn't home. Ordinarily, he'd take her to the park and spend hours watching her toddle around the playground. Usually he was the only father there.

He couldn't sit at the computer like other men and watch the market rise and fall, and phone his broker and make decisions about investments because, of course, The Office handled all that for them.

He should try to rouse himself, take a cab, and go to the gym and work himself up into a sweat. But he was in such a torpor, he couldn't even bring himself to do that.

Federico wasn't naturally lazy. Or maybe he was? He'd never had good marks in school and he'd skated through university. He'd thought of going to law school, but that would be impossible for him in a foreign country. His English wasn't good enough—he'd never score high enough on the LSATs, never pass the bar. Perhaps he could work for the Woodford Foundation, be a program officer. But that would be a conflict of interest. Besides, the program officers were all highly trained in their areas—in education, health care, immigration reform, and all the causes the foundation gave money to. Federico had no expertise in anything.

Maybe he should talk to Henry about it all. But that would be telling his wife's father that he was unsettled and depressed because he didn't have a job; he didn't want to appear weak and cause him worry. To reveal it to Henry would make it seem serious—which it was. And it might make him worry that there was more to it than simply not having a job. Despite Henry's kindly demeanor, he was shrewd. He had to be. He'd been a lawyer, and he presided over the family's financial empire. Henry was of a generation in which people didn't give themselves away, and men didn't reveal their inner thoughts. Though Henry seemed to see everything, Federico thought, he seldom judged people and he presided with kindness over them all.

So here he was, a relatively young man, standing idle in the dark afternoon in front of the fireplace, the flames sucking all the oxygen out of the air, when he should be doing something for humanity. Far too often on these autumn afternoons, when the world was dark, he would sink onto the couch's downy pillows and take a nap. Losing himself in sleep had become his default mechanism. Usually, he napped on the couch in his study, out of sight from everybody, embarrassed to be caught sleeping in the middle of the day, and sometimes in the morning too, when everybody else was going about their business. He fought the urge. Last night, he'd slept a full eight hours, and he'd just wake up logy and useless from oversleeping.

He decided to go down to the kitchen and make an espresso to wake himself. But just then, the doorbell rang. Mrs. Evans wasn't there, so he went down to answer it himself.

The house had an elaborate security system. When he got to the front door, he saw Christina on the video waiting to be let in, her face smudged with rain, her long hair dripping wet and flat on her head. Slowly, with trepidation, he opened the door. Beyond, a cab was pulling away from the curb.

Standing there in the rain, she said to him, "Aren't you going to let me in?"

"Yes, yes." He backed away and stepped aside, letting her pass him, breathing in so she wouldn't brush against him.

"You don't have an umbrella," he said.

"I was in a hurry." She smiled. Her parka was soaked through. She was carrying a cloth bag full of packages. He helped her remove the parka and hung it up to dry on the hall tree, where it dripped onto the floor. She was shivering, her teeth chattering, and she wrapped her arms around herself. Every instinct made Federico want to embrace her, to warm her. It was all he could do not to.

They stood looking at one another. Even unspoken moments between them were coded. "You'd better come upstairs," he said. "I've got a fire."

She was wearing a man's shirt, untucked, and jeans. Christina was a rich woman now, but like Emily she usually wore jeans. All their rich friends wore jeans; they were indistinguishable from those of lesser means, except for their expensive haircuts (though not for Emily), their confidence, their touches of expensive jewelry, their expensive boots.

"It's nice and warm in here," she said as they went into the parlor. The rain had grown heavier on the windows, further darkening the room, screening it from the outside. She went up to the fire and, with her back to Federico, held her hands out to the flames.

"You haven't been out?" she asked him, over her shoulder.

"Where would I go?"

"I suppose that's true." She still knew him.

He sighed. "You've got a lot of courage."

She knew what he meant and she smiled. "I'm braver than you." That was the hard truth. She'd always been the stronger one. She'd had to fend for herself.

He stayed away from her.

"When Emily and Isabella arrived at the house," she said, "I said I had to go do some errands. They didn't care. They prefer being together anyway." She looked boldly at him. "Did she say when she'd be back?"

"No. Probably a few hours. Where did you go?"

"I hailed a cab and I told the driver to just drive—anywhere! I told him I'd give him a big tip. I was going mad with boredom."

"I've been bored too," he said, confessing to her for the first time the condition of his whole life.

"Have you?" she asked, again with a smile of triumph.

"Yeah."

"I ended up at the Museum," she said, "and I bought some books in the bookstore. Then I came here. The three of them are completely happy together at our house."

He said, haltingly, "I don't get them." It was involuntary, more than he'd intended. An invitation, he realized, immediately regretting it. Nonetheless, he went on, "They're very different . . . from me."

They hadn't spoken personally like this for a very long time; it was like the old days. She was so near, and they were alone.

"I'm not different from you," she said, still smiling. "I'm part Italian, too."

In his anxiety, he closed his eyes shut. "Of course. They adore being together with Isabella," he said.

When he opened his eyes again, her face was full of unspoken communication. "I really wanted Henry and me to have a child, you know," she said.

It was as if she'd punched him in the gut. She had to know the effect her words would have on him. It was unendurable. But he had no right. . . .

She went on, "It hasn't happened. Though, maybe . . . who knows?"

A violent feeling came over him.

"I don't think we'd adopt," she said.

"Please. Don't talk about it," he said. "I can't bear it." He took a breath. "I've been desperate. I needed to talk to someone. I wanted to talk to Jean."

"I wouldn't do that," she said.

"Do you think she's ever said anything?"

She thought a moment. "Jean wouldn't want to cause a storm."

They didn't have to articulate it further.

"Henry's one of the finest people I know," Federico said. "He's a good man. I could never hurt him."

"I'm the same. And Emily's an angel."

He wanted to cry.

She stood against the firelight in the gloomy afternoon, the margins of her body lit by the flames. In the warmth of the fire, her skin glowed. Her hair had dried now, and it was full and sun-streaked and flowed down over her shoulders.

Despite himself, he began to move slowly, inexorably, toward her.

"There's no one here," he said. "The woman's out. She's got the afternoon off."

She nodded, her eyes fixed on him.

He touched her waist and then he pushed his hand up under her shirt. At the shock of his cold fingers on her bare warm skin, she drew in her stomach. It made room for his hand to go farther, and she held still and let it happen. After all this time, he felt her flesh, the familiar pulse of her life.

There was no going back.

They were in his and Emily's house. Anyone could come. But Mrs. Evans was gone.

It was wrong, it would destroy his world.

But they were beyond that now.

Later, when Emily returned to the house with Isabella, she asked him, "Did you go out?"

"No. Why?"

"There was water on the hallway floor. I thought you had," she said.

That was where he'd hung Christina's wet parka to dry. It was still wet. "Maybe it was Mrs. Evans," he said.

"Oh, is she back?" Emily asked.

"I don't know," he said. "But perhaps it was her."

# Twenty-One

HE WALKED RESTLESSLY THROUGH THE STREETS, VISITED MUSEums, but saw nothing of the art in front of him. Sitting in coffee shops, he gazed dully out the window at the leaves drifting across the sidewalks, the pedestrians passing by, and he saw nothing. Still, he could feel the shock of that first touch, the moment of contact. He went to the gym and frantically exercised.

But a boundary had been crossed.

It was sunset and Emily had taken Isabella to have an early dinner with a college friend and her own baby. He texted Christina. Just this once, a lighthearted suggestion for coffee. But cell phones had a record of texts. They could be seen by other people. She texted back. "Yes. Where?" He suggested a place, then deleted both messages.

She made an excuse to Henry. There was a hurried meeting in a diner. Then they went into the park. It was early winter, nearly deserted in the cold. The black shapes of the trees loomed; beyond them the sky was a dark red-gray. Without even consulting one another, they found a place on a rise behind a tree. Down below there was a man with a shopping cart sitting on a bench. Two youths were walking down the path. But they were hidden here, and no one could see them.

They felt a moment only of amazement that they, of all people, would be here like this. But the park was a place where all varieties of transgressions occurred after dark—sex, drugs, as long as you didn't get in anyone's way, it was okay. Anyway, their need was so great the danger didn't matter, they couldn't help themselves.

They did it quickly, desperately, up against a tree.

When they'd finished, she said, "I can't do this again. What are we doing?"

"I can't either," he said.

They resolved to stay apart. But after only a few days, the need built up again and it happened once more. In his own house when Emily was gone and wouldn't be back for hours, and Mrs. Evans was out. In the basement in the dark, the boiler clanking beside them, the smell of damp and fuel in the air, quick, and then she was gone again. They took a room in a derelict hotel in Midtown; it was sixty dollars for an hour. There were old people and vagrants in the lobby, the rug was mildewed, and the sink rusted, but the sheets on the bed seemed clean. Neither of them had ever been in a place like this. But they didn't care, they took the risk.

At first, they tried to be careful, not to meet too frequently. But that became harder and harder. He knew she must be having sex with Henry. The thought of it made him sick. She'd guess he was having sex with Emily. But they didn't ask the question of one another. It would be too awful to know the answers.

Family gatherings were a new hell, all of them sitting there together, he and Christina, pretending they hardly knew one another, and that they were a normal, happy family. He sat through these family meals in a state of suspended animation and disbelief, across from his father-in-law, a kind and generous man, and alongside his sweet, birdlike wife. Christina was composed, more reserved than usual. Henry and Emily seemed unaware of what was happening. This was her husband, and his wife. They were intimate with them; they knew them the way husbands and wives always knew their spouses. How could they not notice what was happening right in front of their eyes?

At night in bed, after the lights were out, Federico lay with his back to Emily. In the beginning of their relationship, they used to make love nearly every night. He knew her so well he could sense her desire in the air. But everything had been spent with Christina. He didn't move, his back was a wall between them. He heard her sigh, and she wrapped her arms around him and moved up against him.

He had to respond. How could he not give her what she wanted? He turned over and took her in his arms. She touched him, but nothing happened. She tried to arouse him, using all her gentle skills, and in the past she would have quickly succeeded. Now there was nothing. He was dead.

"I'm sorry," he said. "I think I'm tired from the baby. She doesn't stop moving, our girl!"

She pulled away. "It's okay," she said softly. "Don't worry about it. We'll try again." She kissed him, turned on her side herself, and soon he could hear the distinctive breathing that he knew by heart meant that she'd fallen asleep.

Coming home one evening after he'd been with Christina, he found her waiting for him, strangely all dressed up. She was wearing makeup, which she almost never did, and a new dress, tight fitting and low-necked, accentuating her full breasts and tiny waist. She wore high heels. He'd never seen her like this.

He said, uncertainly, "You look so pretty. Are you going out?"

"I thought *we'd* go out," she said. "I've missed you."

"Missed me?"

She didn't answer, instead she came toward him and kissed him fully on the mouth. He felt her tongue on his lips.

He had no choice but to gather her in his arms and kiss her back. But what if she could smell what they'd done this afternoon, the sex on him, Christina's scent lingering on his skin? He couldn't pull away. Finally, she released him.

He held her at arm's length. "I've never seen you quite like this."

"You don't like it?"

"Of course I do. But it's sort of . . . not like you at all. It's very sexy."

"You mean I'm not usually sexy?"

"Of course you are. But in your own way. A sweet way."

"Thank you. It's for you. I've felt guilty," she said.

"But why!"

"I've been too wrapped up in Isabella. Spending too much time at Dad's."

"Why this sudden realization?"

"Just that . . . as I said, I've missed you."

"That's good," he said, and kissed her on the forehead.

"Now Isabella's getting bigger, I want to restore things."

"Restore?" he asked, though he knew what she meant.

"The way we were together. I feel I've neglected you. Do you like it?" She twirled around, showing off her dress. "What do you think? Christina's been advising me."

"Christina? Why?"

"Why not? Christina's so stunning, she has such simple, elegant taste."

"She does," he said, carefully. "But I like the way *you* dress."

"I could always use improvement."

He collected himself. "Not in my eyes." He sniffed the air. "And perfume? I don't think you've ever worn perfume. And makeup?"

"I usually don't. But Christina suggested it. It's fun."

What was Christina doing? Was it her guilt at destroying his marriage? Was this some sort of weird scheme, to put Emily in front of him, make her seductive, to make him love her again?

"Come," Emily said. "Let me get you a drink. Want me to mix you a martini?"

"I'm a bit tired. It'll make me fall asleep." But he guessed that for her own reasons she wanted to make him a strong drink. "Why not?" he said. It would calm him, anesthetize him. Help him make love to her.

He waited while she mixed the drinks.

Her smile, as she came carrying them toward him, was seductive, not the shy, girlish smile that was her usual expression. "I thought we'd have 'a date.' Go to 'our place.' " The Italian restaurant with its authentic feel and dark intimacy where they often went. "Isabella will be fine with Mrs. Evans."

"I'm a bit tired," he said again.

"Maybe not, then?" she said, accommodatingly as always.

"No. If you want to. Of course. Let me just take a shower."

"Want me to come up with you? Help you unpack?" She took a step forward, hopeful, eager. She wanted to go with him to have sex.

The idea of being naked in front of her before he'd taken a shower panicked him. "No. I'll be fine. I'll just be quick. You wait here."

For a second, she looked disappointed, then she smiled again. "I'll wait for you."

He was being cruel, rejecting her. He took his martini and left her to go upstairs.

In the shower, the water stung his skin. It had been rubbed raw by the lovemaking with Christina. He let it run hot until it burned and scrubbed himself vigorously with the brush. He had to erase all presence of her on his body. The water hurt his tender skin as if it were a flagellation. Federico wasn't religious—if anything he despised the old Church. Though, like most former Catholics, it was still part of him. When he died, they'd have a mass for him because it was his heritage. From early on, he'd been schooled by nuns and priests. The stories told to them about saints whipping themselves bloody in penance for their sins, of St. Paul and St. Rose of Lima with her crown of thorns, had both transfixed and horrified him and all the other boys in the class. Though the stories didn't help much when their testosterone came in. How amazing it was that he still carried them within him, he thought. They would always be there.

He dried himself off and emerged from the bathroom. She was there in the bedroom.

"I feel I want to be with you again," she said, and came toward him. She kissed him, then reached behind and unzipped her dress, letting it fall to the floor. She had nothing on underneath. Her breasts had grown fuller after Isabella's birth, her skin was flawless, young and pale. Usually, she wasn't forward like this. She'd always been a shy but eager lover, and it was he who usually led the way. Now he couldn't refuse her.

He dropped his towel, drew her across the room to the bed and began to make love to her. Her response was more urgent than it had ever been. She took his hand and guided it along her body, and with her own hand she tried to arouse him.

But nothing was happening. She drew back. "What is it?" she asked. "Is something wrong?"

He pulled her to him. "Of course not. You made me that martini. I think that did it."

She tried again to arouse him, but failed. He lay back. "I don't know what's gotten into me," he said.

# Twenty-Two

For the next few days, she didn't approach him. But then he could feel her need once again. She lay on her back beside him, and he could tell that her eyes were open, that she wanted him to make love to her. He began to touch her, her lovely, full breasts, her skin smooth as silk. He tried to remember how good their lovemaking had been at the beginning. Her response to him had been so passionate, thrilling, and unexpected in such a small, demure person. How good it had made him feel that he was the one who'd brought her to this.

He forced himself to remember all of it so he could make love to her now. It took more time than usual, but this time he succeeded. After, he swung over on his back, exhausted from the effort. But she didn't seem to mind, and when they were done, she stroked his cheek and whispered, "I love you."

Why could she at least *not* be pretty, not be an eager lover, or be a wife who wouldn't sleep with her husband? That would justify it. Why couldn't she be sarcastic or unkind? If she were somehow "bad," it would make what he was doing all right. She was none of those things, and it deepened his agony.

The next time he tried, he failed again. Everything had been spent with Christina that day. She had consumed all his desire.

"What's the matter?" she asked. "Is it me? Do you still love me?"

"Of course. Of course!" He pulled her toward him and hugged her. "I don't know what's the matter with me."

He tried to imagine it was Christina beneath him, that it was her pale green eyes looking up at him, her small, firm breasts against his chest, her long limbs wrapped around his body. He tried to hold on to that, and sometimes it got him through.

He was able to do it enough, he hoped, to make her happy. She didn't deserve this, to be unhappy, this good, sweet woman.

When he failed, she asked, "Is it because I'm not beautiful? I'm not a good lover?"

"Don't say that!" he cried. "I want to make you come," he said. And he did.

Afterward, she dozed off, but he lay awake, all his senses acute.

One evening, they were together, and Emily had a book in her hands. "God, there's no one like George Eliot to describe an unhappy marriage," she said.

"What are you reading?" he asked.

"*Daniel Deronda.*" George Eliot was actually a woman, Emily had told him.

"The heroine, Gwendolyn, is married to horrible, cold Henleigh Grandcourt, and she's fallen in love with Daniel, but he can't love her back."

How did Emily even know what an unhappy marriage was? Why was she reading this now? Was she trying to tell him about her own pain?

Christmas loomed, an important holiday for the Woodford family, a time when their full affluence was on display. Before Isabella was born, Emily, in the final month of pregnancy, in anticipation of the holiday, had even gone over Henry's house days before the holiday to decorate it—of course they'd have Christmas at Henry's house because he was the head of the family. She festooned the place with elaborate ornaments, garlands, and fairy lights, inherited over the generations of the family. She'd even bought their unborn child presents, a stuffed rabbit and a doll with real hair and a lace dress—by then they'd known it was a girl. The doll would sit on the nursery bureau until she was old enough to play with it, the embodiment of the little girl to come.

This year, he couldn't bear the idea of being there with Christina, having to gasp with forced delight as she and Henry and Emily unwrapped their gifts. He wanted to give *her* a present, to see her hands receiving it and her expectation as she unwrapped it, to fill her with happiness, to go beyond sex, to be able to love her fully. Instead, he'd have to pretend she wasn't there and endure the charge between them.

He had to get away from her.

Then Emily said, "Why don't we go to Rome for Christmas, just the three of us?"

"But what about your father? Won't he mind your being away at Christmas?"

"I want to be with my father, but you and I need some time together, just us as a family. And maybe they do too?"

Perhaps going to Rome would relieve him of the pain of having to be around Christina, of his guilt at his crime against the person he still loved—and he *did* love his wife—and his crime against Henry.

"We do spend most of our time here in New York with your family," Federico said. "I guess I kind of miss Rome, the old sights . . . I'd like to visit Aunt Celeste."

"Good," Emily said. "Done. I'll tell Dad."

They took a commercial flight to Rome, the big planes being safer crossing the ocean than the smaller, leased ones. The eight-hour flight was tough. The change in cabin pressure hurt Isabella's ears, and she cried continuously. After the lights dimmed and people were trying to sleep, they had to alternate with one another walking her up and down the aisle for hours trying to get her to stop crying, while the other passengers who'd spent a fortune for first class seats glared at them. At last, a children's video calmed her. They'd been keeping her away from "screens" at home because Emily thought they'd stymie her intellectually. Now Federico welcomed the excuse to hold her in his arms while she watched the squawking cartoon figures on the little screen, and to feel her warm body snug against his.

In Rome, they took a suite at the Hassler. The first night they were jet-lagged and exhausted, and to his relief there was no question of having sex.

The next day, as always, they had to give their full attention to Isabella. They took her to see the wavering canopy of rainbow-colored Christmas lights hanging over the Via del Corso, and to the carousel on the Piazza Navona. They waded through the crowds in St. Peter's Square, and he held her up so she could see the nativity. All the while, he and Emily had hardly any time to talk to one another, and he was relieved.

They'd taken two adjoining rooms at the hotel, one for themselves and one for Isabella—Emily's idea. "So we can have some time together," she said, and he knew what she meant.

But just as they were settling into bed, Isabella woke up crying in the next room.

"I'll get her," he said. He went in and rubbed her back in an effort to soothe her. But she was crying piteously, and she wanted him to pick her up.

He brought her into their room. "Let's take her into bed with us. I think she's just scared of the unfamiliar surroundings."

From then on, every night of their vacation, the child refused to go to sleep unless they let her sleep with them, and they gave in to her.

It was supposed to be a vacation to heal their marriage.

They brought Isabella to visit Aunt Celeste at the *casa di riposo*, where she still resided at Henry and Emily's expense. The halls smelled of disinfectant, but they were clean. Aunt Celeste was shrunken, barely able to speak, and deaf, sitting in a chair by her bed, a blanket over her legs.

"This is my daughter, Isabella," Federico shouted. "*Isabella, saluta la zia Celeste. Dalle un bacio.*" Aunt Celeste smiled radiantly up at them, and Federico held Isabella down so she could kiss her. Christmas was about family. Aunt Celeste was Federico's family, and Isabella was the future of his family. And Emily was his family too.

He wanted to introduce Isabella to Padre Matteo. They took a cab to the old church and found the priest in his office. Matteo was still pale and young looking, and still bald. As they sat there in his office, the realization swept over Federico that in the eyes of the church he had sinned. There in the little office, he found himself asking Matteo to bless Isabella. The request was instinctive; he had found himself suddenly uttering it, and Matteo was happy to do it. Out in the main church with its cold, stone walls, the priest dipped his finger in the holy water and painted the sign of the cross on Isabella's forehead. "May Almighty God bless you, my child, for time and eternity . . . " As Federico watched, he thought of asking him to christen her too. She'd already been christened in the family's Episcopal church in New York, but he wondered if she could still be christened in the Catholic Church, and if Emily and Henry, who weren't very religious, would allow it.

Afterward, they had coffee in Matteo's office and Federico asked about the soccer boys—particularly he wondered about Efrem.

"I remember that child," Emily said. "You were so sweet with him."

The priest shook his head sadly. "*È scomparso.*" Efrem had disappeared.

Matteo said Efrem had stopped coming to the soccer games, and he'd gone searching for him. He discovered that Efrem had been squatting in an abandoned building on the Via Curtatone. It turned out the police had raided them. The migrants had nowhere to go and some of them had been sleeping in the Piazza dell' Indipendenza. The police came after them there too with batons and water cannons and drove them away. After that, Efrem's trail had run cold. "*Niente*," Matteo said, shaking his head again. "I hope he's still alive, poor boy."

On Christmas Day, the hotel served a special lunch. They sat silently together in the grand dining room watching Isabella, who was engaged with her food. Gazing out the window at the glorious city, the twin domes of the Trinità dei Monti, the hills and the monuments, Federico understood for the first time what true loneliness was. It was being in the place of his boyhood with his precious child, and the good woman who'd given her to him, and yet feeling far, far away from it all, with his mind drawn to only one place, four thousand miles away, and to one person.

They arrived back to New York just in time for Henry and Christina's New Year's Eve dinner, an event they had to attend because they hadn't spent Christmas with them.

Christina had taken on the role of Henry's hostess and arranged the whole thing, sending out gold-embossed invitations to their friends. There was no way out for him. He was forced see her again.

The house was all lit up and shimmering with lights and silver, decorated with holly and urns filled with white carnations to match the snow outside. A string quartet had been hired from Juilliard and a few guests stood listening to them, but most of them talked and laughed over the music while the young musicians played valiantly on.

Waiters in white shirts and black suits were passing hors d'oeuvres. Henry, tall and modest, greeted the guests, nodding in acknowledgement of their warm words. Mike and Jean arrived.

Federico stepped back and let Emily move forward to say hello to her father's friends, a small figure in her black velvet dress, the only party dress she seemed to own.

Then he saw Christina, taller than most, swimming swan-like among them. Tonight, she wore a diamond necklace and a red, off-the-shoulder dress which showed the delicate bones of her clavicle and the cleft between her breasts. It was impossible to keep his eyes off her.

She spotted him too, and from the other side of the room she smiled her amazing smile at him, unnoticed by the others, daring him. It was as if a light beamed forth from her, and for a moment they were bound together by a golden ribbon pulling them toward one another. She knew her effect on him; he was still dazzled by her. He didn't return her smile and glanced around to see if anyone had noticed the look that had passed between them. But no, everyone was busy chatting with one another.

Tables were set up throughout the house, laid with perfect white linen cloths and sparkling crystal. At each place was a party favor, a jeweled masque which the guests donned, nodding at the person next to them, and then put aside.

Christina presided over it all. His own wife was sitting next to her father, but he noticed Emily wasn't engaging in her usual friendly conversation with the guests. Christina, in her red dress and diamonds, dominated the room. She, not Henry, was the governing presence. Rarely did these people encounter someone like her, a woman slightly exotic, from outside their world, with her tawny skin, her perfect posture and long neck, daring to wear a low-cut red dress, a formal dress, at a celebration in a home.

Federico was seated at another table among the various guests. As they ate the first course, caviar served on silver plates, his neighbors asked him about Henry's museum, and about Isabella. He couldn't concentrate, could hardly hear them, and they had to ask their questions twice.

After the meal, a waiter carried in a New Year's cake on a silver platter and placed it in front of Henry. Christina stood and raised her glass. "Henry has asked me to make the toast for him, to all our dear friends here tonight—you know how he is!" The guests laughed. They all knew Henry's reserved nature; it was a joke among them and they held him dear for it. In the light of his immense wealth, it made him less intimidating. "Happy New Year to you all!" Christina said. She seemed manic, as if she were in a kind of trance, fulfilling her role and acting like a wife.

"And I know you'll join me in toasting my dear husband," she said. She addressed Henry directly. "I'm so proud of you, Henry, with the museum, and the gift you're giving to so many people." Everyone clapped, joining the toast.

With that, Henry began cutting the cake. Bits of it dropped from the knife onto the tablecloth and Christina rushed to his rescue and took the knife from him. "Let me do it," she said. "You go and sit in my place so other people have a chance to talk to you."

More chatter, then Christina announced in a high voice, "Everyone—coffee in the parlor, and more champagne if you want it." With that, the crowd spread out through the double parlor doors, and the waiters began passing coffee.

Federico felt a sudden urge to jump from his seat and run.

# Twenty-Three

Emily was growing more distant. She was irritable in a way she'd never been before; she, who was always so soft and gracious with Federico, and with everyone. In the past, if she wanted Federico to do something, she'd ask him gently. Now she ordered him, "Federico, don't be late for my father's." When Isabella fussed unattended in her crib, she rebuked him. "Don't you hear her? Can you please go up there?" She was even impatient with Isabella. When the child threw a tantrum for some reason or another, she grabbed her and cried, "Stop that! Stop it now!" But then she caught herself, looking distraught at what she'd done, and took Isabella in her arms. "There, there. I'm so, so sorry, darling. Mommy's just a little tired."

They hardly spoke, except about arrangements for Isabella and household matters. He tried to be a good husband, to be attentive. "How is Moira?" he asked her. Moira was her friend. "Does she like being back at work?"

"She's fine," Emily answered coldly.

Unhappiness filled her face. In his guilt, Federico wondered if ever, before this, Emily had thought of herself as unhappy. Yet she seemed to sense nothing about Christina. She was his wife. They knew each other's habits, what even a change in a breath meant.

In the past, they sometimes had the same thought at the same time. Yet she didn't see what was going on! Strangely, this made Federico angry. Was she stupid? So weak she was willing to let this happen? Some sort of saint, unearthly, waiting for him to find his way back to her?

They'd been invited for the weekend to an estate on the Hudson River, by a collector and a client of Jean's, Miriam Alexis. Miriam had specifically asked Jean to invite Henry, Christina, Emily, and Federico to come along. Henry had recognized at once what this was about. He'd never met the woman, but her father had founded a chain of supermarkets and she was a collector of people as well as art. She wanted the prestige of having old money in the group—and, no doubt, a prince—and to oblige her, Jean had facilitated the invitation.

Henry, as always, disliked these social occasions, and he sent his regrets. But Christina said she'd like to go, and that it would be good to get out of the city.

Later, when Federico and Emily discussed the invitation, Emily said, "I can't take Isabella. It'd be too hard on her. There won't be any other children."

"But there'll be the train ride," Federico said. "Isabella would like that. She's never been on a train."

"She can't stay in one seat for two hours," Emily said flatly. He should know that already.

Federico could see her waiting tensely for his response, her eyes on him, studying him. Would he decide to go with them and leave her at home?

He walked away from her. He knew he shouldn't delay giving her an answer and he should insist on staying behind with her. But the possibility flooded through him. For weeks, Christina and he had had only fleeting, furtive moments together. If he went, it would be as if he and Christina were a couple, just for a little while, alongside Mike and Jean, of course. Two whole days, breakfast, lunch, dinner, across from one another—a relief from their strange, miserable hours on family occasions with Henry and Emily, pretending as if they hardly knew each other. And they might steal uninterrupted time alone. Even at a crowded house party, they might be able to go off for an hour or so, and no one would notice or care.

Mike and Jean would seem like their chaperones, even though Federico and Christina were technically in-laws. Of course, it would be perfectly proper for him to accompany his mother-in-law on a weekend away in the country—with other people.

"It would be nice to go to the country," he said to Emily. "It would only be a couple of days."

Emily watched expressionlessly.

"And Jean and Mike will be there to chaperone," he said, with a smile.

"Very well," she said crisply.

"You're not upset, are you?" he asked.

"I'm going to check on Isabella," she said, and walked out of the room.

That night he lay awake, while beside him Emily appeared to be asleep. She seemed not to want sex, but he wrapped his arms around her anyway, as if he were still her affectionate husband.

They decided to take the train up to the Alexis house so they could have "the experience of seeing the river," as Jean put it. On Friday morning, the four of them met at Penn Station. They'd booked two sets of double seats facing one another. As they boarded, Federico said to Christina, "You should take the window, so you can look out." He sat catty-corner from her, opposite Mike and next to Jean. He wouldn't have to look directly at her, so there'd be no danger of giving themselves away.

The train started up and began to leave the station, gaining speed as it lumbered through the suburban straits. Jean was quiet; she seemed preoccupied. Mike was his usual genial and oblivious self.

It rattled along, and their small talk ceased. Soon they were gazing out the window, engrossed in the scenery and the great river flowing by. At first, near the city, the landscape was green, the trees leafed out. But as they moved north, there were still chunks of snow on the riverbanks. There were small islands in the river, and on one of them, an actual castle. The castle was abandoned, Jean said. It had once belonged to an arms dealer.

Lulled by the train's rocking motion, Federico started to fall asleep, and welcomed it.

The next thing he knew, Jean was shaking his shoulder. They had arrived. He must have slept for at least an hour. His first thought was that Christina had seen him asleep. It had been a very long time since he'd slept in front of her. Asleep and unconscious, he'd given her the gift of his vulnerability, as if he were a child.

He stood up and helped Mike grab the suitcases from the overhead rack.

Outside, Miriam Alexis's driver was waiting to take them to the house.

They drove up through the riverside city, along country roads, past fields of withered corn husks sticking up from the snow. After a half hour, they came to a driveway with a metal gate. The driver spoke into his cell, the gate opened, and they proceeded along a private road, through pines and scrub oak. At the end, on the heights above the river, was a big white clapboard house with a pillared porch, and their hostess waiting for them outside of it.

Miriam Alexis was a sweeping figure, sixty or so years old, with dyed shoulder-length black hair, wearing a silvery-colored top with sleeves like wings. "Oh, how fabulous!" she cried in a high throttle. "And you," she said to Federico. "You are *Prince* Federico, I believe."

"Yes," Federico said, embarrassed as always when someone called him that.

The other guests were a curator from one of the river mansions that had been given to the state for a park and museum, and a big, broad man who was, Miriam told them, a famous scientist, accompanied by their wives.

Miriam Alexis was divorced, and no one had ever met her former husband. The house was her pride and joy. She'd bought it from one of the old river families, descendants of the original lords of the manor who'd owned it for generations but had gone broke and couldn't afford to maintain it. It had been built in 1790, she told them, and it was nearly a ruin when she got it. Bit by bit she'd restored it and furnished it meticulously with appropriate eighteenth-century antiques. In doing so, she'd made herself a part of the river families, though few of the original landowners remained and most of the great houses had been taken over and renovated by Wall Street people.

She gave them a tour of the place. There were nineteenth-century American landscapes on the walls, of the Hudson River and the Catskill Mountains and a great waterfall cascading down over the rocks. "Kaaterskill Falls," she told Federico. "It's across the river. The Hudson River artists all painted it." Jean followed along behind, listening studiously to Miriam's descriptions of the provenance of each work, though Jean herself had found most of the art for her and had taught her about its origins.

They were shown to their rooms. There was a mural of a river scene on the wall of Federico's room, and an old four-poster bed; a double bed in which he would sleep alone.

Then came lunch and an afternoon walk. Miriam walked briskly ahead of them along the paths of the estate. She showed them the barn and the path leading down to the river where the railroad tracks ran. But it was too slippery to go down there that day. Out on the point was an ice house. "Ice used to be a big business on the river," she told them. "They used to send it down to the city. Now, of course, the river doesn't freeze over anymore."

Miriam had invited some people from the surrounding houses for dinner. There was no way that Emily could have brought Isabella, Federico thought; they would have had to put her to sleep in an unfamiliar upstairs bedroom, and then would have to sit at the table, unable to hear her if she cried. He would call her later and tell her that.

Miriam sat at the head of the long table, an imperious figure with perfect, pale, smooth skin that made her look strangely young. When they'd finished the first course, before the dessert, Miriam tapped her glass with her spoon, and the talking ceased. "I think each of us should give our opinions on the current situation in Washington," she said. "We have a distinguished crowd here."

Around the table she went, calling out the name of each guest and giving a short description of their affiliations. "Jean, our world expert on art. Christina, who's married to the great collector Henry Woodford. Peter Jones, who's done so well with the Coxburgh estate, and of course, John Elting, our prize-winning scientist."

And then she came to Federico. "Prince Federico, who's a visitor to our country, and perhaps can give us a different perspective on it all . . ."

Once again, he was embarrassed at the mention of his title. People expected some authority, some special intelligence from him because of it. But he had none. He said quietly, "I'm not a citizen yet and I can't vote. I don't really feel it's proper for me to give an opinion." Miriam looked disappointed, but she went on until she'd also let the wives briefly give their opinions, which were more hesitant.

After dinner, when they dispersed to the living room for coffee and cordials, Federico found a seat by himself on a straight-backed chair in the corner. He couldn't bear talking to any of them. As always, he was aware only of Christina on the other side of the room, clad in a white blouse and long blue velvet skirt for the country dinner, talking to the famous scientist.

He saw Jean drawing near. "Are you all right, Federico? You seem down."

He sat up, on guard. In her anxiety, Jean was aware of everything. Sometimes he thought that Jean could see entirely through him.

"I'm fine," Federico said briskly. "Doing well." He didn't move to give up his seat to her. He gave her nothing.

"Federico," she said. "I just have to say this. Please, I beg you."

" 'Beg' what?"

"Please, don't hurt them." The words cut through him. Abruptly, he got up from his chair. She'd managed to dig her way in. Their behavior had been perfect.

He began to leave. She grabbed his arm and he snatched it away. Across the room, Christina had seen what had happened, and she'd stopped in the middle of her discussion with the famous scientist.

"Leave me be," Federico said to Jean, rude to her for the first time, like a child who'd been rebuked by a mother. "You don't know what you're talking about."

He strode across the room to the entrance hall and went out into the night. He stood under the light of the front door, his heart pounding.

A few seconds later, Christina emerged from the house.

"Why are you here?" he asked.

"I know from ten miles away when you're upset," she said. "What happened?"

"Jean. She said something. 'Don't hurt them.' "

"Oh, dear," she said. "Well, she has absolutely nothing to go on."

"That's what you say." There was a road leading from the house up to the barn. He moved toward it and she followed. The road was sheltered by trees. They wouldn't be seen.

"No one's noticed anything," she said.

"Did they see you leave?"

"They don't care," she said. "It's all right. You can't let her see you're afraid. That would be admitting it."

"Sometimes, I just want to die," Federico said.

"Don't ever say that," she begged.

"What are we doing?" he asked her.

"Don't you see?" she said fiercely. "Jean can't say anything. They'd be furious at her for even suggesting it."

"She senses something."

"But has Emily said anything?"

"No. But I know she's depressed. We're just distant from each other."

"In her own way, Emily's very mysterious," said Christina.

"Is Henry different?" he asked.

"You never know what's on Henry's mind. He's so reserved. Sometimes I think he just doesn't notice what he doesn't want to see."

"Maybe Emily gets it from him," Federico said bitterly.

"He's still so good to me," Christina said. She sighed. "*Siamo stati attenti*. We've been careful."

He shook his head. "I want to stop. But I can't." And in the secrecy of the trees, he reached over, pulled her to him, and kissed her.

From the distance came the sound of a train, then down below, the roar of the engine, filling the air deafeningly and cloaking them, at least for a moment, in an illusion of privacy. Then the train clattered past, and the night was quiet again.

She held his head between her hands. "Let's leave early tomorrow. Saturday!" she cried. "Tell them we want to get back to the *sposi*, and go to a few galleries beforehand." They were supposed to stay until Sunday.

"We could have the whole afternoon together," Christina said.

"Real time. Find an inn, then take a later train. We'll still be home a day earlier than they expected."

Federico let out a groan, of pleasure, of pain. "You've planned everything."

"I'm an Anglo-Saxon," she said. "I want it all." She stepped back and laughed, a strange laugh.

Again, he reached out for her. Only with her did he feel whole. "Yes," he said, pushing himself against her. She pressed into him and he met her lips.

Afterward, before he went to bed, he phoned Emily to say good night. He said he loved her, and to give Isabella a kiss for him. And he was careful to tell her that it was wise of her not to have come with them, as it would have been impossible with Isabella in the big house with all the guests. He thought of telling her he missed them so much he'd decided to come home early, tomorrow instead of Sunday. But he didn't. If he told her, it would fix a time in her mind, and it could cut into his time with Christina.

Saturday morning at breakfast, Christina told the others, "Federico and I've decided maybe we better go back this afternoon rather than tomorrow."

Miriam, seeing her party disintegrate, cried out, "Oh, no!"

"Federico really wants to get back to Emily and Isabella, and I feel guilty leaving Henry. I know you'll understand. We thought we'd go into town this morning, maybe walk around for a half hour or so and see a couple of galleries, then catch an early train."

Jean was dismayed too. "We were looking forward to having some time on the train to talk."

"We'll catch up later," Christina told her. To Miriam she said, "I hope you'll invite us back again."

"But this is such a shame," said Miriam.

"We'll see you in the city," Christina said. She was holding out the possibility of an invitation to one of the Woodford homes. That seemed to appease Miriam.

"We've had such a wonderful time," Christina went on. "But Federico really doesn't like to be away from his daughter. And I don't like to be away from Henry."

Federico let her speak for both of them.

After breakfast, they went up to their rooms to pack. Federico was the first to be ready and while he waited for her, he went outside to take in the morning air. The sun shone brightly, the air was crisp and cold. He walked around to the back of the house to better take in the view of the river, and the mountains beyond.

As he gazed out at the scene, he felt a feverish happiness and expectation overtake him. There were no rules.

From above him, there was the sound of a window banging open. He looked up. Christina was in the window, grinning down at him, challenging him. She had a dangerous courage.

"*Sono pronta,*" she cried. "*Sono pronta!*"

# Twenty-Four

WHEN THE TRAIN DROPPED THEM OFF IN THE TOWN THEY waited to make sure it had left and then made their way up the street toward the inn. They stopped briefly at a café just to fill their stomachs and gulp down some sandwiches, hardly paying attention to what they ate, and they each had a glass of wine in preparation. Their hunger appeased, they continued on, past the Greek Revival houses, the galleries and storefronts filled with antiques. The town had once been an industrial hub, made prosperous by its location to the river. But the factories closed, it had gone into decline and was gradually being restored by weekenders and prosperous artists.

Christina, eager to reach their destination, strode recklessly ahead of him. He stayed behind her so they wouldn't be spotted together. Though, in this town, two hours away from the city, they'd hardly be recognized.

She'd found the inn on the Internet. It was on a side street off the main thoroughfare. At the beginning of the block, to be extra careful, he suggested they go to opposite ends so they would enter separately.

The inn was an old house that had been done up and refurbished with terrycloth bathrobes, scented lotions and shampoos; a tourist venue far from the rundown hotels that, in their desperation, they'd frequented in the city.

When they arrived, Federico told the man at the desk that he'd left his credit card at home, and he let him pay cash in advance. There'd be no record of their stay on his credit card report, and the man didn't ask to keep a card as insurance in case they trashed the place. They looked respectable enough. Both wore wedding rings. They could be married to one another, though the man might have intuited from their awkwardness, positioned rather far apart as they stood in front of the desk, that they weren't.

He asked if they needed help with restaurant reservations. Federico said no, they were fine, thank you. They were in a hurry, and made none of the quick chat tourists usually do with concierges, asking about local sights.

Finally, they were in the room. Federico double-locked the door and closed the curtains. They turned off their cell phones. They didn't bother to get into the bed, and they made love, unrushed for the first time in months. When—spent—they finally broke apart, Christina said, "I want to stay the whole night with you. At least that. I want to wake up next to you."

"I know," he said.

"We could say we decided after all to stay longer at Miriam's."

"There's no way," he said. "You know that. We can't."

"Imagine," she said, "that this was our own home together. We could just make love whenever we wanted, eat, sleep together. I want to do ordinary things with you. I want to take care of you. Just simple things: cook for you, do your laundry. The things women do when they love someone. Make plans."

"That can't happen," he said.

As if she hadn't heard him, she went on. "That's what love is. All you want to do is be with the other person every single moment. It's a gift. We know each other better than anyone else in the world."

Then she said, "I wish I could have your child." It was what she'd said that night in Rome years ago.

This time, as before, a feeling like ice swept over him. But it was her right to want his child, the natural consequence of her love for him. All he could say was, "Oh God." He could never gratify her love, this deep, womanly wish of hers.

She buried her head in his neck. He was relieved she didn't cry. He couldn't bear it. They made love again.

Their train was at 4:45 p.m. It would get them to New York at 6:40 p.m.

It was only a ten-minute walk down the hill to the station, and they dragged themselves out of bed.

Downstairs at the desk, they checked out, Federico saying to the man they weren't staying overnight, they'd had a change of plans and had to get back to the city.

Outside in the town, she said, "I wish we could stay. We could at least have dinner."

"We can't," he said firmly.

On the train, they settled into their seats. She draped her shawl over their laps and they held hands underneath it.

The train started up and headed south toward the city.

Then, just as it left Rhinecliff station and they were on their way to Poughkeepsie, it came to a grinding halt. The conductor's voice came over the loudspeaker. "We apologize to our passengers. We're experiencing a delay due to a signal problem. We'll update you when we know more."

The car went quiet. Federico panicked and stood up, dislodging Christina's shawl from their laps, and searched the aisle for the conductor to ask him when the train would start up again. The man was nowhere to be seen. They'd told Emily and Henry they'd be home by 7:30 p.m., which had given them all those hours together in the inn. It was risky enough that they'd left Miriam Alexis's early.

"We'll text them the train's delayed," Christina said. "This train's delayed all the time. People expect it."

Federico took out his cell phone. He'd forgotten to turn it on. "*Madonna!*" he swore. "I can't believe it." He switched the phone on and immediately saw there were three messages from Emily. He listened to them. "Where are you?" she asked. "I called the house this morning."

"She phoned me and the thing was off," he said. "I've got to call her!"

He punched in the landline number. There was no answer. She must be at Henry's. He didn't try her cell phone because then he might actually reach her and have to speak to her. He left a message on the voice mail to cover himself. "The damned train's stalled! I didn't get your message because my phone was in my parka and I didn't hear it. We're going to be late." When he saw her tonight he'd say he didn't call her cell because he didn't want to interrupt them if she was at her father's.

The train's ventilation had gone dead. The car was airless.

He sat upright, tense, no longer under the sway of what had happened at the inn, waiting for the jolt of the engine starting up again, planning ahead what he'd say to his wife.

They had to wait close to an hour before the train started up again and continued on to the city. At eight thirty, he finally got to the house. He put his key in the lock, stepped into the entryway and saw Emily standing there. "Where were you?" she asked.

"It was awful. But you got my message about the train. I thought you'd be over at your father's."

"I called you at Miriam Alexis's. I called at 1:30. She said you and Christina had left early this morning. I tried your cell all afternoon, but you didn't answer. Where were you all that time?"

"I told you, the train was delayed a whole hour. We walked around town and looked at some of the galleries."

"Why didn't you answer the phone then?"

"I just didn't hear it. It was in my coat."

She only looked at him.

"There's leftovers in the refrigerator," she said, turning and walking away. "I'm going to bed."

That was all.

The next day there was the inevitable reunion, the four of them as a family, at Henry and Christina's house for an early dinner, taking Isabella with them. Isabella, of course, had her own child's seat at her grandfather's.

Christina was before Federico again, as Henry's wife. He thought he saw a deep new glow in her eyes. Maybe it was simply an illusion, formed in his memory from the day before.

What had happened had changed everything. Until now, their relationship had been furtive. But those hours together, and being able to have sex twice because they had time and no one could interrupt them, was the first happiness he'd known in months. He could still feel it in his body. It had given everything between them a new, ineluctable immediacy.

In the inn, as they were getting ready, he'd watched as Christina washed herself, put on her underwear, and bit by bit, her jeans, her shirt, and bent over and brushed her long hair. It was conjugal, they were a couple.

Here, at Henry's table, Christina said, "Look, she's feeding herself." Isabella was spooning her food into her mouth with precise, delicate little motions. "She's got such good motor control."

Federico was temporarily distracted by his pride in his child.

Emily interrupted them. With a feverish smile, she said to Christina, "I want to hear everything about the trip!"

Christina came alert. "It was great," she said.

"Which galleries did you go to?" Emily asked.

"Oh, lots," Christina said.

Henry didn't seem to be listening. He was busy tearing off bits of roll and feeding them to Isabella.

Emily persisted. "But what were their names? In case we want to go up there too, so Dad and I'll know which ones to see. I hear the town's getting to be a real artist's center."

He could see by the set of Christina's expression that she had begun to panic. She attempted a smile. "Gosh," she said. "There were several. I don't remember their names."

"You must remember some," Emily insisted, leaning forward, her eyes intense upon Christina.

Christina looked around vaguely for Federico. "I don't know. Do you remember, Federico?"

"They were all rather small," he said. "You just go up and down the main street. You don't really pay attention to the names."

"So, where did you have lunch?" Emily asked.

"Oh, some sandwich shop," Federico said. He couldn't remember the name of the place they'd stopped at, they'd been in a hurry to get to the inn. He came to Christina's rescue. "I think it was some sort of French café at the bottom of the street, near the station. Right?" he asked Christina, addressing her for the first time. "They had crêpes and things."

"Yes—yes," she said. "I remember now. Right down by the station. Across the street from that old converted factory building."

Emily looked from one to the other, smiling, her eyes fraught and gleaming.

# Twenty-Five

On the train back to New York from Miriam Alexis's, Jean had kept to herself, thinking it all over. She didn't say anything to Mike—it was all too awful, and people around them in the car would hear. All the way down, she'd brooded. Was what she saw real?

Later, in the apartment, as they got ready for bed, after they'd lathered and creamed themselves, attended meticulously to their teeth, swallowed their pills and poured their two bedside glasses of water, they settled themselves into the king-sized bed with its gray linen headboard, the honeyed scent of Jean's night cream filling the air between them, and Mike, as usual, switched on the television in time to watch the news.

The room was dark but for the light from the big blue screen on the wall in front of them. Jean couldn't care less about the news tonight, but for Mike the news was a continuing soap opera. Since his retirement, he'd become addicted to it, checking his cell phone every half hour or so during the day for the latest developments.

Jean lay under the heavy gray linen duvet, propped up by her many pillows and cushions and staring straight ahead, heedless of the moving figures on the screen, the journalists with their microphones reporting each moment of the unfolding drama. The

President was giving a press conference on something to do with North Korea.

"I'm now officially worried," she said.

"About?" Mike asked, his eyes on the television.

"Federico and Christina leaving early together."

"I know," he said, still watching the screen. "I don't know if anything's going to come of this," Mike said.

"I can't help it," Jean said.

"Did they get back yet?"

"Please, I hope so. Her face crumpled. "I don't know what's going on." She sniffed. "I don't want to know . . ."

Mike raised the volume on the TV.

"Would you please pay attention!" Jean said.

"This *is* rather important."

"It's not possible," she said. "There *couldn't* be anything going on."

" 'Anything'?"

"You know what I mean," she said.

"Not exactly."

"I mean, between Christina and Federico. How clear do I have to be?" she snapped. "Did you hear me?"

"Sorry," he said, and took her hand.

She smiled, very briefly, in apology for rebuking her big, white-haired husband. "Nothing is happening," she said firmly. "I actually don't think there's anything going on."

"I hope not," Mike said. "Emily said she didn't want to come, right?"

"Yes, but I wouldn't let *you* go away with another woman without me."

"I should hope not." He smiled.

"I don't understand Emily," Jean said. "Is she just totally oblivious? Doesn't she want to guard her property?"

" 'Property'?" Mike said.

"And what about Henry? What's he thinking?"

"He seems perfectly normal and happy to me."

"I'm surrounded by a bunch of optimists," Jean said. "I'm always the worrier."

"That's true," he chuckled.

"I can't help it," she said. "I feel I'm the cause of it."

"You were just trying to do a good deed by introducing Federico and Emily."

"This is awful to say, but it's my livelihood."

"True. But it's only a small part of our income."

"But my work is everything to me—you know that. Henry's my biggest client. And I've done this to him."

"You haven't done anything to anyone."

"There will be consequences."

"But not for you," he said. "You meant well."

Mike lay back in the bed, a great, calming presence into which Jean could always fold herself.

She saw him still concentrated on the television screen. "They're just doing it for show," she said.

# Twenty-Six

He had to get out of the house. "Let's go to the park!" Federico said to Isabella.

Immediately, she ran to her stroller and tried to climb into it.

When Federico was allowed to have Isabella to himself, he could forget everything and concentrate on her. Now that she was older, she was more aware of him and his potential for fun and play. Maybe because Emily was so preoccupied these days, she seemed to crave his attention even more.

The playground near their house was recently renovated with climbing pyramids and a big sandpit, much fancier and more elaborate than the shabby playgrounds he'd grown up with in Rome.

The misery of winter had lifted, and it was spring at last. The air was warm, the leaves on the trees green and tender, the flower beds ablaze with daffodils, the bushes in full flower with blossoms of white, pink, and yellow.

The shrill cries of children echoed off the asphalt and filled the air.

Isabella's first order of business was to make Federico push her on the swing. "*Più in alto!*" she commanded. "Higher!" One moment, it was Italian, the next English. They were the same language to her.

"*Non troppo in alto, tesoro mio!*" he told her. "Not too high, my darling, you don't want to fall out."

Isabella caught sight of her little friend, Milo, who was being wheeled into the park by his nanny. She tottered over to him on her plump little legs, her blonde curls bouncing, crying "My-My!" Milo was almost always there in the afternoon at the same time. The nanny let Milo out and the two of them ran to their favorite place, the sandpit. Sitting down in it, they made sounds at one another that only they could understand and poured sand into a pile and patted it. The sandpit contained who knew what germs and fleas, but Emily said it was okay for her to play there.

Federico sat on the wall drinking coffee, watching her. He lost himself in her, this perfect little being that, by some miracle, he'd helped to create. Her birth had unleashed in him a love he'd never known before.

Despite what had happened with Christina, he did still love Emily. He did. With anguish, confusion, and guilt. But how much of it was admiration for her absolute goodness, his gratitude to her for taking him in, for giving shape to his formless life? And yes, for providing the money so he could quit his job and take care of his mother and Aunt Celeste in Rome. As he sat there, images suddenly came to him in a flash, of Emily screaming at him, and Henry, big and strong, coming after him, trying to kill him.

He didn't deserve Emily. He felt as if he would dissolve into tears.

Watching his daughter in the sandpit, he thought, a little girl is the unsullied embodiment of femaleness, her skin at its most perfect, her hair at its softest. The way a father treats his daughter teaches her of the love she should expect to receive later from a lover or a husband. If she received love from her father, she'd learn to accept nothing less.

If Isabella discovered what he'd done to her mother, she'd hate him for the rest of her life. She'd refuse to see him ever again and she'd be forced to perceive him as a sexual being whose lust had broken their family and destroyed her mother. She'd believe that corrupted love was to be expected from a man, and she would believe she should accept it. It was his daughter, above all—even more than Emily—that he had betrayed.

If Emily left him, he'd lose Isabella forever. Old Washburn, their lawyer who was always so cold and who obviously mistrusted him, would make sure he never saw her again. After he'd signed their prenuptial agreement, on the few times he'd seen Washburn, the man had never let up on his suspiciousness toward him. Washburn was right, Federico thought. He was evil, and he'd taken advantage of the Woodfords.

The sky was growing pink, and one by one, the children and nannies were starting to leave. Isabella and Milo had begun snatching their toys from each other, then Isabella bopped Milo on the head, and he started to cry. The nanny got up to intervene and was trying to force Milo to get into his stroller, and he was kicking and howling in protest.

Federico gathered up his daughter.

# Part Six

# The Princess

# Twenty-Seven

LIKE THE SHADOW OF A CLOUD PASSING ACROSS THE SUN, THE realization had slowly darkened Emily's world.

The day before yesterday, when he'd gone up to that estate with the others, was the first time they'd spent a night apart. As she lay in bed that night, the space beside her was empty and the room so quiet without his breathing, that she'd realized what it would be like if he were gone forever.

She loved him; his slender body, his olive skin, the surprising light hazel color of his eyes. His voice, with its mix of English and Italian was like music to her, the words ending in vowels, the crisp pronunciation. She pictured him in her mind with Isabella, how tender and loving he was with his child. There was good in him. That moment when Isabella was born and Emily was lying on the table in the delivery room while the doctor sewed her up, she'd looked over and seen the nurse hand the tiny bundle to him. He'd taken the baby and gazed at her and wept, and then sang to her, so softly, his song only for her . . .

She'd always believed he had a good heart. The way he'd tried to help those migrant children. In Rome, when she went to that soccer game he coached, she'd seen how much he cared about the boys. He was so full of sorrow that he couldn't save them.

The next morning, she'd had the urge to phone him. He would tell her that he missed her too, that he wanted everything between them to be the way it was before. But the Alexis woman said he and Christina had already left the house earlier than expected that morning and were planning to go back to the city. All day, she'd tried to reach him, but he didn't answer. Not until late afternoon did he call her back, from the train, claiming that he hadn't heard his phone ringing all day. Where had they been all that time, then? She couldn't bear to say it to herself. The possibility was something entirely new in the realm of her imagination. She must be crazy.

But there was this new, awful thing: he'd stopped making love to her. She'd humiliated herself, had asked him why. Wasn't she enough for him? Not beautiful enough? A bad lover? He'd denied all of it and claimed he was just tired from the baby. But from the very beginning, Isabella had been tiring and it hadn't stopped them making love. She was angry at herself for even asking him. She couldn't bear to know the reason and she prayed he wouldn't give it to her, that he wouldn't say it.

Had he ever even loved her? He'd said he did, over and over again. And if he hadn't really loved her, how could he have played the part so well?

She recalled that day last winter, when the sun was bright and she and her father had taken advantage of the warm day to go for a walk with Isabella. On their way home, as they came onto the block, there was the great limestone mansion, its façade gleaming and white and impregnable, and Federico and Christina were standing out on the balcony together, waving at them. The sight of the two of them had struck her, how handsome and happy they were, reborn, satisfied-seeming and free, like two great birds winging over them. Obviously, Federico had gone to visit Christina while she and her father were out. They must have been alone together for at least an hour.

Then, lately, she'd noticed how uncomfortable they seemed

with one another. They never spoke to each other anymore when the family was together. They were so tense and stiff and unsmiling.

Her father, what did *he* think, what did he know? Had he noticed the tension between his wife and his son-in-law, too? How blind could he be? But her father was old—he was wise beyond wise.

People sometimes thought she was stupid. She knew that. But the customs and manners of her world had shaped her. You didn't confront people. Manners were everything. Maybe that was for the better. Her "stupidity," her cheerful, girlish ways were a disguise. It was as if she had a secret life. Her father had insisted she go to a "good college," and she'd devoured her classes, especially the literature ones, and she'd excelled. No one in their circle knew about books. To display knowledge of something others didn't know about was "boasting." The dread of boasting was innate in Emily. Certainly, Federico had none of the knowledge she did. He knew nothing about literature, though he told her he admired her for her education.

When Federico and Christina were upstate, Emily and her father had taken Isabella to the zoo. Her father wanted to show his granddaughter the daily sea lion feeding. Emily had outfitted Isabella in her pink smock dress especially for him. Her hair was growing, and Emily tied a pink silk ribbon around one of her blonde curls.

Her father manned Isabella's stroller as he always liked to do. When they got to the sea lion pond, a crowd of adults and excited children had already gathered to watch. The sea lions, brown coats glistening, knew they were about to be fed and were barking and flapping their flippers in excitement.

The keepers were making their way toward them carrying buckets of fish.

"Look, look, Isabella!" her father said. "They're feeding the sea lions. See." The keepers began pitching the fish at them and the seals leapt up nimbly to catch them as the crowd cheered.

While he and Isabella watched the sea lions, Emily studied

him. If only he realized how closely she scrutinized him, how well she knew the surprising vividness of his blue eyes, the soft fuzz on his cheeks above where he shaved, the threads of gray in his blond hair, the mole on the right side of his neck. And his hands: the hairs on top, the ridges on his fingernails, his strong hands that carried her when she was a child and never dropped her, put together her Christmas toys, and grasped the reins of the horse as she sat in front of him in the saddle and he taught her how to ride.

She knew all his ways, his smiling reserve, and those wonderful moments when some funny remark broke through that reserve and he burst out laughing; how when he was angry, he showed it with just a frown, and his voice was crisp and took on that strong, calm tone that no one could defy.

Was there anything different about him now? Had he registered that his wife and son-in-law had gone off to the country together—even though he said he didn't want to go with them.

But maybe she didn't really know him and could never really know him. There were things about a father that a daughter could never know, and that he didn't want her to know.

The keepers were snapping their fingers at the sea lions and making hand signals and the animals followed them, dodging from side to side. The keepers rewarded them with fish. One of them played Frisbee with them; another, a young woman, leaned down and the sea lion kissed her on the cheek.

"Izzy, can you say, 'sea lion'?" Emily asked.

"Liye—liye!" she echoed.

"She's a very smart young lady," her father said. "Aren't you, sweetheart?"

"I really think she's going to be bilingual," Emily said.

"Is it okay to speak two languages to her so young?" he said.

"Dr. Rose says it's fine. All the research says it doesn't cause speech delay."

Gazing at the scene, her father said, "My nanny used to bring me here when I was a boy." Emily imagined the little boy standing there politely with his nanny, with his trusting blue eyes and his blond hair neatly watered down, and dressed in an oxford shirt and khakis, bearing his circumstances with fortitude. He'd known nothing else—uncomplainingly, he had taken what he could from life, perhaps not even knowing how to complain. Maybe the fact that he was such a perfect, handsome child had saved him.

The sea lions were sated, the feeding was over, and they proceeded on to see the snow leopard. She was a big cream-colored animal with black spots, dozing calmly on a rock, her eyes half shut. "Leopard," her father said to Isabella.

"Lepa!" Isabella reached out to it, wanting to get into the enclosure with the beast.

"Yes, leopard," he said. "Her name's 'Malala.' But you're not going in there with her."

"She's getting so willful," Emily said.

"That's good," her father said. "She's going to be a strong girl."

"Sometimes I think we're spoiling her."

"You can't spoil a child at this age. When you give a child a lot of attention, you're making her more confident, stronger."

"I was spoiled," she said. "I got a lot of attention."

"And look at you," he said. "You're strong and confident, right?"

"I'm not sure about that."

He looked sharply at her. "What do you mean?"

"I don't know. Do I know how to look out for myself?" she asked.

"Of course you do," he said. "Let's go see the pandas." He put Isabella down. She tottered along the path ahead of them and they hurried after her and grabbed her.

Her father took a deep breath, inhaling the fragrance of the new green coming in.

"We're lucky," he said. "We've got everything." Then, suddenly he said, "I'm so glad that I've been able to make Christina happy." It wasn't like him to speak personally like this, about something such as his love for his wife. Emily wondered, was he trying to convince himself?

"Yes." She spoke carefully. "She seems happy." Was he trying to mark his happiness with words because he'd begun to doubt it?

"I used to think you got married for my sake," she said. "So I wouldn't be worried about leaving you to marry Federico."

Her father frowned. "Don't be absurd. I married Christina for *her*, for myself. Where'd you ever get that idea? I can take care of myself." He seldom spoke to her sternly like this and she was intimidated.

"Of course," she said meekly.

She touched his arm. "I'm so happy for you," she said. And that was the end of it.

Later, as she went about her day, she kept seeing images of Federico and Christina in her mind. It was as if there were two photographs, side by side, and her eyes were going incessantly from one to the other—Federico to Christina, Christina to Federico.

# Twenty-Eight

FEDERICO HAD TAKEN ISABELLA TO THE PLAYGROUND, AND THE house was quiet. Emily found herself moving toward his study. It was his private place, one she'd created for him so that he'd have somewhere of his own, of importance, in case he had "something to do."

Tentatively, she opened the door. She almost never came here when he was gone. Usually, when she knocked on the door, he'd have his feet up on the desk, reading *Football Italia* or *L'Espresso* or watching his team, Juventus, on Italian TV on his computer, and he'd smile welcomingly at her.

She was snooping and he'd be angry at her if he knew. Well, he'd have to suppress his anger. After all, she was the one who'd given him this place, furnished it for him with its ormolu desk and an antique picture of Rome.

The air in the room was close. She approached the desk and saw that his computer was open. She sat down, touched the space bar, and the screen lit up. He had a picture of Isabella as his screen-saver, smiling jubilantly with her first tooth.

The little rectangular window appeared on the screen and demanded a password. What would he use for his password? He'd never told her his password, and she'd never bothered to ask. Her own password was Isabella's birthday, 2917. Maybe he used that, too? She typed the numbers into the box and the box shook at her. That wasn't it. Maybe, out of love for her, he used *her* birth date? She tried that. No. Maybe his own birthday? Again, nothing.

From upstairs came the sound of the vacuum cleaner. Mrs. Evans always began cleaning upstairs and worked her way down. She mustn't find her here snooping. Emily pulled down the top of the computer and left the room.

It was inconceivable. There was no proof—nothing. And, if she said anything to him, there'd be no going back. And if it wasn't true, merely asking the question would change their world forever.

He'd leave her, and then, where would she be? She'd be alone and shamed, and she'd have to raise Isabella by herself. She'd be taking Isabella's father away. And if her own father found out that she'd dared to even ask the question, he'd be horrified that she could even think such a thing. That is, if he didn't believe it himself. And if he did, her saying it aloud would force the end of his great new happiness.

She had no one to talk to, no one to ask for help.

# Twenty-Nine

EMILY HAD ALWAYS HAD THE URGE TO THINK OF JEAN AS A KIND of mother, and Jean would like to be that for her, she knew. After Isabella was born, she had told Emily how much she wished she and Mike had had children, that it was an emptiness in her life that had grown more profound as she got older. "We tried. But it just never happened. And we were reluctant to adopt. You don't know what an adopted child will be like. There's the genes, the prenatal environment." Emily was so lucky to have a girl, Jean said. When Emily was old, Isabella would take care of her. If Mike died, Jean would have no one.

"*I'll* take care of you," Emily had said. "But Mike's not going to die."

Now in the bistro, Jean sat across from her, dressed in sharp, gray spring linens today, her dark red lipstick faultlessly applied; a warm, comforting presence.

"How are you, dear?" Jean asked.

"This is so hard," she said. "I've got . . ." The words seemed to choke her, and she couldn't get them out. She gave up. "Oh, well."

"What is it?" Jean asked.

"I guess . . . I've been having these dark thoughts. I feel you're the only person I can go to."

"My goodness!" Jean said. "What's the matter?"

"I've been thinking about Christina . . . and Federico."

"But . . . what about them?"

"You know they knew each other in Rome."

"Yes, of course." There was dread growing in her face.

Emily shook her head. "I don't know."

The waiter appeared and was standing over them. "Can I tell you about our specials?"

"Please no!" Emily begged. She forced herself to glance at the menu. "Just a chef's salad. And iced tea."

Jean hadn't taken her eyes off her. "Same for me," she said.

He scooped up the menus and departed.

Emily said, "When he told me once he'd known Christina in Rome, I asked him if . . . if he'd ever wanted to go out with her."

"What did he say?"

"He deflected it."

Jean pursed her lips. "Well, there you have it."

"Do I?" Emily asked.

"Did you expect more?" But she wasn't giving a flat denial.

"I don't know. It's too awful. I can hardly think about it. And Dad . . . my God. It's unspeakable. Do *you* think I'm out of my mind?" she asked Jean.

"No. But you know, marriage is always an adjustment."

Emily listened carefully. "I was happy when Dad married Christina," she said.

"It was time you tore yourself away from your father," said Jean. "I think he's really found himself with Christina."

"But lately I've . . . felt even more that I have to watch over him."

Jean let out a dry laugh. It was too sudden, exaggerated. " 'Watch over him'? Over *Henry*? He's the most competent person I know. What does he need watching over for?"

"Because, because I'm so terrified for him, of his being hurt again."

Jean was gripping the edges of the table. Emily went on. "It's inconceivable. Too terrible even to think of. Impossible. I can't even say it to myself. What do *you* think?"

"What do I think?" Jean said. "About what?" she asked. "I think the whole thing is too awful to think about, too." She was saying nothing. Maybe it was just as well.

"You're coming to the island, aren't you?" Emily asked.

"Of course," said Jean.

"You have to come. I need you."

The food arrived, and they had to stop while the waiter set the glasses and plates down in front of them.

After he'd gone, Emily said, "What would I do? What would I ever do?"

"I don't know." Jean's voice was weak.

"I'm on my own, aren't I?" said Emily.

"You have me." She reached over and took Emily's hand.

Emily looked hard at her. "Do I?"

"Of course," Jean answered. "Of course you do."

# Thirty

THEY WERE LEAVING FOR THE ISLAND IN TWO DAYS. HER father's birthday was coming up and they'd be celebrating it there, as always. There was nowhere on the island to buy anything so she had to get him something now.

The thought of giving her father a present always filled Emily with warmth and a soft adoration, and now she had a new urgency to make him happy. It would be a temporary distraction.

To buy a present for her father was always impossible. Every Christmas, every birthday, she agonized over it. He had all that exquisite art he'd bought for his museum. But he always pretended anything she gave him was superb.

Time was running out. She strolled along Madison Avenue, hoping for inspiration. It was hot and humid today, like trudging through hot soup, though it was only early June. The sweat ran down her face; she could taste it on her upper lip.

She couldn't buy him something to wear; that was in the intimate realm of his wife, Christina, now. Expense wouldn't impress him.

She walked into one of the galleries. It was deserted, except for a single salesperson, an attractive young woman dressed in black. People had already begun leaving for the country for the season.

How did these places stay in business? The prices were so high, maybe they needed to only occasionally make one big sale to keep the place going. The woman greeted Emily with a relieved smile. At last, someone was coming into the shop who might buy something.

A brief glance around told Emily it was all inferior work, capricious, flat, without inspiration or feeling, just squares and lines of paint and unfathomable shapes. Being around her father all this time and listening to him talk about art, she'd developed an instinctive eye for good work. Who, she wondered, determined this was even art, and who would ever buy it? It was merely something to fill rich people's walls, she supposed, the colors to go with the décor of their apartments. Nothing here would do for him.

Back out on the street, she looked up and noticed a sign on the second floor of a building, EDOUARD GAMAL, ANTIQUITIES. Christina had mentioned a fascinating little shop near them that sold antiquities. "It's full of all these unusual things," she'd said, "the way it used to be with all the little stores, before everything was chains." She'd said the name, it was "Gamal something."

Her father didn't collect antiquities, but there might be something here that would interest him because of its unfamiliarity.

In the entryway of the building, the coolness was a relief. She pressed the button for the gallery, gave her name, and she was let in. Upstairs, there was a small office, and an elegant lady who led her into the gallery, and Mr. Gamal. He was a broad man, with dark, wavy hair, and smiling dark eyes. He was delighted to show her his wares. Like the other places she'd visited today, this one seemed to have no customers.

"I'm looking for a birthday present for my father," she said. "It has to be very special. He's a very special man." She smiled, hoping this would make him more eager to help her.

He smiled back. "*Mais certainement.*" He seemed to take pleasure in her mission.

"You're French?" she asked.

"Actually, no. I'm Egyptian. But I grew up speaking French. We learned several languages."

"That must be a great help in the business."

"It is indeed," he said.

She glanced around at the ancient busts and statuettes on the shelves, and the jewelry in glass cabinets. The busts and statuettes were too big, too dominant for what she had in mind, and she didn't understand their significance or their provenance sufficiently to risk buying one. She wanted to be sure whatever she bought for him had some intrinsic value. Mr. Gamal went over it all, patiently describing everything, obviously enjoying talking about his cherished objects.

Emily sighed. "Oh dear. I just don't know. My father's an expert on art. It has to be something unusual, something that would engage him. So he can look at it and think about us, myself and my husband and my daughter."

"I understand completely," Mr. Gamal said. "Who is your father, if I may ask?"

She told him.

"I've heard of him," he said. In the small world of wealthy collectors, of course her father's name would be recognized. "I don't know him myself," he said. "I believe he collects paintings, doesn't he?"

"Yes."

"Anyway, I'm sure he knows a great deal."

"He knows everything!" she said.

"We fathers like to think our daughters believe that," Mr. Gamal said with a laugh.

"Do you have a daughter?" she asked politely.

"I do," he said. "I think she's about your age."

"I'm sure she thinks you're special, too," she said.

He smiled. "Perhaps undeservedly."

"What does she do?" Emily asked.

"She lives in Paris. She's getting her *Magistère* in Economics at the Sorbonne."

"You must be very proud of her," she said.

"I am very proud," he said.

She continued examining the objects. Everything was too big, or too odd, and sometimes ugly, valuable only because of its great age. There was just nothing suitable. She said to Mr. Gamal, "I'm afraid I'm not getting anywhere."

Mr. Gamal, his hand over his mouth, thought for a moment. "I do have something. Something very sweet, actually."

It was then that he went to a drawer behind the counter and took out a red leather box. He opened the lid and revealed, lying in a satin bed, a small vaselike object. It was glass, with a cloudy green and gold iridescence.

"Is it a vase?" she asked.

"Perhaps."

"It's very sweet," she said. "May I?"

"Certainly."

She lifted it out of its case. "I love the way it catches the light. It seems very old, but the age makes it enchanting." She pointed to where the glass was encrusted with a hard, white substance. "What's that?"

"That's calcification from age. It's actually Roman," he said. "But this one was dug up in Egypt. The Romans were everywhere, of course. It's probably second century."

"What was it for?"

"They're not sure. It might be what they called an *unguentarium*. Possibly used for storing oils for household use. Archeologists find them in ancient household dumps."

"Dumps?"

"They're found in burial sites, too," he said. "Possibly it's what they called a *lachrymatory*, so mourners could cry their tears into them. There's a passage in the Bible: '*Put thou my tears into thy bottle.*'"

"You know the Bible well," Emily said.

"It's my job to know the Bible," Mr. Gamal said. "There are a lot of things here from the first and second centuries."

"What does that part from the Bible mean?" she asked.

"It's from the Psalms. King David is begging God to see how much he's suffering at the hands of his enemies. He's showing Him with his tears how grieved he is by them, and asking Him to store his tears in His bottle."

"Oh," she said. "Tears. I don't know. Sadness. I'm not sure . . ." To give him something sad on a supposedly happy occasion like his birthday. "I don't want to give him anything signifying sorrow."

Then, in the warmth of the man's fatherly kindness, her inhibitions fell away. "I'm concerned that my father may be going through a rough time." It had just come out of her, telling this to a stranger. But . . . he was also a father. She stopped herself.

The man looked stricken. "I'm so sorry," he said.

"He doesn't show it. I don't think he even realizes it yet." She felt tears rise in her eyes and shook her head. "I shouldn't have said anything."

Mr. Gamal looked even more upset, but he was obviously too polite to ask further.

"Whatever it is," he said sympathetically, "I'm sure you're a great comfort to him."

"That's sweet." She wiped her eyes with her fists.

"Remember," he said, "they also think they could have held perfume. The scholars don't really know."

"How would it stand up, though?" she asked. "It doesn't have a base."

"That's characteristic of that period. None of them do," he said. "I can have it mounted for you. It takes no time. I could deliver it myself to you tomorrow."

He had said it might also have been for perfume. It might have had a sensual use. It was unusual, something no one else would ever give him.

"I'll take it," she said. She remembered to ask, "How much is it?"

"Five hundred dollars," he said.

"That seems very cheap. Though I don't know what things cost,

I suppose." She probably shouldn't have said that, letting the man know price wasn't an issue, that she had money. But then, the price *was* low. She trusted him. Perhaps because he dealt in such expensive wares, the little vase or whatever it was, was a trivial thing for him.

"I'm surprised you haven't sold it before," she said.

He nodded, acknowledging that. "Yes." He made no further comment.

She wrote out a check for the amount and handed it to him. He stared at it. He seemed to be hesitating about something.

"The check really is okay," she assured him.

"I'm sure it is." He wavered again, then, "I'll bring it over tomorrow for you," he said.

"Thanks so much!" she said. "The address is on the check of course."

"I see," he said. "And you are very welcome. I wish your father every happiness."

As she left him, he was still holding the check in his hand and looking at it. "I will see you tomorrow," he said.

The next afternoon when he arrived with the package, she led him into the parlor. He unwrapped the box for her and separated the bubble wrap to show her the little vase nestled in tissue paper and mounted on a new black-lacquered plinth. He held it up for her to see.

"That's great," she said. "The stand gives it authority, makes it seem bigger."

He was looking doubtfully at it. "Is something wrong?" she asked.

"No. No," he said hastily.

"Don't you like the way it's mounted?"

"Yes, very good." He put his hand in his jacket pocket, and he pulled out her check. "I am refunding your money," he said.

"But . . . why?"

He seemed to be formulating a response. "You see, my business depends on integrity, on trust."

"Yes, of course."

"The reason the vase is cheap is that there is a flaw."

She squinted at it. "I don't see anything."

"It's a bit hard to see," he said. "It has a crack."

"But it's not visible."

"It's only visible with a magnifying glass. At the bottom, right over the mounting."

She could just make out a faint line on the glass. "Honestly," she said. "You can hardly see it, it doesn't matter. The money is nothing. Really."

"No," he said. He gave her a sad smile. "I am a father too. It's for your father. I can't charge you for something that has a flaw. This amount doesn't mean anything to us." With that, he tore the check in two.

"My goodness," she said.

"It's very nice, in its way," he said of the vase.

"Thank you! I'm putting it up there on the mantel so I can look at it. My father won't be coming here before his birthday."

Mr. Gamal followed her over to the marble mantel and she placed the vase among the family photographs there in their ornate silver frames, the pictures of herself and Federico and Isabella, and of her father and Christina.

He stood there scanning the photographs. His eyes rested on two of them and went from one to the other. He leaned in closer. "That's odd," he said. "I believe I have seen two of these people before."

"You have?"

"Yes. I think they came into the shop awhile ago. I will never forget them."

"Really? I think my stepmother went there once. She told me about the shop."

He pointed to the family portrait of her and Federico and Isabella. He indicated Federico. "I think it was this man," he said. Then he pointed to the other photograph, of Christina and her father. "He was with this woman." With Christina.

"He was?"

"I remember it very well. They were looking for a wedding present. They almost bought this very same thing. They spoke in Italian. They didn't know that I speak Italian. I thought perhaps they were . . . together." He stopped, as if realizing there might be significance to this. "I thought they were . . . married . . . to each other," he said. "They were very emotional together. I remember them because the man was angry with her, and he walked out. I think there was an argument."

"Married?" Her breath caught.

"Madame?"

She flushed and sat down abruptly on a chair. Even after she and Federico were engaged, they'd been together. He'd made it seem that they'd just run into one another now and then. He'd said they hardly knew each other.

Here it was before her, what she'd refused to see, what she hadn't wanted to believe, the truth forming in front of her eyes.

Mr. Gamal asked agitatedly, "Are you alright? Can I get you something?"

"Are you sure?" she asked him. "Are you sure you saw them?"

"Why, yes," he said. "I am absolutely certain."

"An argument?" she said. "They were having an argument?"

"Yes," he said. He looked at her as if understanding that he'd said too much, and he realized that there was even more meaning to this.

# Thirty-One

After he'd gone, she sat in the dreadful quiet, unable to move; the furniture seemed to breathe around her, everything bright and hard.

From here, the thing on the mantel looked tiny. She could just make out its spindle shape in the middle of the photographs. Two happy couples, Federico holding Isabella, and her head resting lovingly on his shoulder. The other: her father with his arm around Christina, who's gazing up at him with a smile.

He'd gone to the gym—so he said. Would he dare? Had he found a way to be with her, even today?

The doorbell sounded. Jean had called and said she wanted to come by for a cup of tea and to see if Emily was alright after their lunch.

Emily started down the stairs to let her in. She gripped the banister as she went.

She opened the door. Jean leaned in to kiss her. Emily let her lips brush her cheek.

Then, like an automaton, she led her up to the parlor.

She lowered herself carefully into a chair, and Jean sank down in the chair next to her.

"I know everything," Emily said. "I know about them."

Jean blinked.

"They were having an affair then," Emily said. "And they're having an affair now."

Jean sat forward in her seat. "What do you mean?"

Emily stood up. "I have proof," she said.

She got up and walked over to the mantel, reached up and took the little vase. Without expression, she brought it back to Jean and handed it to her.

Jean held it out before her. "What is it?"

"It's Roman. Some sort of vase or bottle. I bought it on Madison Avenue for Dad for his birthday."

"It looks very old." Jean handed it back. "But it's not my field."

Emily placed it on the mantel again. "They think it held perfume," she said. "Or tears."

"Tears?" said Jean.

"It's maybe something called a '*lachrymatory*,' to catch the tears of mourners at funerals. Tears. Appropriate, right?"

"I don't understand," Jean said. "What's this got to do with anything?"

"The man delivered it this morning. He recognized Federico and Christina from the photos on the mantel. He said they'd come into his shop a couple of years ago to buy a wedding present. They spoke Italian and they didn't realize he understood them. They were arguing. He assumed they were married." She looked wildly around the room. "I don't know what I'm doing!"

Jean started to go to her. She stepped away.

"But . . . but that doesn't prove anything," Jean said. "I mean about now."

"It all fits together. The way they're so tense together. Going up to that woman's house on the Hudson together. The way Federico's pulled completely away from me."

"But you didn't want to go with us?"

"Do you think I'm stupid, Jean?" Emily said.

"No. Of course not. How could I? Have you said anything to Federico?"

Suddenly, Emily was calm. "I think I'll just wait." Then, fiercely, she asked, "Why didn't you tell me they'd had a relationship? I thought you were my friend."

"It wasn't relevant," Jean cried. "It was over."

"Relevant? That I was marrying a man who'd had an affair with my friend. That my father married a woman who'd had an affair with my husband? And she's having one now. How's that not relevant? Every person who matters to me is lying to me. Who can I trust?" Emily said.

"He pretended to love me. He's the father of my child!" She stopped, couldn't finish. Then, "I didn't want to see it," she said. "I am so screwed up! What do I say to my father? This will destroy him. The idea that this man who's given everything to Federico and me, and Federico is sleeping with his own wife!" She looked hard at Jean. "Now I know you're not my friend."

Jean was about to break into tears. "Oh my God, Emily, I *am* your friend," she said. "I love you. Federico had ended it with Christina. He was lost. I was so glad when he fell in love with you. I knew he'd found the right person in you. And then, with Christina and Henry, it was so great to see Henry happy again. What good would it have done to dig up the past?"

"You wanted to be the matchmaker. Federico was a good catch, a prince for your client's daughter. Are you trying to tell me it's not happening?"

"If your father doesn't know about it, leave it."

"How can I? She's evil! What about me? Us? Federico and me?"

Jean hesitated. "Take your cue from him," she said.

"What do you mean?"

"Henry doesn't want to know. I really think that."

"Everyone thinks I'm stupid!" Emily cried. "Well, I'm not stupid anymore."

"I am so sorry," Jean said. "I made a mistake. I thought it was the right thing to do." She took a deep breath. "This whole thing, it's not happening." She hesitated. "I'm assuming you don't want us to come to the island now?" she said meekly.

"No," Emily said. "You'll come. If you pull out, my father will know something's wrong."

Then she spun around, she walked across the room, and lifted the vase from the mantel. "It's got a crack," she said. "The whole thing's cracked." And with a violent motion, she hurled it to the floor.

Just then, the parlor door opened.

"What's going on?" Federico asked.

# Thirty-Two

JEAN LOOKED INTENSELY AT HIM; SHE WAS TRYING TO WARN HIM.

Slowly, Emily bent down to pick the shards up from the floor. She placed them in a neat pile on the mantel and began fiddling with the broken pieces, trying to fit them back together. It was futile; they were too small.

Federico took off his baseball cap. Emily faced him, her smile delirious. "I broke it," she said.

He looked puzzled.

Jean cut in. "I've got to go, you two. No need to see me out, Emily."

She hurried out.

Federico ventured slowly, carefully toward Emily, then stopped.

She said calmly, "You thought I was stupid." He didn't answer. "Look at it." She threw her arm out toward the mantel. She was flushed, perspiring.

"What is it?" he asked, going up to it and peering at the bits of glass. "I can't see anything. It's broken."

"I broke it," she said again. "It's the vase, or whatever it is, the '*tear holder*,' that you and Christina almost bought from that antique shop on Madison Avenue, before we got married. I went there to buy something for my father—Christina told me about the place—can you believe it?"

He didn't move. More was coming, something grave.

"You and Christina went there before the wedding," she said.

"We did?" His voice was smooth. He was pretending to be confused.

"Don't lie. I've suspected it. You and she were together. And you're together now! I didn't want to see it. I phoned Miriam Alexis's house and she said you'd left together early that morning. I called and called you all day, but you didn't answer."

"What are you talking about?" he said. "We came home a day early because we missed you. The train got delayed. I left a message on your cell."

"Don't lie to me. I've had it with lies."

"Your father—" he began. How much did her *father* know? That's what mattered to him.

She went on. "The man delivered the vase this morning, spotted the photographs on the mantel, and recognized you both. He said when you came into the shop, you were arguing. He figured you were married. You spoke Italian, but he knows Italian."

Federico lowered himself onto the couch. "How much did he charge you for it?" he asked.

"Is that all you have to say?" she cried. "I'm getting much more than it's worth. He said it had a crack. How's that for symbolism? He tore up my check."

He had nothing to say.

"When you got home, I was waiting for you. You didn't want to have sex. You don't want to make love to me anymore!" She spat out the words. "And you couldn't, because you'd been with *her*. And . . . my father . . ." She faltered. "How could she? How could *you?*"

He began walking toward her. "Emily," he said, "I've never loved you more than I do now."

She glared at him. "You're a liar."

"If you'd known about it when we met, would you still have married me?" he asked.

"You would've told me it was over and, like a fool, I'd have believed you."

"It's over now," he said.

"You make me sick!" She spun away.

Again, he asked, "Does your father know? Have you said anything to Christina?"

Emily laughed. "I've told you everything I'm going to tell you. The rest is up to you."

# Thirty-Three

HE WENT INTO HIS STUDY AND STAYED THERE WITH THE DOOR shut. Her anger scalded her. But there was Isabella to take care of. Isabella had to survive, to eat, to sleep. She found some instinctive memory in herself of how to feed her, draw her bath, stir the toys in the water for her, and pretend to play with them, and then get her into bed.

"Da?" Isabella asked. Usually, Federico gave her her bath.

"Daddy's not feeling well. He's taking a nap." That seemed to satisfy her, at least for the moment.

At bedtime, she managed, tonelessly, to sing her lullabies. As always, she listened to them closely, sucking her thumb and watching Emily. She didn't ask for her father again. Maybe she could feel that something serious had happened, that he wasn't going to come, and she'd have to accept her mother alone.

After Isabella had fallen asleep, Emily didn't try to eat supper—eating would make her sick. Federico was still in his office. There was no sound coming from it.

She batted about the house, trying to tidy up. The only thing to do was to go to bed and try and drown herself in slumber. She undressed in the bathroom. When she came out in her nightgown, he was there in his pajamas, which he rarely wore. A new modesty, a defense. They weren't going to make love anyway.

There was a question on his face. He was waiting for his punishment, to find out what she was going to do. So far, she hadn't thrown him out. What now? Were they to sleep in the same bed? She refused to tell him.

Meekly, he took a pillow and blanket from the bed and made a place for himself on the chaise. He was trying to stay in the room with her, to assert that he was still her husband, trying to avoid his punishment.

They lay across the room from one another, wired. From the street came the sounds of spring, footsteps on the pavement, voices, occasional bursts of laughter. Her thoughts raced—she should make him leave. The thought flashed through her—not yet. She wasn't ready. She didn't have a strategy. She didn't have the tools for this.

And how would she explain it to her father? Reveal the truth to him? Her world would disintegrate. Would Federico leave *her*? Would he dare? He'd never see Isabella again—she'd see to that.

The prenuptial agreement. Mr. Washburn would nullify it, he was better than any lawyer Federico could ever find. Federico would be penniless.

There was no way she could sleep. She couldn't even cry. She was alive, paralyzed. He was over there on the chaise, very still.

She knew he wasn't asleep; she didn't hear the regular breathing that always signaled he'd fallen off. The rhythms of his existence were ingrained in her. Coffee first thing in the morning, while she had tea. He didn't eat breakfast, so nothing to eat until an early lunch. His habits of moderation, modest portions of food, hardly any alcohol. The one certainty was that the television would be on. He could find any soccer game in the world on his computer—Germany, Ecuador, Finland, Italy—and sit for hours watching it, sometimes holding the inattentive Isabella on his lap and trying to teach her the rules of the game. "See, the man has to kick the ball down there where those posts are."

Nearly an hour passed of mutual stillness and silence. Then, abruptly, he got up from the chaise and left the room. She heard him going down the hall to the guest room. Trying to be the angry one now, to hold on to his denial, and to his life. She didn't go after him and beg him to come back.

The night surrounded her, the thought of lying awake forever in the infinite, formless darkness terrified her. She couldn't stop the racing of her thoughts. There was a bottle of sleeping pills in the bathroom for when they traveled and had jet lag. She went into the bathroom, found the pills in the cabinet, and swallowed one.

The morning light woke her. As she came to consciousness, she expected to feel the press of his leg against her body as she always did. But he wasn't there. She heard Isabella chirping in the next room. Usually, he jumped up, eager to get her, but this morning he hadn't, and she was still chattering to herself. He no longer had that prerogative, to be the first to get to the baby and hold her and kiss her, to briefly have his daughter to himself.

Her mind was clogged from the sleeping pill. They were supposed to leave for the island and they had to pack. If she could just propel herself on, she could use the preparations to fill her mind.

At breakfast time, he came slowly into the kitchen and went to make his coffee. He didn't look at her, or say anything to her. He only went to kiss Isabella in her high chair and wish her "*Buon giorno*." Pretending all was normal. He was waiting, waiting to see what she was going to do.

She said to him, "We have to pack. You can pack your own things." Normally she'd pack his clothes for him. "I'll do my own and Isabella's."

So, he knew she was making him go to the island, forcing him to see Christina, and show himself to her father. She wasn't leaving him behind to soak in his misery and wonder about his future.

In the bedroom, she found him obediently folding his clothes into his suitcase.

"You can cancel the newspapers," she told him. "And do the mail forwarding thing. You can do it online. As you know, Devlin goes once a day to the mainland to fetch it."

Gingerly, he left and went to his study to do as she directed.

The next day, they continued their mutual censorship, breaking it only to speak about essential things: Isabella, and what they needed to pack. With doglike compliance, he obeyed her every instruction.

There would be two boats, one separately behind them with all their belongings so there'd be room to bring Isabella's tricycle.

As they moved about the house preparing, she wore her frozen smile. A wall to keep him off guard, unnerve him. She was in control, but it was only temporary. Until she fell apart.

Isabella, sensing the excitement of the forthcoming journey, chattered happily and took the things that Emily had packed out of the suitcase and examined them, and Emily had to gently put them back.

Mostly, the child seemed oblivious to the tension, but once she grabbed Emily's face and asked, "Mama, Mama?" as if she sensed something.

"Yes," Emily told her. "Yes, honey. Mama loves you," and Isabella released her.

Emily moved about the house making lists, instructed Mrs. Evans about what she wanted done while they were away, and wrote out checks—though most of the bills were paid directly by The Office. Federico was nearby and she heard his cell phone chime. She saw him glance at the screen and press the red dot. Several more times the calls came, and he did the same thing. Then they stopped. He was avoiding Christina. They wouldn't be able to see each other until they got to the island.

If he put the cell phone down, she could look at the list of the calls he'd received. But he kept it with him, probably so she wouldn't see them. And to know all the calls he'd gotten from her would be too much to bear. He'd probably been careful to erase them anyway.

# Part Seven

# Again, the Island

# Thirty-Four

THE FLOTILLA MADE ITS WAY ACROSS THE BAY, WITH EMILY AND Federico and Isabella in the first boat, Devlin piloting it, and their luggage in the second, with Devlin's brother, Adam, at the wheel.

It wasn't full summer yet and it was chilly on the open water. Isabella's eyelashes fluttered against the wind; she seemed hypnotized by the journey.

As they sped across the bay, their separation was in force. The fuss of packing, the two-hour van ride from the city to the dock, loading up the boats with the suitcases and supplies, and donning the life jackets, had all made it possible to maintain their distance.

She kept her face a mask. Federico was now irritable, abrupt, growing angrier, she saw, that he'd been caught, that he'd been stupid, and because of her cryptic response. He was angry in an effort to deflect her, but she was torturing him and making him wait. Now he'd have to see the others. Christina—who knew what she would do? And her father. The most dangerous one.

Emily was numb, her jaw set, her eyes burning with exhaustion. Keeping him near her—what a punishment, to be stuck with his own wife! For a moment, she actually felt sorry for him, but she caught herself. She refused to cry in front of him, she wouldn't give him that.

When they reached the shore, her father and Christina, who had come the day before to set up the house, were there to welcome them.

Devlin switched off the motor, and there was the momentary silence, the sudden peace of the place, as the boat rocked silently in its wake. Devlin sprang out, tied it off, and helped them disembark. Emily hugged her father, held on to him longer than usual. He was looking beyond her, smiling at Isabella. He seized the child. "Hello, sweetheart. How's my girl?"

Emily nodded to Christina. She saw Federico nod at her too, then turn away. Christina looked baffled. So, he hadn't told her, Emily thought, he hadn't dared to contact her. He'd been with Emily and Isabella almost every minute for the past two days.

When they reached the house, there was the noise and effort of unloading the Jeeps and lugging the suitcases up to their rooms. Then came lunch. She saw that Federico was still avoiding Christina, and with each moment growing more troubled and more subdued.

After lunch, there was the traditional walk to the beach to greet the sea. They went in a group, picking their way down the wooden steps. Her father led the way carrying Isabella, followed by Federico, then Emily. Christina walked last.

There was a cheerful wind on the beach, the sky was blue, with big, white, friendly clouds, the water was blue-gray, the waves small but brisk. The sun gave forth its beam of warmth, the promise that real summer would come soon.

The water was still too cold to swim so they set out to explore the shoreline. Christina still lingered behind. As Emily strolled along the beach, she suddenly became aware that Christina had come to a stop. It caught Federico's eye too. He swung around and looked back at her and Christina stared straight at him, her expression naked, questioning, unprotected, and hurt. She was so desperate she didn't care who saw her, Emily knew. Quickly, Federico moved ahead again with her father.

Everyone proceeded except Christina who sat down on the sand. She pushed her hair back in the wind and picked absently at the fragments of shell and seaweed. She clutched her legs and looked out at the sea, squinting into the sun. Emily's father noticed that his wife had disappeared, and he went back to her, extended his hand, and pulled her up to walk with him.

So, this was to be their awful pantomime.

That evening, Mike and Jean arrived, so there was that distraction, more to pay attention to. Jean was subdued; she seemed thinner, her eyes darting from one person to the other. She was laden with files and plans and catalogues to go over with her father. Mike was cheerful, as if nothing had happened, or he was pretending not to know and trying to smooth things over.

At bedtime, Federico, without discussion, again took his pillow and blanket from the bed, and this time he made a place for himself on the floor. He was forced to stay in the room with her tonight. It would be remarked upon if they slept in separate bedrooms in the house.

The hours passed, the night deepened, the unspoken words hung in the air between them. He awaited his sentence.

At breakfast the next morning, Jean came into the dining room just as Emily was settling Isabella into her chair and tying her bib. "What's going on? I haven't talked to you since the city. What did he say?"

Emily watched as Isabella spooned her porridge into her mouth and smiled vaguely. "I didn't ask him to say anything. He just knows that I know."

"He didn't try to—to apologize?"

"He said it was over. Thank God, no, he didn't try to apologize." She bent forward and wiped the residual porridge from Isabella's cheeks.

Devlin's wife, Maureen, had been tending to breakfast. She came into the dining room and, realizing she was interrupting something, quickly checked the urns and hot plates and left.

"He's staying away from her," Emily said. "She's desperate."

"She seemed incredibly on edge last night," Jean said.

"Federico hasn't said anything to her," Emily said flatly. "She's confused. She doesn't understand what's going on."

"But—how do you know that?"

"Because if he did tell her, she'd completely fall apart, and Dad would know. Everything would break open. That's what matters," Emily said grimly. "Dad. More than anything."

"Surely your dad is aware of something?"

"Maybe. I don't know. My father's the biggest mystery in the world to me. Maybe he does, and he'd keep it from me if he did."

"Your father's brilliant. He's above us all. I think he thinks in a way none of us can understand. You're astounding," Jean said to Emily. "How can you do this? What about *you*?"

"What do you think?" Emily replied. She smiled coldly at her. "You think I'm giving a good performance?"

"You're okay, then?"

"Do you care?" Emily said.

"Oh my God, Emily, of course I care."

Isabella had finished eating and was trying to climb down from her seat.

Emily mused, "Maybe he's thinking, give him time, he'll work it out."

"You'd let him 'work it out'?" Jean began.

"Good morning." It was Christina, who'd come down for breakfast. She poured herself coffee from the urn, took a seat away from them, and fixed her eyes on Emily.

"How're you this morning, Christina?" Jean asked.

"Fine. Thanks," she answered, still focused on Emily.

"Where's Henry?" said Jean.

"He went out early with Devlin this morning to inspect the traps."

"We're supposed to go over things today," Jean said. "I guess when he comes back."

Christina seemed not to hear. She hadn't taken her eyes from Emily. "Is everything okay?" she asked Emily, her voice dry, tentative.

"Great," said Emily. "Thanks. Aren't we, Isabella?" The child was tugging at her shorts; she wanted to start her day. "Off we go," Emily said to her. "We're going to the beach before the sun's too hot," and she took Isabella by the hand and led her away.

This continued for the rest of the day. That afternoon, Jean holed up with Henry in the library, both kneeling on the floor, their catalogues and architectural renderings spread out around them. Then, in late afternoon, Uncle Everett arrived with Aunt Fran for their annual stay, and there was that to focus on.

At cocktail time, Emily came out onto the terrace with Isabella so they could say good night to her. There was the familiar late afternoon music in the air, the tinkling of ice cubes on glass. Her father sat smiling, seemingly relaxed. He'd noticed nothing amiss, or, wouldn't have let them know if he did.

The men were dressed for dinner in summer sports jackets: pale green, pale blue, dark blue. Aunt Fran was freshly made-up and changed into fresh linens and wore a gold necklace with a big purple stone in it. Aunt Fran usually had only one gin and tonic at lunch, but after five, she began drinking more seriously. This didn't stop her from being a rather nice woman. And after dinner, she usually fell asleep in front of everyone, which no one remarked on. Uncle Everett was drinking only soda water today.

Jean sat stiffly, her gray hair smooth, and wearing a fresh white linen top and wide pants. She was talking about the museum, for her father's sake no doubt. It was his passionate interest and she tried to lead the conversation in her practiced, agreeable way, though no one was responding to her. Mike, jovial as ever, chatted on obliviously.

Federico sat quietly among them, holding his glass of wine, his dark hair slicked back from his forehead, looking pale from his evening shower. When anyone addressed him, he answered briefly, or simply nodded politely with a forced smile.

Isabella had had her bath and was dressed in her pink nightgown with the ruffles at the arms and everyone was delighting in her angelic presence, and her shy little smile.

"Oh, she's so sweet!" Aunt Fran cried in her gravelly voice. "Hello, sweetheart!" There were so many grown-ups for the child to take in that she buried her head in Emily's shoulder in shyness. Federico took her from Emily and kissed her, murmuring, "*Ti amo*," into her ear. Then, with a small, sad smile, he released her back to Emily.

Christina arrived late for drinks. She didn't make her usual glorious entrance, glowing from the day's activities. She looked worn; there were furrows under her eyes, and her hair was pulled back tightly in a bun. She avoided looking at Federico and bent down to kiss Henry lightly on the forehead.

Emily said to Isabella, "Can you give kisses good night?" The child toddled obediently from one grown-up to the other and held her cheek up to allow each to kiss her, just so the kiss didn't last too long.

Everett, watching her, said, "I hope there's more where that came from." They wanted her to have another baby.

"We'll see," said Emily.

Federico, glass of wine in hand, gave a strained smile. More children. None of them knew what was happening. Only perhaps Christina knew it.

Emily started to leave to take Isabella up to bed. Federico sat there bleakly and didn't offer to accompany them. He'd been forced to cede that happy task to her as part of his punishment.

After supper, there were cards in the drawing room. Maureen had laid an early summer fire in the hearth and it made a cheery flame. All the lights were on bright for the game. Jean and Mike, Uncle Everett, Fran, her father and Federico sat around the table; all except Emily, who didn't play cards, and Christina, who reclined, legs up on an armchair, paging abruptly through a newspaper, scanning it as if she weren't seeing it.

Politely, Emily circled the players, studying their hands, though giving nothing away. The chips were piled neatly on the table, all were focused on their cards. Two aces for her father, she saw, a flush for Federico.

After she'd completed her rounds, she walked out through the French doors onto the terrace. There was a chill in the air, and she pulled her sweater around her shoulders. She went up to the balustrade, and gazed out at the dark, cloud-filled sky, the edges of the clouds illuminated by the moon. Here and there, a star was visible. Beyond the terrace, the land sloped down toward the allée and the walled garden. On the horizon was the soft, gray line of the sea, and the calm hush of it permeated the still night.

Standing there looking out, Emily experienced an unaccustomed feeling. It was as if she were floating, as if for the first time in her life, she was filled with power.

She walked restlessly around the terrace and peeked in through the window at the darkened library and the dining room. The big table had already been set for breakfast by Maureen before she went off for the night.

Circling around again to the drawing room, Emily saw her father, her husband, and the guests still together at the card table, holding their cards up and concentrating, their faces yellowish in the harsh indoor light. It was all before her in a single scene. Christina, still sitting to the side and holding her newspaper, was searching the room for something. Emily knew that she was looking for her.

She spotted Emily in the window and came out onto the terrace. "I want to talk to you," she said.

Emily tensed. She was going to confront her. But if she told Christina what she knew, it would be out, and they'd be blown apart. She would have to react, to lie, to cry. And Emily still hadn't formulated a plan; it all still whirled within her.

"It's hot in there," Christina said.

"Not outdoors," Emily said. "Do you want my sweater?"

"No. No. I'm fine." She took a breath. "I've got to ask you something," she said. "Are you angry with me?"

"Why? What do you mean?" said Emily.

"There's something wrong. I know it."

"I don't know what you're talking about," Emily said.

"Have I done something?" Christina asked. "I can tell there's something. What is it?" She was challenging her. But she didn't want to know the truth. She wanted Emily to say there was nothing. And then she could go on.

"Of course, nothing's the matter," Emily said.

"I can't help it," Christina said. "You've been different. Promise me?"

"Yes, promise," Emily lied.

"Thank God. I'm glad I asked."

Emily said gaily, "Now you don't have to worry."

Christina sighed. "I had to know."

"Nothing," Emily repeated. Cruelty, a new thing for her. An art she ought to master, a necessary weapon. She was grimly proud of herself.

Christina put her hands on Emily's arms. "Can I kiss you?"

Emily didn't answer. Christina leaned forward and kissed her on the cheek anyway.

As Emily pulled away from her, she noticed through the window that the card players had finished their game and her father was sitting back in his chair and had caught sight of the two of them together on the terrace.

She wondered if Christina had come outside deliberately so her husband would see them together, so that she could show him that things were okay between his wife and his daughter. And in their marriage.

# Thirty-Five

As the days passed, she was aware of their every movement: Federico's, her father's, Christina's. The weather was getting warmer. Today the sun was out, and it was a good day, with just a gentle breeze. But Christina was nowhere to be seen. The others had gone out on their various expeditions. Federico was on one of his solitary walks. Her father and Mike, in their tennis whites, gathered their rackets and balls for a game. Jean shut herself in the library to work; perhaps, Emily thought, to get away from the strained atmosphere. In their eternal relaxation, Uncle Everett and Aunt Fran had taken their usual places on the terrace. "Everett's not supposed to sit in the sun," Aunt Fran explained. "He had a thing taken off his forehead." They were reclined on their chaises from which they would look out for hours at the sea. Emily collected Isabella's bucket and shovel and took her to the beach.

At 11:30, when Emily brought Isabella back for her lunch and nap, she glanced down into the garden and saw Federico and Christina standing there together, in broad daylight. It was the first time she'd seen them with one another since they'd all arrived on the island.

They were standing at the edge of the trees, away from the path that led down to the walled garden. Federico was looking down at the ground, not saying anything. Christina had cornered him. She was talking excitedly and gesticulating and pointing to her chest.

Behind Emily, her father and Mike were coming in from their tennis game, red-faced and sweating, wiping their faces with their towels.

"Whew," Mike said. "The old man beat me."

"Old!" her father cried. "*You're* the old man. You're a year older than me." They laughed.

Her father saw her staring at something out the window and came up behind her. "What're you looking at, sweetie?"

She couldn't speak. He followed her eyes and now, he too saw his wife engaged in a heated conversation with his son-in-law. He stood there riveted.

They saw Federico raise his arms toward Christina and then shrug his shoulders adamantly. He started walking away from her and Christina stepped after him. He said something to her over his shoulder, and she stopped in her tracks. Christina covered her eyes with her hands, and they could see her shoulders shaking. It was clear that she was crying. Federico turned and stalked away from her, head bent and fists clenched.

Standing there and watching, her father asked, "What's going on?" Emily twisted around. She didn't answer him, but she met his eyes. He held her look and said nothing.

He had seen it. If he didn't know before, he knew now.

Federico had disappeared into the woods. Christina, still crying, was walking slowly up the rise to the house.

Her father, his brow furrowed, watched his wife approach. "I guess I'd better go take a shower," he said. "See you at lunch." He hurried off.

He was going up to their room to find her.

For a moment, Emily had forgotten Isabella and she'd disappeared. She went searching for her and found her in the kitchen. Maureen was chatting with her while she prepared her lunch. "Where's Mommy?" Maureen asked her.

"I'm here," Emily said. "Isabella, let's get you out of those wet clothes. What've you made for her?"

"Scrambled eggs and applesauce," Maureen said. "How's that?"

"Great. We'll be back in a minute."

Lunch was, as always, scattered and informal, each person taking what they wanted from the buffet. Her father came in late, showered, and changed out of his whites. He looked grim and he didn't greet them.

"Where's Christina?" Emily asked.

"She said she didn't want lunch. She's going off for a swim by herself."

He looked at her inquiringly. "And Federico?"

"I don't know where he is." She dared to say, "Is Christina okay?"

"Sometimes she goes without lunch when it's hot," her father said quickly. He didn't want more questions, she knew. He would have to guide her, to somehow let her know what to do.

That evening at dinnertime, Christina appeared in the dining room, a gray, silent presence, her radiance gone. She avoided looking at them.

Federico sat, miserable and unspeaking, at the other end of the table. Henry had ordered a special, expensive wine from the mainland for his guests. They savored the first taste and dutifully praised it, except for Uncle Everett who gazed longingly at the bottle but managed to abstain. Christina silently drank a glass, then another.

Federico, his voice faint, asked Emily's father politely, "Did you get any work done today on the museum, Henry?" When he addressed her father, his tone was always careful, respectful.

Her father answered without looking at him. "Not much today," he said briskly. "But we do have to make a plan for the fall auctions."

Jean interjected, "I think the prices are going to be terrible. They're on to a new trick. They start the bidding low, entice people into a frenzy, and drive everything way up. The Asians, from Singapore, Taiwan, Indonesia, the houses thought they wouldn't show up last year because of the economy, but they came. They're willing to pay a fortune for the Impressionists."

Her father nodded absently and unsmiling. Jean kept up her nervous chatter.

Federico and Christina awaited their punishment.

# Thirty-Six

HER FATHER ASKED HER TO GO FOR A WALK WITH HIM. "LET'S GO alone," he said.

At his words, cold fear spread through her body. He was going to say it, bring it out into the open. She was going to have to witness his fury—and his broken heart. Once he spoke the words, there'd be no going back. She was drained, weak. As they set out, she was afraid she wouldn't be able to walk the whole way with him. He would kill Federico, make her leave him, he would throw Christina out on the street. And she would lose control of whatever decision she might make about Federico. Her father would make it for her.

"Like the old days," he said. It had been a long time since they'd gone on one of their walks together, just the two of them.

Christina was somewhere else, apart from everyone.

As always, when they went on their strolls on the island, he carried his grandfather's old walking stick. There was a compass in the handle and when she was a child, it had fascinated her. He'd used it to teach her about North and South.

All she could do was put one foot in front of the other and pray she wouldn't fall.

They entered the cool, dark woods and without consulting one another, automatically took their familiar path through the white oaks, the wild cherries, and the columns of slender white birches. It was shaded here, and the air was filled with birdsong. A hollow drumming sound came from a tree, and a large bird flew out from the branches. They caught a glimpse of red on its head and black and white patches on its body. "I think that's a pileated woodpecker," he said. Her father was good at identifying birds. "It's bigger than the more common species."

As they walked, she waited for him to say it, the real thing. Their feet crunched along the trail, the insects buzzing around their heads as they tried to wave them away. It was a well-worn path, though hardly anyone came here. When she was a child, he'd told her it was probably an old Indian trail, hundreds of years old. "The Montaukett Indians used to be here. This was where they hunted, in the forest, right where we are. And we're the only people who get to walk here now. It's totally untouched. Isn't that amazing?"

"Are the Indians still alive?" she had asked.

"They're not a recognized tribe anymore. The whites drove them out. They say some of them intermarried with the Shinnecock on the mainland."

Always, during these walks, she'd learned from him, pitching her head up to catch each morsel of knowledge, absorbing from him the ways of the world. It was like sipping honey. Then, walking beside him in the woods, she had, even more than usual, his full attention. She was the heart of his universe, and the act of learning from him was a form of loving him, his teaching her a way of his loving her. So much to learn. She was hungry for it. He knew everything. He was never wrong. Now, as they made their rhythmic procession along the path, his tall figure alongside her, she felt the familiar sensation of once again being a child.

They were far away from the house now, and their conversation was muffled by the trees. No one could hear them. What had happened yesterday in their bedroom? Did he know the full story? But if she asked him outright, he'd have to answer, and it would end whatever safety not acknowledging it afforded them.

She was afraid of him, of his strength, his superior mind. If he put words to it, that her own husband had had sex with his wife, if she told him that she knew it, his rage would be overwhelming, like thunder. She'd seen his anger before, at corrupt judges, at the judicial system failing his poor clients. But he'd never been really angry with her. Only once, when she was little and ran across the street without looking, he'd come after her and gripped her wrist so hard it hurt. She'd cried, frightened, affronted. He said it was to make her remember never to step off the curb without looking, and the lesson stayed with her.

He was ahead of her on the path, and she noticed that he was rubbing his shoulder. He'd been doing that a lot recently.

"Is something wrong with your shoulder?"

"I think it's the tennis. The doctor says it's bursitis. Overuse."

"Does it hurt?"

"Nah. Hardly." He'd never confess to pain or weakness to her.

Even something mild that could be a sign of his aging worried her.

"Can you do anything for it?"

"I'm doing the exercises, weights and things. Anti-inflammatories."

"I'm sorry."

"I'll fix it," he said, in his inimitable way. "Not to worry."

They strolled on. Then, in the intimacy of the moment, it burst out of her.

"You understand things," she said, "because you're a lawyer. Sometimes I think I don't see things because I've been so spoiled and overprotected."

"What are you talking about?"

"I'm not sure."

"I don't think you're spoiled. It's true that we've had everything—materially. But we've had plenty of sorrow. What's gotten into you?" he asked.

"Maybe we're too ignorant about the world. Sometimes I'm jealous."

"You mean, jealous about Federico?" He'd caught her. He was giving her the chance to say it now.

"Perhaps . . ." She pulled back. "I'm not, really."

"Then, of what?"

"Forget it." She took a breath. "Are *you* ever jealous, Dad?" she asked, wanting him to answer, yet dreading that he would say he was.

"Of course not! What should I be jealous *of*?" He was lying, giving nothing away. He'd witnessed the scene, Christina and Federico in the garden. Had he confronted Christina? How could he not talk about it now?

She said quickly, "Obviously, you don't have any reason to be jealous of anyone." Let him preserve the lie if that's what he wanted. "You're everything to all of us. We couldn't live without you."

"One day, honey, you may have to live without me."

"That day," she said firmly, "will never come."

"But it will. It has to." He paused. "Federico has seemed kind of depressed since we've been here," he said. So, he had noticed.

"Yes."

"You think he misses home, Italy?"

"I do."

"Maybe you guys should think about moving there?"

"You mean, leave you?"

"Why not? That's Federico's real home."

"He doesn't ask," she said. "But I know he wants Isabella to be Italian too."

"She's such a smart girl. Like her mother."

"I don't think I'm so smart," she said.

"You always underestimate yourself," he said. "I don't know

why. I've never known what to do about it. Maybe if Christina and I left, then the two of you would be free to lead your own lives."

It took her aback. "Where would you go?"

"I'm frustrated about the museum. I'm not there to watch over them. Who knows what's going on? The bills are mounting. Young Mr. Nick's good, but he doesn't have a lot of experience with contractors and things. There are many decisions to make now that the new wing's going up. I feel I need to watch over everything as they go along. I should really be there all the time now. It's a hell of a lot of money."

"You'd move to Woodford?"

"At least for a while."

"What about Christina?"

"Actually, she mentioned it herself just yesterday."

So, that was part of what had gone on up in their room. "She'd move there?" Emily asked. "It's such a—it's such a sad place. What would she do?"

"I know it's sad. But we want to change that. She's really interested in the museum."

"But how long would you be there?"

"Nick says he thinks they'll have the new wing up by fall, and then in winter they can start on the interior."

"So, you'd be there all winter? Like a year or something?"

"Maybe. Yeah."

"It would be just the two of you, then? In that place?"

"Well, there's probably nowhere right in town we could rent a house. It would have to be outside somewhere, but near enough so I could go there every day and keep an eye on things."

"Wouldn't you feel incredibly lonely?"

"For me at least, the project would take up a lot of time."

"But Christina? What would she do?"

"She says she wants to help me." She'd begged him to keep her, Emily realized. She had no other choice now.

"And Pittsburgh's only an hour away," he said. "We could go

there sometimes. The city's really coming back. They've got the museums, the symphony. There's a lot going on at the universities."

"Would you come back to New York ever?"

"From time to time. But if we do move, I'd have to really be there. There's a lot of work to do."

"You'd never see Isabella."

"There's Facetime. We can talk all the time."

"You'd be willing to give her up?"

"I'm not giving her up. I just wouldn't see her almost every day, like I do now."

"We'd really be separated then?"

"We would," he said. "But that might be good. Good for all of us."

She was suddenly dizzy. She rested her hand on his arm to steady herself. "But Dad, who'd take care of *you*?"

"Christina, of course."

"Would she?" She realized what she'd said.

"Of course she would." He spoke with certainty, then looking at her, he frowned. "You sure you're okay?"

"I'm fine," she lied. She resumed walking, a bit ahead of him, to show him that she was all right. "I'm sorry. Just the old daughter jealousy. Stupid. Thinking I could take better care of my father than his own *wife*."

"I can take care of myself, you know," he said.

She stopped. She had crossed the line. "I'm sorry."

"Well, it's a fact," he said quickly, harshly.

She shook her head. "It's like a tearing away. I'm scared to be without you, Dad."

"Without me? C'mon!"

"I'm still a child, I guess."

"Well, it's time you grew up. For your own good." He saw her dismay. "I'm sorry. You *are* grown-up. You're wiser than you know. What about your husband?"

He was saying that she still had a husband. That she could decide to keep him.

"Federico . . ." She caught herself. If she said more, it would be admitting it, what they both knew.

The solution was decided, not to say the words, to leave it unspoken. Could they bear that? Herself, Federico—and Christina?

"Yes," she said. "Federico."

"Your first duty is to him."

"Yes."

"It's my fault. I should've encouraged you both to live your own lives. You're a mother now. A wonderful mother," he said.

"I don't know . . . I hope so."

"How could you be any better?"

She shook her head.

"Honey, you don't need me now. You're a strong girl. You can take care of yourself."

In the shade of the woods, the birds sang and flitted around them. He didn't understand—or did he? If he left, she'd have no one to keep her safe. She would have to find her own way.

But maybe he did understand. This was his solution, what he had decreed.

He stood over her now, her father, whose daughter had been wronged, an older man with a wife who'd had sex with his daughter's husband. He wasn't telling her what he knew—or *if* he knew. They were in a balancing act, as if they were sitting at either end of a seesaw—up and down, each trying to steady the other, to save the other from falling off.

# Thirty-Seven

CHRISTINA'S SHRILL VOICE ECHOED OFF THE WALLS, THE SOUND trailing her as she led the guests through the rooms of the house, pointing out the objects. The members of the Historical Society had come over from the mainland for their annual benefit tour. They were an eager lot. The few people who were ever invited to the island always accepted the invitation. Emily's father did it to keep up good relations with the community. He arranged boats for them and golf carts to take them around, and gave them a traditional summer lunch of salmon and mayonnaise.

Today, before they arrived, Christina had said, "*I'd* like to give the tour. I feel I really know the art now." And Henry had agreed to it.

The Historical Society members were mostly white-haired old women. They wore white or vivid summer blue that matched their bright blue eyes. There were a couple of white-haired old men too, in silk bow ties and pastel-colored jackets.

Christina led them through the house, pointing out the important objects. She halted before the painting of Venice. "That's from the School of Canaletto," she said. "There's the Grand Canal of course, the Campanile San Marco on the left." She pronounced the Italian perfectly. "In the scheme of things this isn't a particularly valuable painting. But my husband has decided it shouldn't be here in this ocean climate and we're donating it to his museum. . . ."

Emily's father stayed in the background watching; Jean followed the group attentively. Federico, hands behind his back, paced at the rear, away from the scene.

In the middle of the lecture, Christina stopped and glanced at him. At that, he left the room.

Christina went on. "It's not dated. But it's probably from the 1760s. It's part of the Woodford family history." Her voice rose a pitch. "Henry's grandmother, Grace Woodford, brought it back from Venice when she made the Grand Tour. They didn't bring postcards or photographs, they brought back art. That's how a lot of Old Masters first got to this country. There's a family legend that Bernard Berenson advised her, but we don't know for sure."

On she went, object after object, like a train hurtling onward and unable to stop.

"These paintings are of my husband's ancestors. Some of them are copies made from old photographs after the fire in the 1950s. They were painted to look old. They're really of no value at all, but we keep them here because it's the family home . . ."

"If you look at them, you can see the frames are pretty much intact, the gold's a bit too bright. Here's one of old Ephraim Consider Woodford." She pointed to a portrait of a wan, small-chinned man with a thin mouth and slightly bulging eyes. He wore a long dark jacket, his hand tucked into the vest pocket, looking out warily at the viewer. "He was the founder of the family. He died in 1919." Emily had always thought Uncle Everett resembled Ephraim. But Uncle Everett was gentle, lovable, and defeated, though cushioned by wealth.

Someone asked, "Why was he called 'Consider'?"

"We don't know," said Christina. "Maybe they named him that because they wanted him 'to consider' something." She gave a quick smile, like a grimace, and then continued monotonously.

"The Edwardian carved mahogany desk there is early twentieth century. This chair is French, carved walnut, upholstered in an Aubusson fragment . . ."

"Would it be all right if I sat down a moment?" an old woman asked.

"Of course," Christina said. She walked on, to the seventeenth-century brass skeleton clock from Maidstone, England, from where many ancestors of the mainland people came, and to Henry's father's silver yachting trophies arranged in a row on a shelf.

They went into the hallway and Emily was left with Jean in the empty drawing room. They remained there listening to Christina's voice as it faded into the distance, describing the amateur seascapes on the walls, painted by generations of Woodfords including the children—another family tradition— in homage to happy summers spent on the island.

"Awful, isn't it?" Emily said softly to Jean.

"Would it be easier if we left?" Jean asked.

"Stay," she said. "I need you to see me through it."

They had ceased all intimacy, but underneath there was still their terrible conversation, the conversation that had no words, the continuous stream of unresolved questions and unmade decisions. The effort to preserve the fiction of their marriage in front of everyone was exhausting, like climbing a rocky slope, the rock cutting into their flesh. She could see that it was exhausting for Christina too, to walk across a room without faltering, to sit upright at the table while the others talked around her.

Federico said, "I'm going into New York for a couple of days." It was a fact. He didn't ask if she'd mind.

"But. . . ?"

Was he finally leaving her? Alarm spread through her.

"What are you going to do?" she asked. It was the most personal thing she'd said to him in days.

"Rodolfo's coming in from Rome. I want to see him." He spoke coldly, the undertone of irritation still in his voice. Rodolfo was the one who'd worked in the gallery in Rome. "I'll be back Saturday," he said.

She tried to remain calm and composed. She held her posture perfectly.

Then, without warning, the words came out of her. "Would you like to go back to Rome? Would you like us to move there?" she said. "I know you're homesick." She was conscious that for the first time in weeks there was emotion in her voice. It was the first vaguely kind thing she'd said to him. She was offering to continue to imprison him in the marriage. But she was also saying she was ready to stay in it too. Something she hadn't even articulated to herself before this.

She saw him thinking over her question. It hadn't occurred to him it was possible, that she might not leave him, she might not divorce him. That he could stay in the marriage and keep his child.

"I'll be back on Saturday," was all he said.

At dinner, when they were mostly together, her father was still quiet and preoccupied. When he was asked a question, or someone interrupted his thoughts or passed him a dish, he woke up and politely thanked them. Mike, in his typical sociable manner, said, "What about a game tomorrow morning, Henry? That court's not getting any use."

"I know," he said. "I've got this damn shoulder," he said, rubbing it again. "The doc calls it 'Toyota Shoulder'—all acceleration, no breaks. I'm doing the exercises, but I don't think I ought to play for a while. He says I should give it a rest."

The next morning, from the window, Emily saw him down below heading toward the woods with his walking stick, poking at the ground.

He wanted to be alone.

Devlin took Federico to the mainland to get the train. He was physically gone, but he left behind his cold presence. He wanted to escape, but he'd be miserable there in the city too, she knew. Was Rodolfo really coming to New York? Was he really going to see him? Christina was here. He wanted to flee from her as well, from all of them. He'd rather be in the empty house in the empty city in the hot summer than with them. Anywhere else.

Without him, their bedroom seemed even bigger. Emily thought of him miles away in the city in his own agony, and, in the other wing, Christina with her father. What was happening between them? What conversations were they having? And at the other end of the house were Jean and Mike, in their loving, settled, and eternal marriage.

Her nightgown stuck to her body in the heat. In the past, on an exquisite summer night like this on the island, Federico and she would have made love.

She went into Isabella's room. The child was asleep on her back, her arms spread out on the mattress, naked but for her diaper—she only wore a diaper at night now. As always, Emily touched her forehead. Was all well? Would sleep carry her safely to dawn? The child felt her touch and sighed, but she didn't wake up.

Emily leaned down and hooked her arm under her body, raised her up, and carefully put her over her shoulder. Still, she slept. She buried her nose in Isabella's hair, inhaling the musty scent of it, then carried her into her own room and lay her gently down on the double bed.

Dr. Rose always said not to let the baby sleep with them because she'd never learn to put herself to sleep. So, dutifully, they'd reserved the treat of bringing her into their bed just for when she was sick and they had to watch over her. Guiltily, they acknowledged to themselves those were delicious times. Now, if she let Isabella sleep with her when Federico was gone, there'd be a struggle when he returned, to get her to stay in her own bed. *If* he came back. If they ever again were to sleep in the same bed.

What did it matter? This was no ordinary time. She was entitled to the solace of her little girl's warm body next to her, the assurance that she still had someone to live for.

She lay down next to the child, and in the half-light from the moon outside the window, she propped herself up on her arm and studied her in all her beauty.

The next morning, when she came into the dining room with Isabella for breakfast, they were the first ones there, as usual. When they'd finished eating, Emily gathered Isabella up to fetch her toys and go to the beach.

Jean and Mike were on their way in. As always now, when Jean saw her, she gave her a worried look.

"Is all well?" Jean asked. "I haven't seen your father or Christina this morning."

"They must be sleeping late," Emily said.

Later, at lunch, Christina was absent again. "She's a bit under the weather," her father told them. "A stomach thing."

That afternoon from the window she saw her father again setting off by himself, this time toward the beach.

Christina didn't come down to dinner that evening either. "She's still not feeling well," her father said. He looked uneasy.

In the morning, Emily found Maureen, Devlin's wife, dusting in the drawing room. "Have you seen Mrs. Woodford?" she asked.

"I saw her earlier on. Mr. Woodford told me to take her breakfast tray up to her room."

Federico arrived back from New York. Emily went to the front door with Isabella to greet him. He'd had a haircut. He gave Emily only a nod, but seeing his daughter, his face lit up and he held out his arms to her. "*Cara . . . Cara,*" he murmured. "I missed you so much."

Isabella shoved her doll at him. "*Guardate! Guardate!*" she cried. Emily had sewn a dress for it out of an old curtain.

"*Un vestito*," he said softly. "*Un vestito*."

He turned to Emily, his features set.

"How was your visit with Rodolfo?" she asked.

"Good," he said, unsmiling, and went upstairs to unpack.

At lunch they were all reunited, her father as always at the head of the big table. For the first time in days, Christina appeared. She sat at the other end, shrunken, stooped, almost disappearing under it. Federico, sitting far away from her, diverted himself with Isabella. The two them, Federico and Christina, seemed as if they were no longer in the same room, so practiced was their game. Or, so fragile their connection. Maybe that was just true of *him*, Emily thought? Maybe she would still die for him.

Jean smiled stiffly, pretending nothing was happening, and Mike, ever optimistic and at ease, was going along with her.

It was then that her father spoke. "Christina and I have an announcement."

He surveyed the table. "We've decided to move down to Woodford and really take charge of things. We've talked it over, and Christina agrees. They really need us there. We just have to go. It's a big move, of course, and we're going to have to go back to New York early to pack and make arrangements."

Jean sat up in her seat and glanced at Emily. Around the table, they were speechless, digesting his words. Christina, still shrunken in her seat, looked out dully. Federico stared at her father.

Slowly Emily repeated, "You're going back early."

Federico took a breath. "I can see the necessity," he said. "Anything we can do, of course, we're here."

"Thank you." Her father nodded formally at him. "As always," he said.

"But when would you have to leave here?" Emily said.

"Very soon," her father said. "I think maybe in a couple of days. We've got to get a place to live down there. There's a lot to do. We'll have to pack up for at least a year."

"But will you leave the New York house empty?" Emily asked.

"For now," he said.

"Will you come back?" she said. She could have asked him that privately, but she had to know now.

"Eventually, of course," he said.

As he spoke, it came to her: life without him, like a piece of her flesh torn away.

"But it'll be just a few months. Right?" she insisted.

"Darling, I don't know," he said. "Quite a few months, I think. We've got this huge thing going on. It's millions—" he stopped himself. "It's a big responsibility. I can't just let it sit there."

"I see," she said.

Christina looked at Emily with a full, hard expression. "And we'll miss you too, of course, Christina," Emily told her.

It seemed that her father had forgiven her. But how could he encompass it, that his son-in-law had betrayed his daughter with his own wife? How could he live with her now?

Because, in the end he had all the power, and he wanted Christina. This was his scheme, his solution; remove his wife who'd deceived him with his daughter's husband away from the scene of her crime, obliterate it. And so his daughter could keep her husband, the father of her child, if she wanted to.

She would never know. He wanted them to choose silence. It was the only way.

For the first time, Christina spoke. "It's for the best," she said faintly, almost to herself.

Her father said to Jean, "As we start working on the interior, I'll want you to come down and help."

"Of course," Jean said.

"Good." He sat back and smiled benevolently, a man with manners, in command of them all.

Upstairs in Isabella's bedroom, Emily tried to put the child down for her nap. She was exhausted from the scene at lunch, and she needed time to think. But Isabella was resisting. "Lie down, sweetheart, just for a bit," she begged. She folded her hands, lay her cheek on them to imitate sleep. "Just a nice sleepy-sleepy," she said. Isabella looked up at her, considering.

"No," the child said firmly. "No nap." She'd begun to give up her afternoon nap, and as a result, stumbled about crankily all afternoon until bedtime. She ran with her doll and put it in its own little crib, so *it* could take the nap.

There was a knock on the door. "Can I come in?" It was Jean.

Jean went to Isabella, who was standing by her doll's crib. "Is the baby sleeping, Isabella?" she asked. The child nodded earnestly. She said to Emily, "I hope you don't mind my saying this, but sometimes I feel like she's my own grandchild." To Isabella she said, "Can Auntie Jean give you a kiss?"

Isabella didn't say "no," so Jean picked her up and held her close and kissed her on her plump little cheek. "Such a good girl," Jean said. "There's nothing like it, holding her." It was true; Jean did seem to really love her.

"You can call her your grandchild any time you like," Emily said. Forgiveness. Jean had withheld the truth. She had lied to her. But Emily would forgive it, warily.

"She's a good girl," said Emily. "If she doesn't go down, we're in for an afternoon of hell."

"I remember my sister's son," Jean said. "It was the same thing. Now he's a lawyer."

"Yes." Emily stared fondly at the recalcitrant child, who was now emphatically covering her doll with its blanket to make it clear it was the doll who was going to take a nap, and not her. "She's my angel," Emily said.

Jean lowered herself onto the slipper chair. "So. They're going."

"Yep."

"Woodford's a pretty grim place," Jean said. "Your father's going to make it better, but it'll take some time."

Emily nodded.

Jean said, "She knows what's in store for her. The whole thing's going to take years. She'll have to be involved in everything. And Federico?" Jean asked.

"If I really knew what was going on with Federico, I think I'd die." Then, "What have I done?" she said to Jean.

"You've done everything you could. Do you think he's spoken to her?"

"Who?"

"Federico. To Christina."

"That's their business," she replied.

Isabella had rescued her doll from her nap and was walking around the room holding the blanketed thing in her arms and singing the approximation of a lullaby to it.

"Is baby sleeping now?" Emily asked her hopefully. Isabella nodded solemnly. "Should you take a nap like baby?"

Isabella shook her head firmly.

"You're amazing," Jean said.

"I'm not," Emily said.

"How much do you think he knows?" Jean asked.

"Dad? He's beyond me." Emily smiled, a small, sad smile.

"Christina—has he said something to her?"

"I wouldn't know."

"She seems destroyed," Jean said. "Whatever happened, I guess that's her hell."

# Thirty-Eight

THE HEAT ROSE. DINNER WAS FULL OF CHAT ABOUT THEIR plans, Federico and Christina barely participating. Nick, the young architect, would help them find a place to live, her father said. Federico interjected politely—would it actually be possible to find an appropriate house in that area? Though Federico had heard that the climate in winter was supposedly more moderate there than in New York City. Trying to be the useful son-in-law, Emily knew, to win Henry's favor.

Afterward, everyone except for Federico, who said he was going to the library to read, retreated to the terrace to take in the cool air, and to watch the Perseids.

The sky was clear tonight. There was a full, spectral moon, its shadowy landscape just discernable. It made a path of twinkling light on the sea. The moon was always something to contemplate this time of year. The air was still, fragrant with the scent of grass and soil, and some night flower and other unnamed things. The noise of the crickets and cicadas and frogs filled it. All around them, the fireflies beamed. Emily sat with the others reclined on their chaises watching the sky.

"There's one," her father said, pointing. It was almost too late to spot the tiny filament of light streaking across the sky. There was a second burst of light. "And another," he said. This time they were focused, ready for it.

"Amazing," Mike murmured.

"They're actually debris from the Swift-Tuttle comet," her father said. "It takes a hundred and thirty-three years to orbit the earth."

"I thought it was stars," Jean said.

Her father commanded the skies.

Christina rose from her chair, saying nothing, descended the steps and began walking down the lawn toward the walled garden.

After a few minutes, Emily got up from her chaise and went after her, picking her way across the grass, the dew soaking her feet.

When she came to the gazebo, Christina was sitting inside on the bench and gazing out into the dark. Sensing someone there, she spun around.

"How are you, Christina?" Emily said.

"I'm glad we're going," Christina said. "Maybe now we can really start our lives together."

So, this was how she was going to solve it. She wasn't going to talk about Federico. She was shifting it, making it seem as if what mattered was her and her husband, Emily's father, not that she'd slept with Federico.

Emily stared at the tall, slender shape of her sitting there in the moonlight. She was unsmiling, her expression rigid. She could feel her hatred, her bewilderment. This was the woman Federico had wanted. But she no longer looked beautiful, only wrung out, defeated. Emily wondered what it would be like to kill her. To strike her and throw her to the ground, to kick her until she was a mass of bloody flesh.

She echoed Christina's words. "'*Our* lives'?" she said.

"Your father's and mine," said Christina.

"I know things are bad," Emily said. She was going along with it, speaking over and around it, letting the focus be her father, not what Christina had done with her own husband.

"You mean *I'm* bad?" Christina said, through clenched teeth. "The two of you, it's always been the two of you together. Now he's going to be with *me*." As if that were the real issue.

Emily answered softly, "And he's leaving me."

"It was completely weird the way you were together. All through our marriage. Don't you know that?" As if that was the cause of what she and Federico had done. The way she was going to formulate it.

Emily didn't answer her.

"You didn't want us even to get married," Christina cried.

"That's absolutely not true," said Emily.

"You were against me from the start!" Her voice was breaking.

Emily could feel her eyes drilling into her. "You know that's not what happened," Emily said. "I was very happy for you."

"Well, you didn't succeed, did you?" said Christina, as if Emily hadn't denied it.

"If that's what you want to believe," Emily replied. She'd let her have that. That was going to be her way out, the way out for everyone.

With that, Emily spun around and walked back to the house.

One of the chaises on the terrace was empty. Her father had gone.

Leaving Jean and Mike to watch the stars, she went up to check on Isabella. Her bedroom faced west, and it was hot. As Emily moved toward her bed, she saw the shape of a figure reclining in the chair at the foot of it. It was her father. He was leaning back, his legs stretched out in front of him. She approached, but he didn't move. Was he asleep? She couldn't tell if his eyes were closed. It was as if he were guarding Isabella, or contemplating leaving her.

He'd always been a light sleeper, and he always came awake at the slightest sound. But he didn't stir. He was awake, she knew, pretending to be asleep. He'd come up here to make sure his granddaughter was safe, the child who was the future. And he didn't want to engage her, Emily.

The decision was made. He was saying, "It's all up to you now." He was freeing her to fly on her own.

That night, she and Federico prepared to sleep in their separate spots, she in the bed, he on the floor. As they got ready for the night, for a moment they stood across the room from one another, unmoving in their estrangement. As if something had to be said.

He was the one who spoke first. "It's probably the only way he can get the museum done."

"Will you miss her?" she asked. She felt the heat of her anger rise in her.

He looked away, crouched down on the floor, and smoothed out his sheet.

"She's seems distraught," Emily said.

"Why do you say she's 'distraught'?" he asked. It was a feint. Then, he said, "Christina didn't understand you."

"I've been good at making her wonder," said Emily.

"Christina isn't very smart."

The cruelty of his words shocked her. "How can you say that?"

Grief washed over her. The woman had loved him, the way she herself had. Christina had lost him, and *this* was what he had to say about her. She was on her way to prison. Day after day, she would have to follow her husband around on his construction site, from dull, unfinished place to dull, unfinished place, in the rain and chill of winter. No one to talk to but him. What had been said between them? Did he tell her that he knew everything, or just part of it—that strong, forbearing man who held sway over them all? Who owned the world around him, whose principal weapon was kindness and generosity? Or had he kept some of it from her to keep her desperately wondering, to hold power over her?

"Christina does know," said Emily. She'd borrowed her father's strength; it was in her now.

"Know what?" he said. He was challenging her, making her say it out loud, with all the words. But he knew she didn't want to.

They were going round and round, her never screaming, "You fucked her!" His never saying, "I didn't," or, "I couldn't help myself," or, "You weren't enough." Because if they said those things, there'd be no going back.

"I don't have to tell you," Emily said. She had all the cards now. Suddenly, the words lashed out of her. "Women always lose!" she cried.

She knew, knew exactly, the other woman's pain. But *she* had won—because her father was rich, and Federico wanted her money and he wanted his daughter, wanted her more than life itself. And he had enough affection left for her, for Emily, to stay. He would make do. The danger had withered his lust.

Federico sighed. "Yes, men are terrible," he said. "But Christina's a survivor."

She pushed him; she couldn't help herself. "Does this mean you realize what I know?"

"Oh, *Cara*," he sighed. For the first time in weeks, he uttered his endearment for her. "I want you to do me a favor."

"What?" she asked him stonily.

"Give me time."

"Time?"

"I want to wait until they leave."

He approached her as if he was going to kiss her, but she stepped away. He didn't force it, but lay down in his place on the floor and covered himself with his sheet.

Christina and her father were leaving, and she and Federico would remain behind, still not saying the full thing, still maintaining the performance of cold anger. But a burden had been partly lifted.

In the next few days, there were even a few pleasant comments as they watched Isabella's antics, a few involuntary smiles. Then they'd realize they had let their guard down and pulled back.

Still, there was expectation in the air, even excitement.

# Part Eight

# Farewell

# Thirty-Nine

In New York, the leaves were beginning to fade, but there was still a golden overhang in the air. When Emily was a girl, the splendor of autumn in the city, and the excitement of seeing her friends again, had cushioned the sadness of leaving the island and having to go back to school and sit through classes and do homework.

The first few days were still blisteringly hot, as it usually was at the beginning of September, just when you thought summer was ending. The streets were filled with the voices of children heading back for the first day of school, dressed in blazers with school logos embroidered on the pockets, the boys in khaki pants, the girls in uniform skirts and knee socks, accompanied by their nervous parents striding along beside them, clutching their hands, or trying to catch up with them.

It was Isabella's first day of preschool. She was a bit young for it, but they'd admitted her because she was so precocious.

In their anxiety this morning, for the first time, Emily and Federico had both woken up before her.

As Federico emerged from his shower, Emily was coming out into the hallway in her nightgown. He was sleeping in the guest room again.

She knew the outline of her body was visible through the thin cotton of the gown. He wore his blue bathrobe, his hair was combed back, and he was freshly shaved. She saw the dark gold skin of his thin, muscled legs, the soft hair on them, part of another memory. For a second, she imagined him coming forward and taking her hand, pulling her to the bed and making love to her, as he used to. She caught herself. How could she even want it? He'd been with someone else.

It had been weeks and weeks since they were last together, but still, Emily knew, he had the invisible remains of another woman on his body. He'd severed the thread of trust between them forever, the trust that underlay her giving herself so completely to him—that first time, his searching eyes conveying to her only love and care.

They faced one another uncertainly.

Isabella hurried out of her room carrying the dress and shoes they'd let her choose for herself the night before to wear the first day of school, which they had carefully laid out for her.

"Isabella!" Federico cried. "Isabella's going to school. Hooray!"

Isabella pulled her new pink gingham dress over her head herself. Emily only had to button the back and stuff her backpack with her doll, Gigi, so Gigi could accompany her to the first day.

The school was in the Community House of the family church where Emily's father and Christina had gotten married, only ten blocks north of their house. But still, it was as if Isabella was going far, far away. It was the beginning of their separation from her. They knew they were typical silly parents. Nonetheless, it was inescapable.

As instructed by the school, they'd brought her there in advance to show her the space and to meet her new teacher, Nigel. They'd pointed out to her all the great toys to play with, the interesting pictures on the wall. Nigel had asked them carefully about Isabella's various likes and dislikes and they had carefully briefed him. "For some reason she doesn't like yogurt," Emily told him. "She's the only child I know who doesn't like it. And she's very stubborn about her nap."

"Not to worry," Nigel said. "We just have quiet time. They lie on their mattresses, and they can have a stuffed animal or a book if they want."

There was a line of strollers on the sidewalk at the entrance to the school. They waited at the door with the other parents as Nigel greeted each pupil one by one, reaching out to shake their hands. Would Isabella cry? Refuse to go in?

They led her into the classroom. There were brightly colored child-sized tables and chairs, a giant rainbow painted on the wall, and rows of letters and numbers in different colors. The minute they entered, Isabella spotted Milo, her friend from the playground. They'd learned from Milo's parents that he was enrolled at the school too, and it had finalized their decision to send her there.

At the orientation, Nigel had instructed them, "It's best to make your goodbyes brief. You might point to a toy to distract their attention. Remind him or her that you'll be back very soon, and then quickly leave."

Isabella was already a few feet away from them, engrossed in discussing something with Milo. She'd forgotten them. The moment had come.

The first day was only forty-five minutes long. "Bye!" they cried, but Isabella merely glanced at them, and continued talking to Milo. She seemed not to even realize they were leaving—Nigel had warned them that could happen. Paradoxically, he said, it could be a defense. They kissed her quickly and departed.

Instead of going home, they waited in the coffee shop around the corner from the church. Sitting across from one another, they reverted to their usual stance, eyes averted. Federico opened his newspaper and concentrated on the sports page. He looked at his cell phone, probably, as usual, searching for the Italian soccer scores. Emily reminded him that the Spectrum man was coming this morning to fix the cable. Mrs. Evans would let him in and she'd instructed her to make sure to demonstrate to him that both televisions weren't working. This afternoon the electrician was arriving to give an estimate for new lighting for the kitchen. Emily should be there for that.

Federico didn't look up. "Okay," he said, studying his cell phone. "Good."

Emily looked at her cell. There was an email from her father saying they'd be over tomorrow at three o'clock to say goodbye.

Directly after her father and Christina had made their announcement and gone back to the city, they'd flown to Pittsburgh and driven down to Woodford. They'd found a house to rent a half-hour from the museum site. Her father had sent her an email with a photograph. It was a large, faded, yellow brick house that had previously belonged to a state senator. The photo had been taken in winter and it seemed bleak and isolated, the garden around it brown and untended. Emily tried to imagine them there. They'd had the place painted and sent furniture down from the New York house, which they were leaving unrented. Emily had asked if she could help with the move, but he said no, everything was under control and he and Christina were managing fine. Besides, Emily had enough on her hands with Isabella starting school.

The two of them had flown back to New York for a few days to make the final arrangements for the move. It was left unclear whether they'd return to the city for Christmas—maybe they'd go to the Caribbean for the holiday to get out of the cold, her father said. In the mystery of his wisdom, the immeasurable greatness of his soul, Emily thought, he knew they had to stay apart. It was the best way, the right way.

Now, in the coffee shop, she interrupted Federico and showed him the email. "They're coming to say goodbye at three."

"Will they be staying for dinner?"

"I don't know. Maybe Dad will want to take me off somewhere. You can take care of Christina."

He only looked at her. He, too, had learned the value of saying nothing.

# Forty

THE FOLLOWING AFTERNOON, AS THEY WAITED FOR THEM, Federico paced, looking at the floor. The window was open, letting in the warm September air. Every few moments, he stopped to look down at the street. Emily had asked Mrs. Evans to pick Isabella up from school today and take her to the park to give them all some time together. Then she'd bring her back so they could say their farewells to her too.

"What if Christina asks—" Federico said.

"What?"

"If she wants to know what you know . . ." Still, he didn't say the exact words. But neither did she. They'd said enough. They only spoke around it.

"Let her think I'm stupid," she said. "I don't care. Let her wonder for the rest of her life and suffer." She heard herself—"Let her suffer"—and still, she felt empathy for Christina's suffering.

From the window, she saw the black limousine pull up below. She raised her hand to Federico in warning. "They're here." They went downstairs to greet them.

They only wanted coffee, they said. Their plane was at 7:10 and they couldn't stay; they had to get going to avoid rush hour. Christina was flushed, dressed in a T-shirt, jeans, and sneakers for the trip. Her father was dressed uncharacteristically "young" as well, in a sweatshirt, jeans, and sneakers.

As they were seated around the coffee table, Christina chattered at them manically, suffused with excitement. "Celia McKay's found us a Thomas Hart Benton, a perfect one your father wanted." Federico sat stonily across from her. "We're still not sure we can get it, but we're going to try our best."

"And—guess what?" she said. "We've discovered a whole new collection of old photographs of Woodford in the town library. From the turn of the last century. The town was so alive then, people on the streets . . ." Her eyes moved to the wall behind Federico. She wasn't speaking to any one of them anymore. Emily's father watched her intently. She was overshadowing him, and he seemed not to mind. "All the old cars, the men in hats, a drugstore on Main Street, all sorts of shops. They really tell you that the place was part of America, and the town was flourishing."

Her father rose and began to walk slowly around the parlor with his coffee mug. Emily went after him, leaving Federico and Christina a few feet away, and Christina talked on, filling the emptiness, not looking at Federico. As if he weren't there and she no longer saw him. Or, as if she couldn't bear to see him.

Her father studied the family photographs on the mantel. "You need a more recent one of Isabella," he said. He scrutinized the art on the walls that he'd given them as presents over the years: the Degas sketch of a ballerina, a Picasso lithograph of a mother and child. Finally, the dear little Flemish painting, the girl-like Madonna with her baby at her breast.

"It's really special, isn't it?" he said to Emily. "Where's my Isabella?" he asked.

"Mrs. Evans is bringing her home at three-thirty. She'll be here, I promise."

"Perhaps you guys should think of moving too, to Italy," her father said.

"That's a possibility. It'll be hard here without you and Christina.

Christina's wonderful," she said. Lie to him, ease him, support him, whatever it was he knew. Their usual way, nothing declared. The best way. The only way.

"That she is," he said. He put his arm around Emily. "It's going to be okay," her father said.

He looked back at his wife in the parlor, still talking intensely to the wall behind Federico, who was silently watching her.

"It's worked out," said Emily.

"Yes."

They were interrupted by the clatter and piping cries of Isabella's arrival from the park with Mrs. Evans.

"There she is!" her delighted grandfather cried, his arms wide open and ready to embrace her. Isabella ran to him and allowed him to sweep her up and hug her.

"Grandpa will see you soon," he said. "Only now it'll be on a screen. Magic! Grandpa will be in another city, and you'll see me, and Grandma Christina, and I'll get to see *you*. Is that okay?"

Isabella nodded. She was playing with the neck of his sweatshirt, maybe wanting to hide that she understood he was leaving her.

At last, the goodbyes, hugs all round. A brief one, lasting only a beat, between Christina and Federico. Emily's own hug for Christina, breast to breast, stone to stone. Finally, her father's warm embrace, and she was once again small and sheltered in his great, all-knowing arms.

Isabella seemed to realize they were leaving and burst into tears. Federico went to hold her. "No, no, *Cara*. You'll see Grandpa soon," he reassured her. "I'll take her down and get her a cookie. Cookie, Isabella," he said. "*Papà ti darà un biscotto . . . Papà ti darà un biscotto*. I'll say goodbye for now," he said to Henry and Christina, and he carried her out of the room, the sound of her wails fading as they disappeared.

The three of them were left.

Emily followed her father and Christina down onto the street.

One more hug. The chauffeur opened the limousine door and they climbed in.

The car pulled gracefully away from the curb. They were leaving her. Emily waved, but because of the tinted window, she couldn't tell if they waved back.

Federico returned from the kitchen without Isabella, who was with Mrs. Evans again.

"It's done," Emily told him. "They're gone."

"I know how hard this is for you," he said.

"Yes."

"Yes," he echoed, his attention fully on her now.

"We did it," she said.

He nodded and looked into her eyes. "And it will be okay," he said.

Uncertainly, she looked back at him.

"Don't you think?" he said.

She stood there, her arms at her sides.

He stepped toward her, and for the first time in weeks, she didn't pull away.

# Endnote

This novel is intended partly as an homage to Henry James. I've borrowed some of the storyline and the structure from his greatest work, *The Golden Bowl*. I hope he will forgive me.

# Acknowledgments

Many thanks to my editor, Jeannette Seaver, for her astute insights that have helped make this a better book. And to Joy Harris, my indefatigable agent, and her associate, Adam Reed. Thank you also to Elena Silverberg at Arcade, for good-naturedly shepherding this novel through copyediting and many other tasks; to Joshua Barnaby, the production editor; and to Brian Peterson for the beautiful cover design.

Thanks also to Hilma Wolitzer, Katherine Bouton, and Brooke Allen for their helpful suggestions. And to Anne Navasky and Gioia Diliberto for their friendship and steadfast support.

But especially, as always, my gratitude goes to my husband, David Nasaw, without whose patience, affection, and sense of humor, this novel would not have been written.